There was a dip  me. I was going u something. I stumbleɑ, ᵖᵗᶜʰⁱⁿᵍ ᶠⁱorward to the ground. I managed to break my fall with my hands, but the impact jarred me. My head throbbed with pain. Screw it, I thought.

As I was getting to my feet, I swept the beam of the flashlight across the ground hoping to see what I had stumbled upon. It was a shoe. A bone-colored running shoe. There was still a foot in it. Then I realized there was a whole person lying there on the ground. I moved the flashlight to get a good look and something shiny reflected the beam back into my eyes. Chain mail. The guy was wearing chain mail.

In the light of the flashlight, I took a long look at Dirk LeGrand's closed, blackened eyes, and at the bruise marks I had left on his neck. I knelt down next to the body. There was a hole about the size of a half-dollar in his bare chest, a circle burned into his flesh around the hole. Unlike Gilroy, it wasn't an arrow that had killed LeGrand. It was a bullet. Someone had shot him at close range. And I knew that everyone was gonna think that it was me.

The Cough of Birds

by

Brian Anderson

The Lyle Dahms Mysteries, Book Two

The Cough of Birds

Contact Information: info@thewildrosepress.com

Cover Art by *Kim Mendoza*

The Wild Rose Press, Inc.
PO Box 708
Adams Basin, NY 14410-0708
Visit us at www.thewildrosepress.com

Publishing History
First Edition, 2023
Trade Paperback ISBN
Digital ISBN

The Lyle Dahms Mysteries, Book Two
Published in the United States of America

Dedication

In memory of Richard Gatten--musician, artist, armorer, and my guide into to the world of Renaissance Festivals.

Acknowledgements

Many thanks to my editor Kaycee John and the entire team at The Wild Rose Press for giving me the opportunity to bring this novel to print. As always, I am deeply grateful to my critique group of the last twenty-plus years—Jessie Irene Fernandes, Diane Spahr, Roger Schwarz, Mark Knoke, Meredith Fane and Nik Joshi—fine writers all—who have generously shared their advice and support.

And most of all, I am thankful to my family—my better half Sue and daughters Nicole, Sydney and Miranda who daily fill my life with joy and purpose.

As far back as I can remember, I've loved mysteries. Beginning with the Adventures of Sherlock Holmes, my interest eventually grew to more contemporary writers—many of whom were represented on my father's bookshelves. A prodigious reader, Dad's collection included John D. MacDonald, Robert B. Parker and Sue Grafton, among many others. We lost Dad a few years back, but those volumes still line the shelves at my boyhood home, waiting to be taken down and enjoyed once more. I'd like to think that were he still with us, the Dahms novels would have found a place there as well.

Chapter One

The front gates of the festival grounds were flanked on either side by twin towers festooned with brightly colored banners. Despite the early hour, costumed revelers stationed atop the towers raised clunky ceramic goblets, boozily haranguing the crowd gathered below.

"You, sirrah!" a man's voice sounded above me. "What bringest thou to good King Henry's realm? Is it to make merry or dost thou harbor ill intent?"

The voice belonged to a young man standing on the tower to my right. Surprisingly slender given the resonance of his voice, he wore a baggy red shirt that hung low over a pair of sea-green hosiery. His long brown hair spilled out from under a leather cap adorned with a day-glow orange ostrich plume.

Before I could be certain he was speaking to me, I was knocked back a couple of steps by an elderly woman standing entirely too close to me who began frantically digging through her purse. It took her a while. The purse was so big it could be repurposed as a keep for a mob of wallabies. When I was able to turn my attention back to the man in the plumed hat, he was looking directly at me.

I tried ignoring him, but he was an obstinate fellow. "You, sirrah!" he repeated. "Prithee, tell us what bring you to these gates."

I decided to move on to glaring. I'm pretty good at glaring and for a moment it looked like he'd let me pass without further molestation, but the young woman in a low-cut blouse who had draped herself around his shoulders wouldn't have it. "Ah! A saucy knave!" she shouted. "Take care, sir, lest thine insolence lead thee to misfortune. Such ill humor could land you in the stocks—or worse."

"'Tis true, my lady," the young man said, rejoining the sport, "but by his sizable girth I'd reckon our visitor a wealthy merchant—a man, perhaps, unused to being accosted in the street. By faith, I warrant he has servants employed to be accosted in his stead."

He laughed at his joke, his mouth open wide, and his head thrown so far back that the tip of his plume tickled his rear end. The people around me ate it up. Drawing back, they snickered and pointed.

"Yes," agreed the woman with the cleavage, "he does present an exceedingly well-fed appearance and yet, the King's stocks have oft entertained even those of his eminence."

It was bad enough to be made fun of by strangers, but what made it worse was—perhaps owing to my inexperience with men in tights and their busty doxies—I found myself uncharacteristically at a loss for words, unable to come up with anything even approaching a decent comeback. In the end, I could but walk lamely away, the laughter of the crowd trailing after me. I was not happy.

Held every summer in the small town of Little Crow, some twenty-five miles south of my home in Minneapolis, the Midwest Renaissance Festival was billed as a full day of family fun, an opportunity to turn back the clock and visit a bygone land of knights in armor, wandering jugglers, lusty wenches, strolling minstrels, and eerie magicians wielding strange and mystical powers. I'd long maintained that I'd rather spend a day staked to a red-ant hill with my eyelids sewn open than spend it baking in the heat of an old cow pasture with hundreds of people playing out their fantasies from *Dungeons and Dragons*.

But after years of near constant cajoling from my friend and housemate, Stephen Edgerton, who worked at the festival's armory, I'd finally agreed to come out and visit him, provided that he get me in free and keep me well supplied with liquid refreshment. However, if my greeting at the front gate was any indication, I'd made a strikingly bad bargain.

It was partly my own fault. Although Edgerton had told me to avoid the main entrance, curiosity had convinced me to take a quick look. Now I was tempted to simply slink back home. Of course, I knew I couldn't. I could never admit to Edgerton that I'd gone all the way down there only to be driven off by two Shakespeare wannabes. So instead, this time I followed his directions and went around to the rear of the festival site where he'd said I would find another tower. He said I couldn't miss it. There was a large, working cannon sitting on top of it.

The ground was spongy, owing to some rain the night before, but the precip had done little to mitigate the extreme heat from which we'd been suffering the past few weeks. Although late September, summer's heat stubbornly lingered, unwilling to yield to the more temperate embrace of autumn. I hate hot, humid weather in the fall. I'm not real fond of it in the summer either, but at least it's supposed to be hot in the summer. By fall, heat and humidity are simply no longer welcome. Like the morning breath of a lover that you picked up in a bar the night before—heavy, stale, and oppressive, but still wanting to snuggle.

I slogged onward, my shirt already clinging obscenely to my skin. The site had been designed to look like a fourteenth century walled city. Along the perimeter stood a wall of spiked planks nearly fifteen feet tall, the weathered gray boards cordoning off about ten acres in a sloppy circle, several sections jutting out at odd angles. I followed the outer wall until I found the promised rear tower, at the bottom of which was a door inexpertly cobbled together. It was ajar, hanging crookedly on its hinges, and it screeched like an angry barn owl when I pushed it open. I entered a dark, cramped passageway. On the right, a narrow flight of stairs led to the top of the tower; on the left, light was leaking in through spaces between the planks in the wall. Ahead was another door, this one closed. I shrugged and pushed that one open as well.

Stepping through, I found myself standing alone behind a counter looking out upon a kind of open-air weapons mart. On the counter before me was an array of daggers with one nasty-looking mace intruding among the more elegant blades. Several large broadswords, battle-axes and long bows hung on the wall behind me. I hoped to sneak away unnoticed, but a man about forty years old, wearing a pair of pleated beige shorts, a ratty baseball cap, and a T-shirt that read, "Old Fishermen Never Die; Their Rods Just Go Limp," approached me.

Grinning excitedly, he pointed to one of the broadswords on the wall. "How much does something like that weigh?"

I stared at the broadsword. "I don't know. Looks pretty heavy. You gotta figure something like that runs six, maybe seven pounds."

The man's grin became a puzzled cipher. He paused, taking his time looking me over. Finally, he said, "You don't work here, do you?"

I glanced down at my blue jeans and my black T-shirt that read "Piggy's got the conch." and smiled. "No, I don't work here."

The man backed slowly away.

To the right of the counter, on the other side of a narrow wall, I spotted an open area where a tall, broad-shouldered man stood. He had long red hair and wore a leather apron. On the ground in front of him, another man crouched, turning something in the coals of an open fire pit. On a bench nearby, a third man sat holding a crossbow in his lap. Fumbling slightly, he laid an arrow into a groove on top of the stock before fitting it to the bowstring. Beside the fire pit, the crouching man raised a hand, and without looking, pulled a cord that was hanging above his head. This pull brought down an angled wooden arm, which operated a large bellows. The coals glowed a brilliant orange. The crouching man raised himself and looked my way. It was Edgerton.

"Hey, Lyle. You made it," he called to me. "Did you have any trouble finding the place?"

"No," I replied, finally extricating myself from behind the counter. "You were right. The cannon on the tower was a dead giveaway. I'm guessing it's the only cannon in the greater Little Crow metropolitan area."

Edgerton chuckled. "Actually, there's one at the front gate, but we like to have our own. You know, just in case."

"In case of what?"

"One never knows, does one?" Edgerton replied, as

5

he motioned for me to join him at the fire pit.

As I approached, the tall man bounded over to stand beside Edgerton, while the man with the crossbow placed it on the bench before getting to his feet. "This is my friend Lyle Dahms," Edgerton told them. "I've been after him for years to come out and see what we do." He paused, his mouth crooking into a smirk. "Feel honored. I know I do."

The tall man pulled a heavy leather glove off his hand and reached out to shake mine. It was a strong handshake and he paired it with a broad smile. "Donald Hess," he said, introducing himself. "It's a pleasure to have you with us, my good sir. Stephen has spoken of you often."

I dredged up a smile of my own. "If he's spoken of me often, it's a wonder that you're happy to meet me."

It wasn't much of a joke, but Hess laughed heartily, nonetheless. Although I had no memory of Edgerton introducing us before, something about Hess seemed warmly familiar to me, as though I'd known him a long time. Then it hit me. Hess looked like Edgerton. Not exactly like him, but close enough that they could be brothers. Both had enormous amounts of curly red hair spilling to their shoulders and both had neatly trimmed beards and mustaches. But Hess was the bigger man. His thick arms seemed made to heft the broadswords and axes that I'd seen displayed behind the counter. Edgerton was slighter, and where Hess had a broad face, a ready smile and a merry glint in his eyes, Edgerton was more feral, with quick, intelligent eyes and a smile that hinted that he knew more than he was letting on.

Edgerton then turned me toward the final member of their guild. "This is Jason Gilroy," he said, pointing to the man who'd been handling the crossbow.

Gilroy was shorter than average, with a slight paunch, dark, receding hair, and a bruise, mostly faded, high up on the left side of his head. He took my hand in a brief, weak handshake, his palm a bit on the dewy side. "You're the P.I., right?" he asked, smiling eagerly.

Too eagerly, I thought. It was a nervous smile, wide and brittle. The kind of smile that needs to be approached gingerly. A smile threaded with tripwires. The kind of smile that goes with my job. It happens all the time. Even though they've no more to hide than the next guy, some people I meet just get wary, as though they think that because I'm an investigator I'll have a preternatural ability to divine their secrets with a glance.

"Yeah," I said glumly, "and it's every bit as glamorous as you've heard."

Gilroy let out a quiet sigh. "Pretty boring, huh?"

"Yeah. Pretty boring."

Gilroy held my gaze as though expecting something more. I let my eyes wander. The silence grew awkward.

"Come on, Lyle," Edgerton said at last, "let me show you around the armory."

"One of you guys might want to hang out a little closer to that counter of yours," I suggested as we all walked away from the fire and back into the main display area. "Someone might take off with one of those daggers."

"Do not worry yourself, good Sir Lyle," said Hess. "There isn't much crime in King Henry's realm. And if some varlet does commit offense against the king's peace, he will find us defenders of that peace strong, resolute, and..." he paused, "heavily armed." With that Hess snatched a broadsword from a rack on the wall and raised it, with a laugh, high above his head.

A nearby group of customers stepped back in alarm and Hess quickly replaced the sword. He turned to the group, shrugged his shoulders, and bowed his head, peeking out at them with the look of a little boy who knows he has done something wrong, but also knows that he will be forgiven. Then, smiling his enormous smile, Hess clapped one of the men on the back, ushering him closer to the display. The rest of the group followed. Gilroy drifted along with them.

Someone pointed, asking "How much does that weigh?"

"You would like a tour, wouldn't you, Lyle?" Edgerton asked me. His tone indicated that "no" would be a most unacceptable answer.

"Sure," I replied, conjuring up as much cheerfulness as I could. "I mean, 'when in Rome' and all that."

"Actually," Edgerton said, "we're some one thousand to seventeen hundred years after the height of Roman power. It's hard to be more specific since the timeline is a little…Shall we say a little fluid around here."

"Fluid?"

"Yeah. They call this a Renaissance Festival which you might think would mean that the site tries to recreate life in the Europe of the fourteenth to seventeenth centuries, but that's really not true. For example, in addition to Renaissance arms and armor, Don and I also re-create medieval arms, that is to say the arms and armor of Europe from about 476 AD when Romulus Augustus, the last Roman emperor was deposed, to about 1453, when the Turks conquered Constantinople."

I stared at him. "You know, it sometimes frightens

me that you never seem to need to look any of this stuff up."

Edgerton snorted. "How long was the *Fibber McGee and Molly* show on the air?"

"Twenty-one years," I replied. "1935 to 1956. Twenty-two if you include the short-lived TV show. That only lasted one season. 1959."

"See," Edgerton said, "you think it's scary that I can remember a few historical tidbits while you retain minutiae concerning decades old TV shows that only ran for a single season."

"Point taken."

"I'm just trying to tell you that if you came here for a history lesson, you'll be disappointed. Our stand at least strives for authenticity, while as far as the powers that be are concerned anything that predates *Fibber McGee & Molly* qualifies for inclusion in this so-called Renaissance Festival. That is, as long it makes money, and the proprietors toss out a few 'thees' and 'thous' and promise to shout 'huzzah!' as they ring up each sale."

"What powers would that be?"

"Midwest Renaissance Festival Incorporated. It's the company that runs the show. They grant concession contracts, hire the entertainers, and all that."

"You mean," I said with a mock sob. "You mean King Henry isn't really in charge?"

"No," Edgerton said. "He is not."

"Next you're gonna tell me that there's no Barney or Big Bird."

"Well, I don't know about Barney, but there really is a King Henry. He's just not in charge. He's an actor. His name is Otis. Otis McInerny. For as long as I've worked here, Otis has played King Henry, each year with a new queen. You know, the many wives of Henry the Eighth. That kind of thing. You're bound to run into him parading around out here playing lord of the realm and goosing whoever is unfortunate enough to be this year's Queen. The fellow's a pompous gasbag if you ask me." Edgerton chuckled. "Yeah, we can thank the gods that at least old Otis is not in charge. It's bad enough that he thinks he is."

Hess had managed to pilot a few lookee-loos from the weapons display down to the cashbox at the end of the counter. To avoid the crowd, Edgerton led me to the opposite end of the armory, there to show me some of their other wares. What first caught my eye was a wooden mannequin, torso only, dressed in a chain mail coat. I recognized the coat. I'd watched Edgerton make it. He'd spent innumerable hours, sitting on his bed with his legs curled pasha-like under him, winding heavy gauge wire into long springs, then snipping the small rings from the spring, and finally soldering the rings together. Completed, the fabric resembled woven iron.

"That's your coat," I said, pointing.

"Yeah. It's more of shirt really. It's called a hauberk."

"You wouldn't sell it."

"Why not?"

I shook my head. "Because it took you the better part of your life to make the thing, that's why not."

Edgerton smiled. "You're right. I wouldn't sell it. Don just asked me to bring it out here as part of our display. We got all sorts of things here that we don't really expect to sell. Out here people mostly only buy the small stuff, daggers, and the like. Occasionally we sell a sword or a mace, but things like the chain mail coat or even this Saxon half armor or that German cuirass over there." He pointed at other pieces of armor displayed around us. "Well, it wouldn't be real smart to shell out big bucks for authentic armor unless you were sure it was going to fit you. And in order to be sure it will fit, you have to have it custom made. We have examples of that kind of work out here and if someone is really interested, we hand them our catalog and have them call us at our workshop."

"So, this stuff is worth big bucks?"

"Yep."

"How big?"

"Pretty big."

"So how come I'm always buying you beers at McCauley's?"

Edgerton laughed. "How many people you know are willing spend a sizable portion of their hard-earned scratch on suit of custom-made armor?"

"Not many."

"Me neither."

"You know," I said, turning back to the mannequin, "that chain mail shirt of yours would look better with a head."

Edgerton hummed. "You know, you're right. And I think…I think I have something…" he said looking around. "There it is. That old barrel helm. That'll work."

Edgerton crossed the armory to the opposite wall where a flat-topped helmet with long, thin eye slits hung from a nail. He brought the helmet over and placed it on top of the mannequin. Taking a step back, he smiled.

"You're welcome," I said.

Edgerton rolled his eyes. "You'll be flouncing around the house putting doilies under tchotchkes next."

"You think?"

"I'm sure of it. Want to go look at the rest of the festival site?" Once again, it was more of a command than a question.

Catching Hess' eye, Edgerton told him he'd be taking off to give me a quick tour. "Go," Hess replied, sweeping his muscular arm expansively before him. "Go and partake of the pleasures of the kingdom. Sample the wares of a hundred nations. Lose yourself in the splendor that surrounds you. Yet mind that you return before our demo at eleven o'clock."

Edgerton nodded, then removed his apron. Underneath, he was costumed simply in a plain maroon woven shirt and a pair of beige twill pants, each of his legs wrapped with straps of cloth cross-gartered to the knee.

"I always figured that you guys wore armor while you were out here," I said.

"Not very often. It's too heavy to work in and way too hot. We put on some armor every day, but usually not for very long. Today, however, we'll be armoring up a bit more than usual."

"What's that mean?"

"I'll tell you later."

"Tell me now."

Edgerton smiled but made no further comment.

As we turned to leave the armory, I caught sight of Gilroy across the crowd. He'd retreated to a corner and seemed to be in deep conversation with a man who, from his costume, I took to be another festival employee. The other man stood a head taller than Gilroy, had dark wavy hair and was wearing leather breeches and a silvery chain mail vest which was open to reveal a muscular upper body. Gilroy stood with his back to the wall, the other man leaning in only inches from his face. Gilroy was smiling, but there was no mirth in his eyes. Far from it. He looked like a guest at a dinner party who's just bit into something rancid but is too polite to let it show.

I wanted to ask Edgerton about this friend of Gilroy's but was interrupted when a rotund man in a pair of lumpy, khaki shorts that had to have been two sizes too small for him came bulldozing our way, apparently bent on sizing up Edgerton's chain mail coat. After stepping out of his way, I turned back to find that the man with whom Gilroy had been talking had disappeared and Gilroy himself was coming toward us. "Are you two knaves taking your leave?" he asked.

"Yeah," Edgerton told him. "I want to take Lyle on the grand tour, and judging by the way he's sweating, he might need a cold one. Maybe even one of those turkey legs the yokels like to gnaw on."

Gilroy stared. Behind his vacant eyes the wheels in his head made an almost audible whir. At last, he cocked his head and blinked rapidly several times like a flirtatious pigeon. "'Tis strange, sir knight," he said stiffly, "but methinks that thy very manner of speech has been affected by the appearance of this gentleman. Your discourse has become littered with expressions that those of this land knoweth not. Perhaps this be not the friend you think, but rather some magician of ill intent who has taken the form of your friend."

Edgerton responded with a deep, obsequious bow. "Forsooth," he said, his voice now syrupy with sarcasm, "I did forget myself. Let me repeat that it is my intention to show Sir Lyle some of our happy land. Perhaps on this journey we might stop at an ale house for a libation or some roasted capon or other fowl."

Although Edgerton had clearly meant it as a joke, Gilroy lowered his eyes immediately and seemed to shrink within himself, clenching up like a nudist in a snowstorm. Noticing, Edgerton forced a smile and, although not normally demonstrative, he placed a hand on Gilroy's shoulder. "We'll be right back, Jason."

Walking out into the sunshine, Edgerton said, "Both Don and Jason are always giving me a hard time because I don't like to speak the lingo. I used to think it was a hoot, but I swear, the next time someone in costume walks up to me and, for no particular reason, says "'Tis strange, 'tis passing strange, I think I'll gut him."

I glanced back to the armory. Gilroy had disappeared among the customers, swallowed whole by the swirling crowd. Strangely, I found his absence soothing. Everything about Gilroy struck me as out of place. It wasn't his fault, but he made me uncomfortable. For their part, Hess and Edgerton seemed to have been born to their roles, ordered up from central casting to play their parts in this odd mixture of history and make-believe. Not so with Gilroy. His nearly palpable anxiety set me on edge. He just seemed to be trying so very hard. He could hit his marks; he could say the words, but like the lead in a high school production of King Lear, fresh-faced behind a false beard, the role simply wasn't in him.

I didn't have long to ponder it, however. When I turned back to Edgerton, I found him nearly a dozen paces away, cresting the rise of small hill opposite the armory where sat a lovely cottage with thick walls and a thatched roof. I had to break into a little jog to catch up with him.

You'd think that having pestered me to join him out

there, Edgerton would have played the excited host, showing me around and pointing out the many delights that the festival offered. No such luck. Instead, he led me about the grounds treating me to a running commentary on how inauthentic everything was and how everything disgusted him. There were six stages positioned about the grounds where various performers appeared hourly, and although the crowds gathered at each seemed quite pleased, Edgerton refused to let me stop, characterizing all the festival's entertainment as troops of amateur jugglers and so-called minstrels doing Led Zeppelin tunes on lutes.

Passing the numerous booths where potters and glassblowers, jewelers and leather workers demonstrated their crafts to clusters of rapt customers, Edgerton complained that everything was overpriced and groused that he could never understand why anyone with any sense would pony up sixty bucks just to get into a place where the main source of entertainment was to spend too much money on things that nobody really needed. He had particular disdain for a booth displaying gold and silver chain mail garments that he dubbed "the kinky sex chain mail shop." Behind the counter, a tawny blonde— her shining locks, I thought, more a product of chemistry than heredity—modeled a gold, chain mail bikini. An underwire version judging by the way the gleaming brassiere lifted and separated.

"No way that stuff is gonna protect you in combat," Edgerton opined.

"I don't think that protection is exactly what they're marketing over there."

We were about to move on when a man joined the blonde behind the counter. It was the same dark-haired man I'd seen speaking to Gilroy back at the armory. He spoke briefly to the blonde, took a moment to straighten a few items on the counter, then looked up. To my surprise, when he spotted us, he scowled unpleasantly.

Turning his beak-like nose to the air, he sniffed like a finicky crow refusing a piece of carrion. "You there," he called to Edgerton. "You tell that friend of yours I've got his number."

In his congress with the world around him, my friend Edgerton had two basic modes. He was either fascinated or completely disinterested. And while he was able to get worked up enough to decry the lack of utility that distinguished the booth's under-protective chain mail, Edgerton had no time for the man who purveyed it. He didn't so much a break stride or give the guy a second glance.

The guy in the chain mail clearly wasn't used to being ignored. Flushing a shade of aubergine usually reserved for garden vegetables, he rose to his feet, shaking an impotent fist after us and shouting, "You just tell him! You just tell him!"

Edgerton simply kept walking.

"What was that about?" I asked.

He shrugged. "I have no idea."

"Whose number does he supposedly have?"

Edgerton shrugged again. "I've seen him with Jason a couple of times."

"Okay," I pressed. "But that sounded a whole bunch like a threat. Doesn't that worry you?"

Edgerton shook his head. "The guy's just a blowhard."

"You're not even a teensy bit concerned that he might be a problem for Gilroy?"

Edgerton stopped for a moment. "We work in an armory, Lyle. We're surrounded by heavy weapons. Who'd be stupid enough to come after one of us?"

He started walking again. "Besides," he said over his shoulder, "now we have you."

Although the chain mail guy apparently didn't interest him, something else evidently did. For most of the tour I'd had the impression that Edgerton was content to lead me aimlessly about the grounds, but I began to get a sense that our journey wasn't aimless at all. There was something, I realized, that he wanted to show me, and after a sweep past several food stands—including one from which, despite the supposed Renaissance setting, wafted what my well-tuned Minnesota State Fair senses told me was the unmistakable fragrance of corn dog—two small-scale castles came into view. Each was complete with rounded towers and spires from which flew colorful banners. Tapestries embellished with intricately rendered coats of arms hung from the walls and one of the castles featured a drawbridge spanning a gravel-filled faux moat.

Edgerton paused, his lips drawn together tightly as though fighting back a smile. "See that building over there? They call that castle Joyous Guard, home of the legendary Lancelot du Lac, the most accomplished knight in Christendom."

"How 'bout the other castle? Who lives there?"

Edgerton frowned briefly. "That's King Henry's place. But this one over here, this one belongs to Lancelot."

"I thought Lancelot worked for King Arthur. What happened? Did King Henry offer him more money?"

Edgerton nodded. "Turned free agent. Just ain't no

loyalty in the joust game."

"The joust game?"

"Yeah. Lancelot and his cronies don't just hang out here at the Guard, staring at each other across the round table and squirting libations into their gobs from wineskins. No, this year they hired some big bruiser of a thespian to play Lancelot on the back of a horse. He's going to joust with Don. Twice a day. This weekend only. At least to start. They might make it a regular feature if it makes a big enough splash."

"This place never had jousting before?"

"Yes, Lyle, they had jousting before," Edgerton said patiently. "But this is different. Used to be they'd have horsemen tilting at rings or making passes at a burlap effigy. This year we're going at it *mano a mano*."

"We?"

Edgerton nodded. "Jason and I are going to be Don's squires, sworn to serve Sir Donald of Hess, to attend him during his duel with Lancelot and, if necessary, to clash with the opposing squires."

"Sounds dangerous."

"Not really. I mean, it would be if both Don and the guy playing Lancelot weren't both experienced in this sort of thing. Heck, they've even jousted each other before. At some Ren Fest down in Texas." A slight frown passed over Edgerton's features. "Don doesn't seem to like this Lancelot much though. We've all met a couple of times to plan this thing, but other than that Don hasn't been much interested in paling around with him."

"So, these guys armor up and gallop at each other holding lances?"

"That's how it begins. Yes."

"Sounds dangerous," I repeated.

"Oh, it's all choreographed down to the last detail. They make a few passes at each other. Finally, one of them falls from his horse and both end the combat on foot with broadswords. Jason and I get to exchange swipes with Lancelot's guys and, of course, good triumphs over evil."

"Who gets to win?"

"That would be telling."

"Give me a hint."

"Well, Lancelot is the greatest knight in the history of the world, while Don's character is nicknamed the Black Knight. Suffice it to say that the Black Knight doesn't get to kick butt over the defender of all that is noble and pure."

"Damn. Ain't that always the way."

Edgerton snorted. "Come on. I'll show you the jousting ring."

A few paces from the castles, we rounded a large elm tree and came upon a clearing where a fence of rough-hewn logs enclosed a rectangular field about fifty yards long. At one end of the field was a podium with a small stand of bleachers and two thrones in the center. In the middle of the field, a ring hung from a pole about five feet from the ground, and on the other side hung an effigy of a knight made of stuffed burlap.

Edgerton stared at field with a wistful shimmer in his eyes. He'd drawn his lips together in a rigid line, the corners of his mouth curved ever so slightly upward.

I chuckled. "You're not looking forward to this, are you?"

Edgerton kept up the struggle to hold back his grin. The grin won. "You know, every year I tell myself that I'm not going to do the festival anymore. Every year I complain about the heat or the cold, about the stupid questions and the stupid exhibitors, the overpriced food, and the whole tackiness of it all. But every year something comes along to make it worthwhile. Some years it's just the people. I've made a couple of real friends out here. But this year it's this joust. I can't believe I'm admitting this, but I'm really pretty excited about it. Donning armor. The clash of steel. The splintering of lances. Locking swords with my opponent as a crowd of spectators munches on fried cheese curds. It's pathetic."

"I promise not to tell anyone. I wouldn't want to ruin your reputation."

We continued on and soon came upon a small, two-wheeled, wooden cart with a banner that read "Elephant Rides." At first, I thought it was some kind of medieval joke—the plague years in particular being known as an era of wacky cutups—when on the other side of the cart I spied an actual, honest-to-God elephant tied to a post. Nearby, a small oval track had been scraped into the ground. Next to the track a medium-sized man with a slender, muscular build, was kneeling and talking to a young boy in a wheelchair. The man, shirtless but wearing an open yellow and white striped vest, was laughing and pointing at an older boy who, limping slightly, was leading yet another elephant around the track. The boy in the wheelchair and two tow-headed youngsters seated atop the elephant were also laughing.

"Those are the Petersons," Edgerton told me. "Really nice people. The little one has some kind of brittle bone disease. The older one has one leg shorter than the other. They don't seem to let it bother them much, though. The older kid, Jack—helluva video game player."

I hadn't immediately noticed, distracted as I was by the sight of mounted elephants disporting themselves in suburban Minneapolis, but we'd completed our circuit. Both the armory and the small cottage opposite it were within clear sight of the elephant track.

"What is that cottage for?" I asked.

"They call it the Irish Cottage. It's pretty, but it doesn't serve much of a function. Occasionally an event is staged in there, but it's often just empty."

"Pity," I said, "nicest building out here."

"Nicer than my armory?" Edgerton asked, his voice rising in mock agitation. "Them's fightin' words!" He swiveled around comically. "And me without my trusty sword."

I glanced back toward the elephant track. The older Peterson was gone. His youngest son now sat alone, still smiling, watching the older boy.

Hess was still working the crowd at the armory. As we approached, he took a broadsword from the rack on the wall and handed it to a customer.

"It makes me a little uneasy to see you guys handing over weapons to just anybody who walks up and asks," I told Edgerton.

"Don't worry," he assured me, "we don't sharpen anything until we actually sell it. The edges of the swords are blunt."

I looked at him skeptically.

"Well," he admitted, "we do sharpen the daggers, and of course, the maces are bit on the lethal side, but the swords are dull and the display arrows—they're called bolts really—are plastic. In my ten years out here, we have never had an accident."

Gilroy was waving to us from the fire pit. We waved back as he walked out in front of the building to greet us. He was smiling, standing with his back to the armory's wall when I heard it. A hissing sound, as loud as a striking cobra, whistled past us, followed by a sharp knock like a hammer striking a board.

Startled, I whirled to see where it came from. Spotting nothing, I immediately turned back toward Gilroy. He was still standing, but his knees had buckled. He slumped, his back against the wall, as if he was trying to sit, but something prevented him. His smile had tightened into a wince. His eyes were wide and there was surprisingly little blood flowing from his neck where a still quivering arrow pinned him to the wall.

Chapter Two

Cops don't like me. They ask what I do for a living, and when I tell them that I'm a private investigator, they get this look. It's like I'm telling them that they're not doing their jobs or something. Like if they worked harder, I wouldn't have to be an investigator. I could be a circus geek or a bank foreclosure specialist, something more respectable. The cop I spoke to didn't like me. His name was Thompson, and although I answered his questions honestly and completely, he kept calling me "fella." Finally, he told me the chief was definitely going to want to speak to me later. As he finished and went to interview someone else, he backed away carefully, stroking his goatee, and eyeing me like I was something he didn't want to step in.

I went over and stood next to Edgerton who sat on a bucket just outside the armory, his head in his hands. It was early afternoon and a shadow had covered the wall where Gilroy had died. The county coroner's office had already come and gone. Though Gilroy's body had been removed, a police photographer continued to take pictures. The popping of his flashes was joined by the flashes of the cameras of festivalgoers who were not about to go home without capturing the image for their memory books.

Just outside the tape that the cops had strung to cordon off the crime scene, four local TV crews fought over the best spots to do their standups. They kept yelling at us to come over and talk to them. Several people who were in the area when Gilroy was shot had already been interviewed, many by each of the news crews. Most told their stories with that same weird mixture of horror and joy that comes when, despite describing the grisly scene that they had witnessed, they realize with excitement that they are going to be on TV that night. Both Edgerton and I avoided making eye contact with the TV people, hoping that if we ignored them, they would go away.

"You gonna be all right. Stephen?" I asked.

"Yeah," he replied without raising his head. "It's just a helluva thing, you know?"

"Yeah. I know."

"You, fella!" Officer Thompson called. "Get over here. And bring your friend."

Next to Thompson stood a tall blond man in uniform. About forty-five, he looked like he knew his way around the gym. He had a massive chest and impressive shoulders, but his head looked a little too small for his weightlifter's body, as though by inflating his shoulders and chest he had mistakenly let a little air out of his skull.

When we reached them, Thompson pointed at my friend and told Mr. Olympus, "This one is Edgerton, he worked with the deceased. The fat fella is Dahms. I told you about him."

"Only nice things, I hope," I said.

"Shut up, Dahms," snapped the big man. "I'm Chief Dunstable and you're going to tell me everything you know."

"I told your Officer Thompson everything. What? Is he keeping stuff from you?"

Dunstable just stared at me. "I checked you out, Dahms. I talked to the Minneapolis PD. They just love you over there. Hell, I talked directly to the head of your freakin' fan club, a homicide cop named Augustus Tarkof. He told me that you're too stupid to keep from meddling in police investigations. He says if I want to make things easy on myself, I should drop you in a hole somewhere. Says if I invite him, he'll bring a shovel."

"Augie's just a little miffed because even though he sends flowers, I can never find the time to call."

Dunstable grunted. "Just what the hell are you doing here anyway?"

"Like I told your officer, I came out here for a day of merrymaking. Just like everyone else. My friend Edgerton here works at the armory, and he asked me to spend the day with him. I met Gilroy for the first time today. Then I got to see him die."

"Where were you when you saw him die?"

"We were approaching the armory from over there, over to the left, between the jousting ring and that cottage to the right. The arrow came from behind us to our left. If I had to guess, I'd say the shooter was over by the cottage."

"I didn't ask you to guess," Dunstable said. "Did anyone see you at the time the arrow was shot?"

"Gilroy. He was walking out of the armory."

Dunstable grunted again. "Anybody else?"

"Maybe Dick Peterson," Edgerton replied, still hanging his head.

"Who?" asked Dunstable.

"Dick Peterson," Edgerton repeated. "The guy in charge of the elephant rides. I remember we were looking at him just before we heard the arrow go past.

25

He could have seen us."

Dunstable nodded. "Anything you can add to this, Dahms?" he asked, a corner of his mouth curled into a sneer. "We're real lucky to have had a professional like yourself on hand when this happened. With your powers of observation and all, I'm sure you saw something that's gonna crack this thing wide open for us."

"Can the sarcasm, Chief," I said. "Somebody just died. His friends are within earshot. Quit the crap and start doing your job."

Dunstable tried the cold stare again. "Just remember that it is my job, fat boy. I don't want to hear that you've got anything more to do with this."

"Bite me."

Dunstable chuckled and started to walk away.

"Chief, one thing puzzles me," I called after him. "Why haven't you shut this down?"

The chief turned around. "Shut what down?"

"The festival."

Dunstable looked puzzled. "Why would I do that?"

"Jeez, Chief, I don't know. Maybe because you've got a killer loose?"

He gave me a patient smile tinged with menace. "The killer's gonna be miles from here. These people pay me to protect them, not shut down their businesses."

Dunstable loped away. Thompson gave me another long look before trailing after his boss.

Edgerton suggested that we go into the armory to get away from the crowd. "There are a couple of rooms in the tower. Or we could sit on the balcony. Let's just get out of here for a while."

"Yeah," I agreed, watching Edgerton closely.

He was very quiet, rarely looked up, and moved in a

slow shuffle as if his legs had become too heavy for him to walk with his normal gait. He was obviously in need of some comfort. I tried to think of something to say but couldn't think of anything. I was going to put my hand on his shoulder but hesitated just long enough for him to move out of my reach. Instead, I stuck my hands in my pockets and followed him toward the door behind the armory's counter.

We were nearly there when Hess came out. His eyes had lost their former gleam, but unlike Edgerton, he held his head high—his expression somber but alert, as though he didn't want to miss anything. As he emerged from the building and saw Edgerton, he immediately reached out and put his arm around my friend's shoulders and ushered him through the door. I took my hands out of my pockets and stared at them uselessly before I followed the men inside.

It took a couple of seconds for my eyes to become accustomed to the darkness within. The two men had gone upstairs, and I followed them to the top of the tower. There, on either side of a narrow hallway, were two small rooms. Through their open doors I could see that the floor of each room was nearly covered by bedding. What little space remained was taken up by neatly folded clothes and scattered paperback books. In one of the rooms, a couple of long dresses hung from nails on the wall.

As I stepped out onto a balcony, a woman rose from a chair and crossed toward the two men. As she neared, Hess removed his arm from Edgerton's shoulders just as the woman spread her arms to embrace him. She held him tightly and his face disappeared into her cascading curls of long blonde hair. Although Edgerton's arms encircled the young woman's slender frame, he held her only weakly, as though his strength had been drained from him. She held him even more tightly before she released him and took both of his hands in her own. She turned her beautiful face toward him, tossed her head slightly, and attempted a smile. She had been crying. Her blue eyes were rimmed with red.

"A terrible thing," she said, her voice cracking. "I can't believe he's really…"

She didn't finish the thought.

Hess looked at me, then glanced at the woman and smiled slightly. "Lyle Dahms," he said, "this is my wife, Julia."

Julia let one of Edgerton's hands drop and reached out to take mine. "A terrible thing," she repeated.

I nodded silently.

Three chairs crowded to one side of the balcony and a twine hammock took up nearly the entire opposite side. Hess reached out and directed his wife to a chair, then sat in the chair next to hers. Edgerton took a position cross-legged on the floor, and I sat in the remaining chair. No one spoke. Hess held his wife's hand, Edgerton stared at the floor, and I found myself wondering if I was sitting in Gilroy's accustomed place. I wondered how many summer weekends he'd been in this chair, looking out at the view of the festival site, his eyes shielded from the sun by the shade of the awning, a slight breeze cooling him as it tickled through his thinning hair. I thought about where he was now. I sat looking out at the sunshine and thought about the darkness of the morgue. Gilroy had no need for a breeze. In the morgue you ain't nothing but cold.

"Our crossbow's been taken," Hess said, breaking

the silence.

"Did the cops find it?" I asked.

"If they did, they didn't show it to me."

"They would have," I told him. "They'd have wanted you to identify it."

"Jason and I made that crossbow," Edgerton said quietly. "Mostly Jason. He's much better working with wood than I am."

"Anything else missing?" I asked.

"I took a look around," Hess said. "Everything else seems to be here."

"No arrows missing?"

Hess eyed me knowingly.

"It wasn't one of ours" he told me. "And technically they're bolts, not arrows. We use plastic target bolts. The bolt that killed Jason had a wood shaft and an aluminum tip." He winced, shook his head. "Nasty thing. That police chief…What's his name? Dunstable?"

"Dung-stubble," I corrected.

Hess made a guttural noise. It could have been a laugh.

"Dunstable showed me the bolt."

Nobody talked for some time. The news crews were still milling around below us, and a couple of cops were posted around the yellow cop tape that fenced off the part of the armory where Gilroy had died, but the crowd of festivalgoers huddled at the death scene was thinning out. Beyond the armory, the festival continued. Children scampered across the open field beyond the cottage where a man in what looked like a corduroy loincloth was throwing a boomerang.

I was about to suggest that I go fetch us some beers when I noticed a group of people in costume approaching the armory.

"Oh, great," Edgerton muttered. "Here comes Otis."

Leading the troupe was a rather stout, middle-aged man with a dark brown beard and mustache wearing a purple robe edged with white fur, a pair of maroon tights, and tall black boots. He had a gold crown perched solidly on his head and as he walked, he held his left hand out oddly at a ninety-degree angle to his body as if he had lost track of the hand and it was now acting independently of the rest of him. Holding on to the fingertips of the outstretched hand was a young woman in a light blue silken dress, a purple robe also draped across her shoulders. She wore a much smaller crown and an expression on her face like she was hoping that no one she knew would see her in this company.

Behind the King and Queen, three men in armor clanked along. The first was a big man, about six foot five with shoulder-length brown hair and a blank expression on his handsome face. Although he wore no helmet, he wore a full suit of gunmetal blue armor that squeaked loudly at the joints as he moved. Behind him were two smaller men who wore only breastplates but were outfitted with visorless helmets with long nosepieces extending between their eyes. The two guys in the rear carried long wooden pikes.

"I suppose we better go down," Hess said, without stirring.

The costumed visitors had reached the armory and were busily shuffling their feet and trying to decide what to do next before Julia rose, took her husband's hand, and led him toward the door.

"Try to be nice," she said. "They are likely here to offer condolences."

Hess nodded at his wife, but there was something in his eyes that glinted like steel.

We went down to greet our guests.

When we reached them, no one spoke. They just continued shuffling and looking at the ground, except the King, who cocked his head and let his eyes wander the armory as if he were checking for spider webs.

Finally, Julia broke the silence. "How good of you to come to offer your sympathy. It is really very kind of you."

Otis puffed himself up. "It is surely the least that we can do. This has come as quite a shock, you know."

"For all of us," Julia said.

"Yes. Yes..." stammered Otis. "Well, I-I mean, we knew so little of your friend. We had no idea that this sort of thing might occur. It certainly is a dreadful thing for the festival."

"It wasn't such a great deal for Gilroy either," I said.

Otis flushed. "Well, I didn't mean that...I didn't mean to say that...It's not like I'm insensitive to the fact that...I mean..."

"Keep at it, your highness," I suggested. "You're bound to finish one of those sentences sooner or later."

Otis flushed even deeper and looked to his companions for support. One of the pike bearers struggled to stifle a smile. The others were silent.

Otis turned to Hess. "Who is this man?"

"He's my guest".

"I don't like his tone."

"I get that a lot," I told him.

"I mean," Otis continued, "I come here with the intention of offering you my sympathy at the death of your comrade and I am treated rudely by this gentleman and coldly by the rest of you. I really don't know what I've done to deserve—"

Julia stepped forward. "I'm sure that no insult was intended. It's just been such a very bad day. Perhaps it would help if we all knew each other."

She pointed to me. "This is our friend, Lyle Dahms. Lyle, this is Otis McInerny, our King Henry. This is Candace Kincaid, our lovely Queen Anne, and this is our…" She paused and even seemed to blush slightly. "This is our Sir Lancelot, Gregory Eckels."

I looked at each of them and, without smiling, made a little bow. Evidently the two-foot soldiers did not merit an introduction. If it bothered them at all, they didn't let it show.

"A pleasure, sir," Otis said to me. "I apologize for taking offense. I realize that this has been a terrible day for all of you. And for all of us."

"Yes," Julia replied, taking Otis by the arm. "We cannot imagine why anyone would…Why anyone…" She broke into sobs. Otis, looking embarrassed, started to back away. Eckels stepped forward and laid a hand on Julia's shoulder. She lifted her face, her teary eyes thanking him for his sympathy, but then her expression clouded, and she stepped away.

I looked over at Hess. His face registered nothing as he coldly observed the scene.

Julia went to her husband and leaned against him. Hess put his arm around her and softly smiled as she placed her head against his shoulder.

Otis again let his eyes wander about the room. Then he inhaled deeply, as though mustering the courage to say something. "Even at times such as this," he said, "we cannot allow ourselves to be overcome. We have to look to tomorrow."

"What do you want to say, Otis?" Hess asked.

"Well," Otis began, looking first at his feet and then glancing carefully at me. "I've spoken with the festival organizers, and they have agreed that there is no question of our proceeding with the planned joust today."

"No question," Hess agreed.

"But they point out that this joust has been heavily promoted and that it is important that we not let this unfortunate tragedy ruin the festival. Not after all that we, all of us, have invested in it. All the work that we have done. All of the hopes that we have maintained. We must…We must try to focus on the good of all. I think that is what…uh, that is what…" Otis paused. "That is what Jason would have wanted."

Edgerton's head snapped up, and before any of us could react, he sprang toward the King, and reached out quickly to take the actor by the throat. "Shut up, you asshole," he said, his voice strangely, even eerily calm. "You don't know shit." He fingers tightened, but I noted, without exerting real pressure. "What Jason would want most right now is to draw breath. He's past caring about your goddamned make-believe kingdom."

Otis, bug-eyed, searched wildly around for help. Eckels stepped forward, but I got to Edgerton first. I reached up and removed his hand from the royal throat but could not resist winking at the frightened monarch as I led Edgerton away.

"Perhaps this is not the time," Eckels said, as calm returned. "We can talk about this later." He turned to Hess. "Perhaps you could come by the office later this afternoon. Nothing's written in stone. We can talk about it with the festival organizers."

Hess nodded but said nothing.

As the costumed troupe departed, I turned to Edgerton. Not really angry, he seemed a little more alive, not quite as listless as he had appeared since the murder.

"Feel better now?" I asked, not entirely able to stifle a smile.

"A little."

"Nothing like roughin' up some blowhard to perk up the blood."

"I don't think I've ever done anything like that before."

"'Bout time," I told him. I turned to Hess. "Is there any place around here where we could get some beers?"

Hess nodded. "The Cock and Bull. They have beer and wine. Music sometimes." He looked at his wife, saw something there, then shook his head. "You go," he said. "Maybe we'll catch up with you."

Hess took Julia gently by the arm and led her back into the armory.

"There's something going on there," I told Edgerton as we walked to the tavern.

He crinkled his forehead at me. "What do you mean?"

"I'm not sure yet."

"You gonna find out?"

"I hope not."

****

It was after lunchtime and the tavern was crowded with customers. A young man and woman, he with a guitar and she carrying a basket of flowers, took a standing position just inside the tavern and began to perform what I took to be a medieval English madrigal. The woman sang lead and the man joined in on harmony.

34

The occupants of a table at the rear of the tavern moved forward to hear the music better, so I was able to plant Edgerton there, before going to the bar for our beers. When I returned, Edgerton drank deeply, looked up at me, inhaled, then paused and took another draught of beer.

"It wasn't really Otis' fault," he said.

"What wasn't?"

"It wasn't really even Otis that I got mad at. I'm not sure what made me do it. I guess this thing's got me all screwed up."

I nodded.

"I mean," Edgerton continued, "this morning I was so psyched about the joust. I mean really excited. It seems so stupid now. I feel so…foolish."

"Death changes things."

Edgerton closed his eyes and shook his head as though trying to shake loose a thought. "That sound," he said.

"Sound?"

"Yeah. The sound of that arrow striking the wall." He paused, then looked up at me. "That fucking sound. There's this Old English verse fragment. Most scholars call it *The Fight at Finnsburg*. You know it?"

"No."

"There's this line. Gathered in the hall, a group of warriors are waiting for dawn and a battle to come. One of them, a young man anticipating how at sunrise their position will be attacked first with a volley of arrows, says, 'Soon shall be the cough of birds, hoar wolf's howl, hard wood-talk, shield's answer to shaft.' That's the sound. The whistle of the arrow flying past. The knock of the arrow against the wood as it pierced Jason's neck.

That 'cough of birds.' I'll be hearing that cough for the rest of my life."

I sighed. "Let's have a couple more beers."

Edgerton nodded. "Let's have a whole bunch more beers."

Chapter Three

We had a whole bunch more beers. We drank while the crowd thronged around us. We drank as jugglers passed through the room and minstrels wandered by, playing instruments I had never even imagined. We drank as men pounded beer steins on the tables and pinched women in long dresses and who displayed wondrous cleavage. We drank as the men were slapped, and laughing, stumbled away toward the privies. We drank as the crowd thinned out and we were still drinking when dusk settled and the cannon at the front gate boomed thunderously to signal the close of the festival.

Even though the taps were off, and they were cleaning up around us, no one working at the tavern asked us to leave. I looked around blearily and every time I caught someone's eye, they gave me a sympathetic smile and a nod of the head. Finally, a tall, young woman carrying a wash rag approached our table. She wore the requisite low-cut peasant dress and had a scattering of freckles across the top of her breasts. "We need to be going now," she informed us gently, "but you guys can stay here as long as you like. We all know what happened today and how you must be feeling."

She looked kindly at Edgerton, then knowingly at me. Her mouth was a tiny red bow between two chubby, freckled cheeks, which in turn were framed by great waves of unruly, red hair. I tried to focus on her eyes but found myself drawn to her mouth. It was really too small, not so small that it ruined her pretty face, but small enough to make it distinctive, intriguing. I wondered if she would mind my kissing her.

"It's okay," she assured us, "stay as long as you want. Lots of us gather here every night after dinner anyway." I imagined she was looking at me intently as she said, "You won't be alone tonight. That is, unless you want to be."

"Thanks," I muttered. "It's not good to be alone."

As she left, I found myself fervently wishing that I hadn't had quite so much to drink. I glanced at my watch, but it was too much of an effort to make out the hands. I reached for my beer cup but knocked it over. No matter, it was empty. I looked up and saw that Edgerton was leaning back in his chair, eyes closed, his head tilted at an odd angle. "Stephen!" I called, more loudly than I had wanted to. "Closing time. Let's go get something to eat."

Edgerton sputtered a bit but stood up without protest when I tugged at his sleeve.

Not really knowing where to go, I led my friend back toward the armory. As we walked, I noticed that a large tent was being erected atop a low rise behind the Irish cottage. Several men worked to set the poles and pull the ropes taut while one tall, rather stout man strolled aimlessly around them, holding something large close to his body. He fiddled with it for a while, then raised a long black stem to his mouth. The stillness of the dusk was broken by a shrill whine that cut through my beer-addled brain, dizzying me. Then a melody appeared, on top of the whine, clearing my thoughts and carrying me along the way that fallen leaves bouncing in the eddies of a backwater are marshaled into a stream, flowing slowly at first, then rushing happily along with the lilting rhythm of song.

"Bagpipes," someone close to me said.

Startled, I whirled around to get a look at who was talking and lost my balance. Before I could fall, Hess' firm grip on my shoulder steadied me. "Bagpipes," he repeated. "Celtic funeral music. I think Jason would have liked that."

Hess released me and draped an arm around Edgerton's shoulders. "Let's go back to the armory," he said. "Julia's fixed us something to eat."

Soon we were all once again sitting on the balcony, balancing paper plates ladled with canned pork and beans and grilled sausages on our laps and drinking strong black coffee out of Styrofoam cups. The bagpipes eventually died away replaced by the booming bass of rock music drifting over from the Cock and Bull.

Julia wordlessly offered us more food, and when we had eaten our fill, silently removed the plates.

Hess leaned back in his chair and in the dim light of the electric lantern I could see that he was trying to find the words to tell us something. "I talked to the festival organizers this afternoon," he said. "They want us to joust tomorrow. I told them I would ask you, Stephen."

We waited for Edgerton to say something. "I don't see how we can, Don," he said at last. "The whole thing is worked out for three. Without Jason it just won't be the same."

"No," Hess replied. "It won't be the same. And it won't be the only thing that's different now that he's gone. But it can be done."

"How?"

"Well. We can do it with just two. Me on the horse

and you on the ground."

"Eckels will have two men with him," Edgerton noted. "It'll lack…it'll lack symmetry."

"Who needs symmetry? I'm not worried about symmetry. What I'm worried about is that if we don't at least try to function normally, we may never get over this thing."

Edgerton locked eyes with Hess. "Jason's barely cold and you're ready to be over this?"

Hess waited a couple of seconds. "No. You know me better, Stephen. But you also know that you are not acting like yourself. You've barely raised your head all day, except when you went after Otis. You spent the day drowning your sorrows and that's fine. It's fine as long as you don't do the same thing tomorrow and the next day and the next. You need something to help bring you back. This is all I could come up with."

Edgerton said nothing.

"If you'd rather not do this thing tomorrow, that's your call," Hess continued. "If you want to go home and get away from all of this for a while, that's your call, and it's perfectly understandable. But I think we should do this. I think it might help."

"I'd feel too alone on the ground without Jason. You'd be on the horse. I'd be alone. Vulnerable."

"That's fine, Stephen," Hess said, rising. "I'll tell them we won't be able to do it."

"No, we can do it."

"But you just said—"

"But I won't do it alone."

"Who can we…"

"Lyle will do it," Edgerton said. "Lyle will take Jason's place."

"What?" I exclaimed.

"It's no big deal," Edgerton told me. "We'll give you a little instruction beforehand, dress you in something." He paused. "Oh, we'll find something," he continued, shaking his head. "It'll be okay."

"I haven't the least idea what—"

"Yeah," Hess interrupted. "It'll be okay. Don't worry.

I started to protest, but Hess cut me off. "It's nice of you to do this for your friend. Thanks, Lyle."

My brain was still wrapped in a beer fog. "Yeah," I agreed, "it'll be okay."

Fires twinkled invitingly all over the festival site. Although I wasn't much in the mood for more liquid refreshment, I also wasn't in the mood to go to sleep. In fact, I had no idea where I would sleep. The largest fire and the largest conglomeration of people was over at the Cock and Bull, and I decided that I would wander over there before figuring out the sleeping arrangements. I invited the Hesses and Edgerton to join me, but they declined.

"I won't be long," I told them.

"Take your time," Hess said. "But I'm afraid we won't wait up."

"No need," I assured him as I stood up to leave.

"Lyle," Julia.

"Yes."

"I know you're an investigator."

"Yes."

"Will you try to find out who killed Jason?"

"The cops specifically requested that I not do that," I told her.

"Yes," she said, her eyes tearing, and her bottom lip

quivering slightly. "But will you try?"

I stuck my hands in my pockets and searched Julia's eyes for a clue as to how to respond. "Private investigators don't solve murders," I said. "Private investigators follow cheating husbands for jealous wives. They maybe find a missing person, if that person doesn't mind being found. They provide bits of information that people may find helpful, but they don't solve murders. That's what cops do."

"But you could try."

I looked to Hess and Edgerton for assistance. They both sat with their heads lowered.

Julia walked up to me and extended both of her hands. I took my hands out of my pockets and took hers in mine. "You could try," she repeated.

"I could try," I agreed.

As I was leaving, Edgerton told me that when I got back, I could bunk with him in the bedroom opposite the Hesses' room. I went downstairs and stepped through the doorway of the armory into darkness. The air smelled of freshly cut grass and charcoal lighter fluid. I turned back to look up at the little group on the balcony, still sitting in a circle around the steady yellow light of the electric lantern. The darkness surrounded me like a sadness. I felt terrible. I told her that I would try. I wasn't going to try.

I headed for the fire burning ahead of me at the Cock and Bull. It wasn't as easy as I'd hoped. The coffee had helped to steady me, but I was still drunk. I stumbled over something on the ground and had to take several steps sideways to maintain my balance. A couple of people rushed past me in the darkness, giggling. I turned, but could only make out their indistinct forms, as if I had been passed by laughing specters. Lurching, I reached the tavern and stepped from the darkness into a halo of light cast from the tavern's lanterns.

The tops of the heavy wooden tables were littered with fast food hamburger wrappers and cardboard pizza boxes. Most of the company was drinking beer from plastic cups. There was a sixteen-gallon keg surrounded by ice cubes in a large green plastic garbage can by the bar. Although some were still in Renaissance costume, most of those gathered had changed to jeans, shorts, and T-shirts. A radio someplace close was playing the doo-wop classic "Maybe" by the Chantels, and I was starting to wonder why I was there.

I made my way through the crowd and headed toward the beer keg. I took a plastic cup and was reaching for the tap when an unpleasant feeling in my belly reminded me that I had already had quite enough to drink. I replaced the cup and shook my head.

"Would you like some coffee?" a woman's voice asked me.

It took a couple of seconds for me to locate the person speaking. It took a couple more seconds for my eyes to focus on the woman standing next to me. "If you'd like some, it's no trouble," she said. "I have a fresh pot right over there."

"Still working?" I asked, finally recognizing her as the young woman who had earlier told Edgerton and me that the bar was closing.

"No," she said, smiling, the bright red lips of her small mouth opening like the petals of a blooming flower. "I just thought you looked like you needed some help."

"I do," I admitted. "That is…I, uh…I could use some coffee. Thanks."

I tried to smile but became suddenly aware that the muscles of my face were simply not reacting normally. It was as if my lower lip had been injected with Novocain and when I tried to smile all I could manage was a crooked leer. I rubbed my hand over my mouth to make sure that I wasn't drooling.

She led me to the end of the bar where a large stainless-steel coffee urn sat next to a stack of Styrofoam cups. She filled two cups, handed one to me, and said, "My name's Naomi. Naomi Miller."

"Dahms," I said, and took a sip of coffee to cut the cotton on my tongue. "Lyle Dahms."

She no longer wore the long peasant dress. Now she had on a simple cotton pullover, light blue, its top two buttons undone. The shirt was too short to be tucked into the pair of cutoff blue jeans that she wore, and as she moved, I caught a flash of skin. When she moved again, I noted a small mole just to the right of her bellybutton and a blush of freckles. She was nearly as tall as me, and though shapely, was solidly built. Her arms were muscular, yet round—comfortable arms that could hold you firmly, yet gently. Suddenly, I felt incomplete. Like something was missing. Something I needed. Then I knew what it was. I needed those arms around me.

I raised my head to look into her eyes, but again was distracted by her mouth. I couldn't keep from wondering how it would feel to place my lips on hers. Again, I rubbed my hand across my mouth, this time to keep my lips from pursing.

When I did meet her eyes, I found them gazing thoughtfully at me, but also gleaming playfully, as though something delightful was never too far out of her thoughts. She smiled, then turned away, tendrils of red

44

hair sticking to her sweat-glazed temples.

"I want you to know how truly sorry we all are about your friend's death," she said at last. "I knew Jason slightly and I know he was a good person."

A flush rose on her freckled cheeks.

"I'm sorry too. I'm sorry I didn't get to know him better. I just met him today."

"But I thought…I thought you must be old friends…I mean, the way you two were drinking. And I know that the other guy is from the armory."

"He is. I came out here today to visit him. I'd never met anyone else from the armory before."

"Then you weren't—"

"Drowning my sorrows. No, I just didn't want to leave my friend alone as he drowned his. His name's Stephen Edgerton. You've probably seen him out here. He's worked here for years."

"This is my first year, but, yes, I've seen him. I've visited the armory quite a few times over the past few weekends. Everyone over there seems so nice. Especially Jason."

We nodded at each other, then fell silent. We continued to stand together at the bar for some time, looking at nothing in particular, and listening to the loud buzz of conversation around us. I refilled my coffee cup and was beginning to feel awkward. Naomi, I decided, was likely trying to think of a polite way of ditching me.

I was about to take my leave when she reached out and grasped my hand. "Let's find a place to sit down."

I looked around for an empty table and spotted one on the other side of the room. I took a step toward it, but Naomi pulled me gently back and led me in the opposite direction. I followed her toward the edge of the circle of light that bathed the inside of the tavern.

My mind was blurry, my thoughts as indistinct as the now muted conversations of the crowd behind us. There is nothing rarer in my world than a pretty stranger taking me by the hand and though certainly intrigued, my eyelids were becoming heavy. With my free hand, I rubbed my eyes, trying to drive away a strong desire to just lie down and go to sleep. Then, suddenly, I was jolted alert by the loud voice of a man coming from the tavern behind us. Heavy footsteps came fast toward us. I let go of Naomi's hand and turned.

He was about my height, but a few years younger, and the arm that reached out to stop Naomi was well muscled. He had dark hair, a couple of days' growth of beard on his square jaw, and a thin mustache. He was wearing a vest of ornamental gold chain mail, open to reveal his well-defined musculature. Although he had obviously been drinking, there was clarity in his angry brown eyes, and I guessed that he'd not had as much to drink as I had. The long day's drinking had left me detached. Instead of feeling my heart race and breath quicken, I found myself wondering if he dressed like that to entice women or to intimidate other men.

"Where the hell are you going?" he shouted. "You were supposed to be with me tonight."

Naomi tossed her head. "I get to decide that."

"What do you mean by that, bitch?" the man demanded, seemly oblivious to my presence.

"Sweet," Naomi replied. "That's the way to melt a girl's heart. You call her a bitch."

"I'll call you anything I want. You were coming on to me back there. You said you were just going to talk to this guy. You said you'd be right back. You can't just walk out on me."

Naomi smiled. "Oh, can't I?" she asked, turning her back on him.

The guy was shaking with anger. He pointed at Naomi, his hand covered by a fingerless, chain mail glove. His hand became a fist, and he shook it furiously at her. It was then that I realized that this was the guy who ran the chain mail shop—the kinky sex chain mail shop that Edgerton held in such disdain.

"Hey, I know who you are!" I exclaimed in a dopey slur.

If he heard me, he gave no indication of it. He took two quick steps toward Naomi, both arms reaching for her as she was walking away. Before he could touch her, I stepped between them.

"Out of my way, asshole!" he thundered. "The bitch is mine tonight."

"I don't think so," I said.

"You don't, do ya?"

"Look, I don't want any trouble with you," I told him. "It's just that…It's just that we both know that it doesn't matter what she told you before or what you thought was gonna happen later. She's saying no to you now and that's gonna be the end of it."

"Get out of my way," he muttered, trying to step around me.

I blocked his path, bobbing slightly to keep my balance. "Come on," I said. "Let's be reasonable. How 'bout we go get you another beer?"

"How 'bout if I kick your ass?"

"How 'bout that beer?" I asked, pointing back toward the tavern.

He didn't say anything else. Instead, he hit me. He

was trying to nail me on the chin with a quick right jab, but he missed and slammed me hard in the shoulder. He moved in with his left, but I pivoted and hit him square in the nose with the heel of my open left hand. Both of his hands went up to his injured nose, and I watched the blood start to flow between his fingers. I balled my right hand into a fist and drove it hard into his midsection. The air left his body with a loud whoosh, and he crumpled face first to the ground. I rolled him over with my foot and watched his eyes as he struggled to draw a breath. It took a while, but finally he started breathing again.

Naomi took my arm and we headed into the darkness. We were silent as she led me across the field. I was in a kind of dream state. I didn't have any idea where I was or where we were going, but I liked the way I felt being with her. Wherever she wants, I thought, I would follow.

The muscles in my legs quivered as we walked up a low hill, and then back down into an even deeper darkness. Going down the hill, I lost her arm and could just make out her outline before me. She was carrying a large canvas bag, the strap over one shoulder, and the bag bounced lightly against her backside as she walked. I kept my eye on the bounce.

A bench came up out of the darkness and Naomi guided my hand to the back of the bench and urged me to sit. When I'd taken my place, she sat next to me, pressing against me, settling her head on my shoulder. Her freckled face nestled against my chest like that of a child seeking sanctuary in an embrace. I looped my arm around her shoulders as if this was the most natural thing in the world.

"Lyle," she said.

"Yes."

"I need to be with someone."

"I'm your guy," I said, with a chuckle that struck me as inappropriate the instant it escaped me.

She said nothing. She barely moved. I could feel the gentle rising and falling of her chest as she breathed. After several minutes I began to wonder if she had fallen asleep. My eyes closed and I caught the low hum of a sigh that, barely audible, seemed to draw me closer to her, as though it had come from both, rather than just one of us.

Naomi chuckled. "Don't fall asleep on me now," she cautioned. "Or if you do, just don't snore."

I smiled and opened my eyes as she turned to kiss me. The lips of her small mouth pressed gently against mine. She buried her face back into my chest, and I ran my tongue lightly along my lips, tracing a memory of her kiss. My eyes closed as I tightened my arm around her.

I must have nodded off. When I awoke, she was still nestled against me in the darkness. A pale blue light had begun to rise in the eastern sky, and I realized that Naomi was awake. She turned her head and, through the fabric of my T-shirt, gently bit my nipple. She raised her face and, inching away from me slightly, laid my hand on her breast. I turned toward her, but she moved away, pulling me off the bench and onto the ground. I lowered myself gently on top of her and pressed my dry lips against hers. Her tongue slipped moist and delicious into my mouth.

We made love in the grass.

When it was over, I held her mostly naked body against mine and tried to think of something to say. I cleared my throat and sighed heavily.

"You're welcome," she said, chuckling.

I smiled and started to laugh. Her chuckle tumbled into laughter, and we rolled apart unable to contain ourselves. She let out a harsh snort and in the dim blue light of the pre-dawn I saw her eyes flash with alarm. But as her eyes met mine, we both got the giggles again.

Finally, our laughter quieted into smiles. "I get this reaction from all the women I make love to," I said. "My motto is, if you can't be good, be funny,"

"You were wonderful."

After we'd put our clothes back on, we walked aimlessly, hand in hand, in the field. Although dozens of festival workers were staying at the site, all was quiet. We had the kingdom to ourselves, and though I might not be a knight in shining armor, the young woman with the chubby, freckled cheeks was certainly my lady fair.

We sat on the ground and watched the sun come up together. Around us we began to hear the sounds of people rising—the early morning sounds of throats being cleared and noses blown, of grunts and small groans as folks stood and stretched and tried to get the kinks out of their bones after having spent the night sleeping on the ground. We held each other and listened as bodies slipped into clothes, and coffee was measured into pots, and doors and tent zippers opened, and figures paraded into the indigo morning on their way to the bathrooms.

"I had a nice time with you tonight," Naomi said.

"I had a nice time, too."

"I feel like I need to explain something to you."

"You don't."

"Maybe I want to."

"If you want."

"I really needed to be with someone last night. I've been out here for three weekends and you're not the first guy I spent the night with out here."

My arm around her, I gave her a reassuring hug.

"My first weekend here I slept with Jason Gilroy."

I looked at her, smiled sympathetically, and touched her cheek lightly.

"I don't normally sleep around like this. It's just...It's just."

"You shouldn't feel like you owe me an explanation."

Resolve shown in her face. "I don't want anyone thinking that I'm a slut."

"I don't much care for labels, Naomi."

"Good."

Before long the festival site was abuzz with activity. The stalls and stores were opening up, wares were being displayed, and from somewhere I could distinctly smell bacon frying. We stood and Naomi said that she would walk me back to the armory. In the distance, I could see Dick Peterson leading an elephant in through a gate at the back of the site, near the armory.

"I never asked what you do, Lyle."

"People never seem to know how to respond when I tell them."

"You're not a state senator, are you?"

"No, I'm a private investigator."

"Really?"

"Yes, really."

"So, you're one of those wretched little men who spend their days peeking through windows trying to get the goods on cheating wives?"

"I'm not so little," I pouted.

"No," she laughed. "You're not. You're my knight in shining armor."

"You want to see me in armor?"

"Oh yes!" she exclaimed. "I want to see you shimmering in the sun, a lance in your hand, astride a brilliant white horse, defending my honor."

"Okay. How 'bout today at noon?"

"You're not serious?"

I gave her a serious look.

"You are serious."

"Yeah. The guys at the armory have a joust scheduled today at noon against Sir Lancelot and his boys. They needed another body, and I'm the only guy they could get with no notice."

"Will you be defending my honor?"

"I'll be lucky to get out of there with my pride."

"I'd be honored to attend. And don't worry about your pride. No matter what happens, I'll be proud of you."

"I'll bet you say that to all the knights."

She laughed.

"You said that you guys are going to fight Lancelot and his men?" she asked.

"Yes."

"That could be interesting."

"Why?"

"Well, it's not really my place to say this, but..." She paused and looked at me narrowly. "You're not investigating Jason's death, are you?"

"No. The cops have suggested that it would not be in my best interest to do that."

Naomi stood in thought for some seconds. "Well, I guess it can't hurt if I tell you. I mean, it's not really much of a secret anyway."

"What's not a secret?"

"It's something that Jason told me a couple of weeks ago. I don't even know why he told me. It's not like it was any of my business. And according to him, the whole thing is over now anyway. I think he just told me to try to convince me that everybody sleeps around a little at these festivals."

"Are you going to tell me, or should I wait for it to come out in your memoirs?"

"Jason told me that Don Hess' wife, Julia, had an affair when they were down at a festival in Texas earlier this year."

"Go on."

"Jason told me that she slept with Gregory Eckels. You know. Sir Lancelot."

I thought for a moment.

"You're right," I said. "Hess and Eckels facing off, both on horseback, both aiming potentially lethal weaponry at each other, and Hess probably knowing that Eckels has been with Julia…Yep, that could be interesting."

Chapter Four

When I got back to the armory, Julia was making breakfast and coffee had already been brewed. She smiled as I approached and offered me some of the coffee. I thanked her, rubbed my eyes, and yawned loudly. "Where are the boys?" I asked.

Before she could answer, I heard the sound of clanking metal and both Edgerton and Hess emerged through the armory door carrying armloads of armor. "Good morn to you, Master Dahms," he boomed. "Or perhaps I should call you Sir Lyle, as you will soon be transformed from your piteous, lowly condition to that of one high-born, and fitted to do battle for God, king, and country."

Hess and Edgerton tossed the armor loudly in a great pile on the ground.

"Something here has got to fit you," Edgerton said. "Even if we have to piece a couple of things together."

"Can I have my breakfast first?"

"Certainly," Julia chimed in, as she flipped pancakes on a cast iron skillet perched on a grate over the fire pit. "And it's nearly ready. Go, all of you, and wash up for breakfast."

"Oh, Mom, do we hafta?" Edgerton replied with a mock pout.

Julia raised her head. Her blue eyes twinkled with joy spoiling the stern look she tried to give Edgerton.

And when she glanced toward her husband a luminous smile spread across her face.

"Yeah," Hess added with a whine, "do we hafta?"

I found myself staring at her—at her high cheekbones and at the line of her jaw, at the slight flush of her cheeks, and at her gently upturned nose. It was a good face. Beautiful and strong; playful and caring.

She stood looking down her nose at her disobedient boys, shook a spatula at them and ordered, "Now, you two just scoot before I have to take a switch to you." She looked at me and winked. "You, too. Get washed up or I'll feed your breakfast to the elephants."

"Yes, ma'am," I replied, returning her wink. Then we all hurried off to the nearest privy, giggling like morons.

Well-scrubbed, we returned to a hearty breakfast of pancakes, eggs, bacon, and, most importantly for me, lots of hot, black coffee. I was bone-tired; my head was thick and throbbed dully. Edgerton, however, showed no signs whatsoever of a hangover.

I yawned, sipped at my coffee, and sighed.

Edgerton gave me a sly smile. "Did you sleep well last night?"

"I got a couple of minutes."

We ate mostly in silence, but occasionally, Hess and Edgerton would look at each other, then at me, then shake their heads slightly.

Anxious little flutterings started to contend for space in my belly with the eggs and pancakes. In the sober light of morning, the idea of participating in the joust didn't seem quite as wonderful as it had the day before. I could go home, I reminded myself, but I realized that I couldn't just leave. Despite my best intentions to stay out of it, I'd begun to wonder about Gilroy's death. There were so many questions. Questions that were best left for the cops to answer.

Why did the killer target Gilroy? Where was the killer now? Was Gilroy the only intended victim or were the Hesses in danger? And what about Stephen? We'd all done our best to leave off thinking about the murder we'd witnessed, but that couldn't last. Not for any of us. Still, I tried to push these thoughts back into a quiet place, for butterflies or not, I'd have to play my role in the joust. If for no other reason than to keep an eye on things. I got up and poured the last of the coffee into my cup. "You know the kinky sex chain mail guy?" I asked Edgerton.

"Yeah."

"What's his name?"

"LeGrand. Dirk LeGrand."

"Dick LeGrand? Didn't he play Peavy the druggist on the old Gildersleeve show?"

"I said Dirk, not Dick," Edgerton said.

"I heard you."

After breakfast, I offered to help with the dishes, but Julia said that she thought there was something else in store for me.

"Time for your fitting, Sir Knight," Edgerton said with a bow.

He led me over to the pile of armor and we tried on different variations for what seemed like an eternity. We had a problem.

"Why isn't this working out better?" I asked.

"We, uh...We don't have a lot of, uh..." Hess began, rubbing his beard.

"We don't have anything big enough for you, Lyle,"

Edgerton said. "Has anyone ever told you that you could stand to lose a few pounds?"

The size problem was complicated, I was told, by the fact that both Hess and Edgerton were going to be wearing 16th century Saxon armor. I actually fit into Edgerton's chain mail shirt, which he had designed to hang loosely about his spare frame. Although it did not hang at all loosely about me, I had managed to squeeze into it. But after some discussion they decided that they couldn't allow me to wear it.

"The chain mail hauberk is really pretty twelfth century," Hess assured me. "Chain mail was around after that but was used in conjunction with articulated plate armor. No, we're gonna have to do better. "

Finally, after several more trips back to the storeroom, they found a simple breastplate that they were able to cinch around me. When I told them that it was a trifle tight and that breathing was maybe going to be a problem, they assured me that unless I fainted the audience probably wouldn't notice. They slipped a chain mail hood over my head and topped the outfit off with a visorless helmet—a bowl with a broad rim around it that I thought looked like a stainless-steel version of Oliver Hardy's bowler hat. I fought off the desire to declare that this was another fine mess that Edgerton had gotten me into. A pair of what Hess called greaves were added to cover my arms. These were made of sheet metal and were hinged both at the shoulder and elbow to allow movement. I kinda liked the way they squeaked as I moved my arms.

Having fitted me with armor, they turned their attention to the rest of my outfit. For some reason they didn't think that my T-shirt and jeans were the appropriate undergarments. Hess tossed me a simple cotton, long-sleeved shirt of deep burgundy that he said would match those that he and Edgerton would be wearing under their armor. He told me that it wouldn't fit but if I could just get my arms into it, I needn't worry about buttoning it.

"The breastplate should hide the fact that it's open in front," he told me.

"Whose shirt is this?"

"Jason's."

I decided there was no way I was going to get my beefy thighs into a pair of Gilroy's pants, but it turned out Julia had spent the previous evening adding material to the side seams of a pair of light brown trousers that had belonged to the dead man. They asked me if I would like to add leggings to the ensemble, but I declined. I was afraid that I'd look ridiculous enough without elaborate garters. A pair of leather booties sewn together with rawhide provided an adequate covering for my tennis shoes.

Hess had me put on the whole outfit and handed me a pair of padded gloves. Then he, Edgerton, and Julia stood back and looked me over carefully. They stared at me silently for some time, looking at me the way the way that parents look over a strange boy who has just arrived to take their daughter to the junior prom.

"Could be worse," Edgerton said at last.

"Can't do better without more time," Hess noted.

"You look wonderful," Julia said.

She was probably lying, but I preferred her assessment.

Now, I knew what I was to wear, but I had no idea what I was to do. Edgerton and Hess went to arm themselves, and when they returned, Hess was carrying two broadswords, each nearly four feet long. He handed one to me and I took it in both hands, surprised at the heft of the thing. "How much does this weigh?" I asked.

"About seven pounds."

"And we're going to take swipes at each other with these things."

"Well, yeah. Sort of."

"Did I tell you that I'm self-employed and have no health insurance?"

"You'll be fine," Edgerton piped in. "Probably."

Hess led us out into a clearing and spent the next half-hour showing me how to go at someone with a broadsword. First, he hacked at Edgerton, who, I gotta say, really knew how to hack back. Despite the weight of their weapons, and the two-handed grip needed to handle them, both men were able to use the long blades with surprising grace. The air resounded with the clash of steel on steel. Their agility and power were striking as they swung the heavy swords with tremendous force over their heads, from below, and from each side, setting off sparks bright enough to be seen even in the sunlight.

My favorite move was when Edgerton was able to avoid a blow by locking Hess' blade with his own, twirling around and forcing Hess' sword to the ground behind his own back. When it was my turn, Edgerton turned over a metal bucket and took a seat well away from us.

"What you doing way over there?" Hess asked.

"Just want to be out of harm's way when that blade comes flying out of Lyle's hands."

"Why, I'll moider ya," I said, taking a step toward him.

"First, let me show you how to use that thing," Hess said, grinning.

I've got to give Hess credit. He stuck with it for at least twenty minutes, showing me where to place my hands on the hilt of the sword, how to swing it offensively, how to counter defensively, never showing any frustration as I bungled each attempt to do as he asked. He barely let out a whimper the time he asked me to try an overhand attack and the sword slipped from my hands and thunked against his leg. Finally, Hess told me to just stand holding the broadsword in both hands in front of me while he pushed my blade around with his own.

"It'll be okay," he said. "Most people are going to be looking at the horses anyway."

It was time for the festival to open and Hess and Edgerton went up into the tower to ready their cannon. They waited to hear the cannon at the front gate sound before Hess touched the armory's cannon with a glowing punk setting off the charge. As the echo from the first cannon shot was just beginning to reverberate across the site, the second cannon roared. And as the echo of the first cannon died away, the second echo passed like a shiver over the landscape.

"Pretty cool, huh?" Edgerton called to me from the tower.

"Pretty cool."

We still had to go over the sequencing of the joust with Lancelot and his men. Julia assured her husband that it was early enough that she could handle any customers by herself. Hess, glancing at me, told her that he didn't really know how long it would take, but that we would be back as soon as possible. He gave her a nice, husbandly peck on the lips as we prepared to go, but then turned back to his wife. He took her in his arms and kissed her again, long and deep.

"I love you," I heard him say.

Her eyes gleamed as she looked at him. "I love you too," she said.

When we got over to Joyous Guard, we found Eckels and his men in full armor, lounging on benches in front of the building, drinking coffee from Styrofoam cups. We waited briefly as they finished their coffee, then began to go over the choreography for the joust. They explained to me that the men on horseback would make two passes at each other with lances. Eckels' lance was scored so that it would break away when he struck Hess on the second pass. Hess would be unhorsed. Eckels was then to dismount and ask Hess to yield. Hess, villain that he is, would spurn this attempt at mercy and both men would be given swords with which to continue the combat. After much clashing, Eckels would best Hess, but spare his life. As Hess departed, he was to vow to return to continue their quarrel at another time.

All I had to do was stand in front of one of Eckels' men with my sword out as if keeping him from unlawfully assisting his liege lord. Or he was keeping me from helping Don. Something like that. Anyway, the upshot was that we only had to clash once, right after Hess is knocked from the horse. Hess told my chosen opponent that I wasn't exactly experienced with the broadsword and asked him if he could just kind of clink my sword as I held it out. The guy said he would do his best to make it look good and he winked at me. I smiled at him, wishing my parents had had the good sense to force me into broadsword lessons when I was a kid.

Hess and Eckels barely spoke to one another. Edgerton, on the other hand, was quite animated. He asked myriad questions, insisted on exchanging blows over and over with his opponent to determine what moves would be the most dramatic, and reviewed every detail time and time again. You'd have thought that he was preparing to stage a full-scale reenactment of the Hundred Years War rather than ten minutes of "Let's Pretend" with five other guys. After the first run-through, frankly, I'd checked out entirely. Instead of listening to Edgerton repeat everything, I studiously picked at the dirt under my fingernails and ran my tongue over my teeth wishing that I had been able to brush that morning.

Besides the prospect of really bad morning breath, another thing had begun to disturb me. No one at the rehearsal had mentioned Gilroy. He was to have been an integral part of the joust, and no one had said a thing about him. It's not that he wasn't missed, and there was certainly no way that anyone had managed to forget about his grisly demise. No. Instead, I thought, no one mentioned him because in this world they'd fashioned for themselves—a playful world of blunted swords and choreographed battles—death, real death, simply had no place. In the other world, the world to which they would return the next day, their colleague's death would cause definite ripples.

Finally, even Edgerton was satisfied that we had reviewed enough. He went up to Eckels, and then to each of his confederates, shook their hands, and wished them good luck. I managed a limp wave good-bye. Hess merely turned and left.

"I'm psyched," Edgerton admitted as we walked back to the armory.

"Not really," I said. "You'd never know it."

Hess' good humor returned as we walked, and he and Edgerton talked about how good it would be for business to have more jousts. Hess mentioned that he knew several people who he could train to help out, and that it would really be better if he was allowed to use people with a background in historical reenactment, rather than local stage actors like Eckels. Edgerton agreed, apparently without realizing that Hess had a special reason not to want to work with the handsome, ersatz Lancelot.

We passed the front gates, and I spied my two verbal assailants from the day before, still greeting those streaming in through the turnstiles.

"Those two on the gates gave me quite the time yesterday morning," I told them.

"What, those two?" Hess asked.

"Yeah."

"Well, it's all part of the so-called merriment," Edgerton said, a sour smile on his face. "You just have to give as good as you get."

"I'm afraid I just couldn't think of a comeback."

Edgerton straightened. "We can't let that stand," he said, exchanging a look with Hess. "Come on."

We drew closer to the gates and Edgerton addressed the young man with the ostrich plume first.

"You, knave!" he called. "Yes, you that dost hang like a scarecrow from our battlements. How come you to such work?"

Both the young man and woman turned to face Edgerton. "I serve the king, my lord," the young man answered.

Edgerton pointed to the young woman beside him.

63

"What dost thou say, my lady? Does your man serve the king?"

"Yes, my lord," she answered. "He seeks to bring joy to those who are visitors to our land."

"It is good," Edgerton said, "that he has found such an outlet. One so afflicted should make the most of his situation and serve where he can."

"I don't take your meaning, good sir," the young man called. "How do you imagine that I am afflicted?"

"I shudder to imagine it at all," Edgerton replied. "Yet it is quite well known within our kingdom that you raise yourself atop these walls to serve the king to compensate for your inability to raise anything with which to serve your lady there."

As the young man reacted with exaggerated shock and the members of the crowd began to chuckle, Edgerton shakily began to raise his arm, his face contorted as if with great effort. But before it was completely raised, he dropped the arm, letting it hang limp before him. The crowd around Edgerton erupted in laughter.

Atop the wall, the young man slumped down holding his hands to his chest. "Behold, I am slain!" he shouted.

"Suggesting that a man is impotent is real big around here," Edgerton told me as we walked away. "Gets 'em every time."

"I thought you didn't go in for all this…uh, Renaissance lingo."

"I said I didn't like it. I didn't say I wasn't good at it."

We all laughed. It felt good, even warmly familiar, as if the three of us had been together forever. Then it hit me, hard enough to freeze an unnatural smile on my face. I wasn't supposed to be there. Gilroy was supposed to be there. And I couldn't help but wonder if he was watching, staring enviously out at us as we walked in the warm sunshine while he shivered in the cold grasp of death.

Chapter Five

When we got back to the armory, we found Julia tending to a few customers. Many more people were gathered just outside, pointing at the wall where Gilroy had been killed. A couple of uniformed policemen stood nearby but they didn't seem to be doing anything besides adding to the scenery.

I just wanted to take off my armor. I hadn't drawn a deep breath since I'd put it on. But when I told them that I was going back into street clothes, Edgerton balked. "Come on, Lyle. This is the only chance you're going to have to spend any time out here in costume. Make the most of it. Shout 'huzzah!' with the rest of us for a bit."

"You told me that you guys never parade around in armor all day," I protested.

"True. But Don asked me to clank around here until after the joust to help drum up interest, and if I gotta, you gotta."

"I hate this," I muttered.

Edgerton approached me and tinged a fingernail against my breastplate. "Look at it this way. Girls can't resist a guy in uniform."

"Yeah. But they have no trouble resisting a dork in a tin can."

"Say! How much does this weigh?" a customer interrupted, pointing at the chain mail shirt that had been set back up in the front of the armory.

Edgerton left to speak with him while Hess and Julia busied themselves with the customers. I milled around, hoping that I looked fierce enough to slay any dragon that happened to wander by as well as to dissuade any customer that might want to chat with me. Before long I thought maybe I'd mill around someplace else. I adjusted my helmet, stretched my arms just to hear the protective greaves squeak, and headed outside.

To my left were the elephant rides; beyond them, the Irish cottage, and the tent I had seen being pitched the evening before. I glanced back to the armory and decided that no one would mind if I took a little stroll. My first thought was to introduce myself to the Petersons, but both father and older son looked pretty busy. Each led an elephant around the oval track—the boy's elephant carrying two youngsters, the father's carrying a pretty girl about sixteen who feigned fright while her boyfriend watched impassively from the sidelines. The youngest boy was also occupied, manning the line of waiting riders. As I passed them, the elder Peterson looked up at me and smiled. I waved and kept going in the direction of the cottage.

The leather straps that held the breastplate tight against me were digging into my sides. I grunted loudly as I walked up the low rise to the cottage and stepped inside. It was dark and completely empty. I stepped to a window and tried to span the width of the windowsill with my hand. I couldn't do it; the walls were too thick. I walked over to the window that faced the armory. From there I could see the wall Gilroy was standing against when he was shot but decided that the killer could not have fired from that window. The angle was wrong.

I stuck my head out the window and saw that a

shallow wooden structure was attached to the left side of the building. Probably for storage, like a big closet, I thought. The shed was wide enough for a man to stand inside facing the armory, but I didn't see any windows that faced the spot where Gilroy was shot. I was going to go outside to examine the shed closer, but I looked down and spotted a cigarette butt squashed into the dirt. I knelt, picked it up, and read the words "Pall Mall" in a circle around the filter. I stood and tossed the butt back to the ground. I reached into my pants pocket where I had slipped my own pack of cigarettes, lit one, put the pack back into the pants pocket. Not my pants, I remembered.

"Dead man's pants," I said aloud.

"That would be a good name for a rock band," someone said behind me.

Startled, I turned to face a tall man with dark brown hair, well salted with gray, who had entered the cottage behind me. He was about thirty, broad-shouldered, barrel-chested and, like me, had a substantial waistline. He stepped forward out of the shadows and into a beam of light that streamed through a window into the darkened cottage. He looked at me somewhat guardedly, but a smile played about his lips. He ran a hand through his hair, then tugged at the green plaid wool that crossed his chest. He was wearing a kilt.

"It would be a good name," I said, recovering. "Maybe we could put something together. You could play the bagpipes."

"Sounds good," the man said. "What will you do?"

"I could front the thing. You should hear me sing."

"You any good?"

"Is that required?"

The stranger's smile broadened. "Not really."

68

I offered the guy my hand. He took it in a firm handshake and looked me directly in the eyes. "Dahms," I said. "Lyle Dahms."

"I'm Max Wiseman."

"Was that you I heard playing the bagpipes last night?"

"Yeah," he said, glancing around. "The Clan got here yesterday afternoon. Supposed to be here earlier, but we got delayed. Seems we missed the excitement. Guy got killed, they tell me."

"Yeah. Right over there," I said, pointing.

"Yeah, that's what I heard. You know the guy."

"I'd met him."

"Sorry."

"What clan?" I asked.

"Oh, I'm here with a historical reenactment group. We call ourselves Clan Highland. It's Scottish."

"So, I gathered from the kilt."

"What do you do here?" he asked, pointing at my armor.

"So far all I've done is look stupid. But I'm doing a remarkable job if I do say so myself."

"That's okay. I don't mind if you brag a little. But where do you mostly practice this looking stupid?"

"Over there at the armory."

"Oh, then you make armor."

"No."

"You just help out over there?"

"Not so far."

Wiseman raised an eyebrow. "Then you just engage people in meaningless conversations, refusing to actually answer any of their questions."

"I am answering your questions. You're just not

asking the right ones."

"You could just tell me."

I smiled. This guy was persistent, I thought. That wasn't necessarily suspicious. If someone had been killed near where I was camping, I'd be a bit snoopy myself.

"I came out here yesterday to visit a friend who works at the armory," I said. "When another guy that works there got killed, they asked me to stay and replace the dead guy in a joust they had planned for today."

"The guy got killed and they're still going on with the joust?"

I shrugged. "What do you do besides play the bagpipes?"

Wiseman stared at me a moment before returning my shrug. "When I'm out here or at a rendezvous, I toss a caber or two, maybe do a Highland Fling. The dancing thing only comes out after a bit of the single malt and a couple of pints. In the real world I work for an insurance company."

"In the real world I'm a private investigator," I said.

Wiseman raised his eyebrows. "Really. Are you trying to find out who killed the guy at the armory?" Nothing in his expression betrayed any great anxiety behind the question.

"A natural question," I said. "No. I'm not."

"Then what are you doing?"

I crushed my cigarette out on the ground. "At the moment, I'm hiding."

"You gonna be doing that much longer?"

"No. I'm just about done."

Wiseman and I stared at each other for a couple of awkward seconds. I was pretty well convinced that he was just a regular guy showing a regular interest in what had gone on the day before, but tendrils of suspicion still tickled within me. I shouldn't care, I told myself. I wasn't working the case anyway. Wiseman turned away first. "I'll leave you to it then," he said, stepping toward the door.

"Wait," I said, maybe a little too eagerly. "You want to walk around a bit?"

The questioning aspect reappeared in his eyes. "Sure," he said.

We left the darkness of the cottage and stepped into the bright morning. It was going to be another hot day. I could feel the humidity rising by the moment, each breath of air a little heavier in my lungs. The shirt under my breastplate was already soaked with sweat. I looked over at Wiseman and his heavy woolen kilt. "That thing as warm as it looks?" I asked.

"Probably every bit as warm as what you're wearing."

"Except you're sleeveless and your skirt only comes to your knees."

"True."

"You get a good breeze up that thing and you'll be downright cool."

"You'd think so."

"Say, what do Scotsmen wear under their kilts?"

"How should I know?" he replied. "I'm Jewish."

We rounded the corner of the cottage, and I was able to take a good look at the shed adjacent to it. At first glance I thought there were no windows facing the armory, but when I got up close, I discovered a closed access panel built into the side. I pulled open the panel and stared into the darkness within. When my eyes had adjusted to the dimness, I saw that the shed was empty, except for some boards, a couple of rakes, and a coal shovel.

"Whatcha looking at?" Wiseman asked me.

"Nothing. Just wanted to know what's inside."

"What is inside?"

"Couple of rakes and a shovel."

"Probably for cleaning up elephant poop," Wiseman said, nodding toward the nearby elephant track.

"Probably."

I peeked around the corner of the shed, and by the front door found another cigarette butt on the ground. I stooped to pick it up but was able to read the words "Pall Mall" without having to actually touch it. I reached into my pants pocket and pulled out my pack of Merits.

"Cigarette?" I offered Wiseman.

"No thanks," he said. "I don't smoke."

I put the pack back in my pocket. "So, tell me about the Clan."

And he did. For the next twenty minutes or so we walked around and through their encampment. Wiseman told me briefly about the history of the Scots from Roman times, when they were known as Picts, to the present. He talked about the wars against the English, and the Middle Eastern origin of the bagpipe, and about the importance of the clans in Scottish history.

I waited for Wiseman to finish telling me the difference between a great kilt and a modern kilt before I suggested that we go get something to eat. The smell of cooking was everywhere, and I am not really given to resisting the temptation. Wiseman agreed and we went off in search of victuals. Then it was my turn. I talked about investigatory work, about how most of it involved using various databases to track down addresses for people or waiting around hoping to get evidence of someone's infidelity or other dishonorable behavior.

"I bet your job has really changed your opinion of people in general," Wiseman said.

"Nah. I've never really been a huge fan of other people." I smiled. "Sometimes I make an exception."

On the way to a cluster of food booths, we passed the kinky sex chain mail shop. The blonde woman I had seen the day before was leaning with her elbows on the counter showing a man in a loud Hawaiian shirt a pair of silver mesh panties. The man was working hard at it but was unable to stop staring at her cleavage. I spotted her partner, LeGrand, coming out of the back of the shop, his eyes blackened, cotton balls in both nostrils. I smiled and waved at him, the screeching of my greaves turning a few heads in the crowd around us. Maybe it was the armor, but LeGrand didn't seem to recognize me.

Wiseman suggested that I try something called "Scotch Eggs," and I figured that since I was strolling around with a guy in a kilt something Scottish was probably in order. They were actually pretty good—an egg cooked hard inside a ball of nice, spicy sausage—and they certainly fit in well with the low cholesterol theme of all my other meals since I had been at the festival.

A large crowd had gathered in front of one the festival stages, and as we passed, we heard the crowd roar its approval of the entertainment. I craned my neck to see above the crowd and saw that a team of jugglers had taken the stage. One man was standing center stage juggling three flaming batons and trying to maintain his balance atop a large ball, while two other men stood on either side of him tossing what looked like bowling pins at one another. Each man would occasionally declaim something loudly and the crowd laughed, but we were too far away to hear what they were saying. We skirted the crowd and passed a large oak tree in a small clearing at the beginning of a row of stalls. There was a tree house built in the gnarled branches of the ancient oak. I'd been leading Wiseman around the tree, but I stopped to look more closely at the tree house. Wiseman kept going and was nearly out of my sight when I heard him yelp. I raced around the tree and found him standing stock-still, staring wide-eyed at something out of my view. His arms hung motionless at his sides.

I broke into a trot, the leather straps of my breast plate gouging into my sides and the greaves screeching like a rusty weathervane. As I circled around Wiseman, my helmet slipped over my eyes. I had to push the helmet back on my head to see what was in front of Wiseman. It was LeGrand, brandishing a baseball bat.

As I entered into view, LeGrand's eyes left Wiseman and settled on me for only an instant before he rushed toward me with a yell, the bat held over his head. I planted myself firmly on my feet and braced for the assault. He never reached me. Something glinted in the sun just to LeGrand's right. I noticed but didn't want to take my eyes off the charging LeGrand. A gloved hand appeared grabbing the barrel of LeGrand's baseball bat from behind. LeGrand was abruptly pulled backward. I finally took my eyes off him, and saw that a tall man in full armor, his visor open, had taken ahold of the bat and was swinging LeGrand around as he held stubbornly to the handle. It was Eckels.

Eckels turned the bewildered LeGrand around so

that they were facing each other. In the instant that it took LeGrand to reorient himself, Eckels was able to twist the bat from his hands. Eckels let the bat fall to his feet and took hold of LeGrand by the shoulders.

"Settle down, sir," Eckels told LeGrand.

His rage seemed to have left him. LeGrand just stared at Eckels, his mouth open.

"Just settle down," Eckels repeated. "Now, what started all this?"

A small crowd began to gather around us. An audience in place, Eckels was now every bit the medieval marshal—Matt Dillon sheathed in steel, keeping the peace in the streets of the fiefdom of Dodge. I hated him for it. I'd have vastly preferred to handle it myself.

"Look at my eyes," LeGrand said finally, passing a hand across his face. "Last night this prick sucker punched me and gave me two black eyes."

Eckels looked at me.

"I don't have to explain myself here," I said. "I'm not the one with the baseball bat."

Eckels drew a deep breath and looked down his nose at me. "You don't have to explain yourself to me, but there are several policemen about, and I should think that you would rather explain yourself to me than to them."

I grunted.

"Besides," Eckels added, "I just saved your life."

"Let me just make a couple of things clear, pal. In the first place, I never sucker punched this dickweed. Last night he was making unwanted advances on a young lady, and when I suggested he stop, he hit me. I hit him back."

"Whore!" LeGrand shouted, his fury returning.

Eckels held him firmly as he squirmed.

"And," I continued, "although I'm grateful to you, you didn't just save my life. If this bag of dung came at me with a howitzer, I'd still send him running home to mommy."

Eckels chuckled. "Well, you certainly have a high opinion of yourself. Especially for someone who—"

"Finally," I interrupted, "I resent your attitude. You've no right to pretend to that you're in charge here. You're just an actor for God's sake, not the Sheriff of Freaking Nottingham. You've no right to question me."

Eckels grinned. "Pride a bit hurt?"

I resisted the impulse to fling myself to the ground in a tantrum, screaming, "You're not the boss of me." Instead, I managed a tiny smile. "Yeah. Maybe a bit."

Eckels turned to LeGrand. "You going to be a good boy?"

LeGrand said nothing. Instead, he looked at the ground.

"I'm going to let you go now," Eckels told him. "I don't want you to try anything stupid."

LeGrand responded with more silence.

Eckels looked first at me, then at over Wiseman, whom I had nearly forgotten was still there. Eckels looked one more time seriously into LeGrand's eyes, then let him go.

Eckels smiled. "Now, let's all be friends."

"Yeah," Wiseman said, also smiling. "How 'bout a hug?"

"How about—" LeGrand began, but he never finished the sentence. Instead, he stooped quickly and snatched the bat from the ground. Eckels made a grab for him but was too slow. LeGrand rushed toward me swinging the bat over his head as he ran, his face contorted with hate. I tried to sidestep the blow but wasn't quite quick enough. But I got mostly out of the way and the barrel of the bat glanced off my helmet. A bell went off inside my skull, but I was otherwise unhurt. LeGrand's momentum pulled him off balance, and the bat hit the hard-packed ground with a sharp crack. LeGrand tried to stay on his feet by leaning against the bat like a crutch. As he tried to steady himself, I moved behind him, punching him hard in the kidney. I really got my weight into the blow, spinning him around to face me. The sound that issued from him was beyond pain. It was the sound of anguished legions roaring full-throated from within the yawning pit of hell.

I looked into his senseless, bulging, blackened eyes and gently took the bat from his hands. "Let's go," I said to Wiseman.

All eyes were on us for a couple hundred feet or so as we left LeGrand and Eckels behind us, but soon we found ourselves once again anonymous amongst the crowd. I removed the helmet and found only a small dent where LeGrand had hit me with the bat.

"That guy don't like you," Wiseman said.

I nodded. "He likes me even less now."

Chapter Six

I walked with Wiseman back to Clan Highland's encampment. It was almost time for the joust and, as I was leaving, Wiseman told me that he wouldn't miss it. Then he smiled a disappointed little smile and shook his head almost imperceptibly. I got the impression he didn't much approve of the way I'd handled LeGrand.

Returning to the armory, I began to feel worse and worse about the whole thing. I shouldn't have played the tough guy with LeGrand. Like Cagney in *Public Enemy*, I knew I wasn't so tough. LeGrand wasn't as tough as he made out either, but he couldn't help it. He just didn't know what to do with his rage. He was used to thinking of himself as fearsome and some fat guy had stolen his date and roughed him up—twice. I could have played it differently. I could have apologized and diffused the situation. Instead, I set him down. I could have come across the cool diplomat. Instead, I proved myself the goon. I hate being the goon.

When I reached the armory, Hess and Edgerton, still dressed in full armor, had stowed all their wares away in the back, and Edgerton was hanging a sign across the counter that read, "Closed for Combat. Will Return, God Willing, Neither Bloodied, Nor Bowed."

"Are you ready, Sir Lyle?" Hess called to me.

"As surely as the morning sun rises to vanquish the dark of night," I said with a smile. "So am I ready to do battle with thine enemies, my lord."

"Hey!" Hess exclaimed. "You've been practicing. I think that deserves a hearty huzzah!"

He looked over to Edgerton.

"Uh, yeah. Huzzah, dude," Edgerton said.

Hess handed me a broadsword.

"Any words of wisdom for us, coach," I asked him.

"Try not to hurt yourself, Lyle."

Hess disappeared behind the armory, shortly reemerging through a nearby gate leading a horse. There aren't a lot of horses in my neighborhood, so I don't know if it was my lack of familiarity with equines in general or if it was that horse specifically, but this struck me as very big. It towered over me—its great, heavy hooves scraping the sunbaked ground viciously, deep rumbling noises issuing from its huge head. It wore a mask, like an equine version of Batman, sporting a sheet metal cowl that covered its face from just above his nostrils to the top of his head, complete with pointy little protectors for its pointy ears. Its back was covered with an embroidered blanket and its saddle was specially designed with raised sheet metal plating that would help protect the rider during combat. Hess climbed easily into the saddle, and Edgerton handed him up his helmet. Stephen then donned his own helmet, securing his visor in the open position.

On horseback, Hess set off slowly across the field, Edgerton behind him on foot. He motioned for me to follow. I swallowed hard, hoping to tamp down the anxiety that was rising within me. It seemed impossible, I thought, but we were really going to do this thing. How did Mother Dahms' little boy ever find himself in such a ridiculous situation?

But, as we walked, a strange thing began to happen. I started to get into it. I couldn't help myself. There was something positively cinematic about it. The three of us, heavily armed, setting out to do battle against a similarly armed foe. It was just cool.

I had the heavy broadsword strapped to my left side with the tip pointed to the ground. The weight of the thing felt potent and powerful as it swayed against me. I turned to see the joy in Edgerton's eyes as he tried to maintain a stony expression as befits a warrior entering a fray. He was not able to keep from smiling, however, when I turned back, and the point of my broadsword caught something on the ground. I tried to dislodge it, but mistakenly shifted my weight to the left, impaling the sword into the earth. Then I tripped and fell face forward with a great clanking sound. I looked up at the departing rear end of Hess' horse, and as I was picking up my helmet and pulling the sword point out of the ground, the metaphor was not lost on me. I felt exactly like the south end of a northbound horse.

My mood did little to brighten as we reached the jousting ring. A large crowd of spectators had already gathered, lining the fence three and four deep. That's when it dawned on me that I was going to be doing this in front of actual people. I envied Hess and Edgerton their helmets. At least they had visors and could hide their faces. My helmet was open. I prayed that no one I knew would be in the crowd. Then I remembered that I had stupidly invited people to this thing.

At the head of the jousting ring was a reviewing stand and all but the seats at the very center were filled with costumed tournament fans. I looked around for our opponents, but they had not yet arrived. I scanned the faces on the reviewing stand and then along the fence until I spotted Naomi. She smiled brightly and waved. I was about to return the wave but decided that knights probably didn't do that. Instead, I bowed in her direction.

Hess dismounted as two men carrying long, straight trumpets entered the ring from each side and blasted the approach of the King. Otis and his queen led the party toward the empty seats in the middle of the reviewing stand. Joining them were various courtiers and bringing up the rear were our opponents. Eckels was flanked by his men, but tall and singularly imposing in his blue tinted armor, he didn't look like he would be needing any help to win the day. He stared across the ring at us with his clear blue eyes and perfect features—every bit the legendary defender of the realm. Hess dismounted and took his place next to Edgerton. They stood to meet Lancelot's challenge. Grim visaged, their long red hair blowing in the warm, humid breeze, perhaps they did not cut as imposing a figure as Lancelot, but all knew that they were not to be trifled with. I took my place next to them. I tried to look fearsome, but tubby and decked out in ill-fitting armor, I felt like the comic relief.

A man in a long brown robe and purple stole, wearing what looked like a wadded-up towel on his head, stepped forward for the formal introduction of the combatants. Hess was introduced first. The guy with the towel on his head was not a big fan of Don's. He introduced him as Sir Donald the Black, a first-class despoiler of women, beater of children, and kicker of dogs. He was said to be the leader of a gang of ruffians so vile that the very sun that shone so brightly on King Henry's lands, shunned completely the environs of Sir Donald's fiefdom. As the ring announcer was heaping derision on him, Hess seemed to become Sir Donald. He remounted his horse and galloped the length of the jousting ring, sneering malevolently at the crowd. The crowd lapped it all up. Loud howls of contempt echoed around us from all sides.

Next came the introduction of Lancelot, the noblest knight in Christendom, the champion of everything good, pure, and Christian in a world buffeted by the dark and seductive forces embodied in the ring by the evil Sir Donald and his vile minions. By the end of the introduction, even I, one of these vile minions, wanted to see Sir Donald defeated, Lancelot's boot across his neck. I was just glad that my mom wasn't there to see what a lowlife I had become.

Cheers erupted as Lancelot mounted his horse, nodded to the crowd, and turned to boldly face his villainous opponent.

Edgerton went to the side of the ring where a long wooden lance lay on a bench. He returned and handed the lance up to his liege. Sir Donald turned his horse to face a similarly armed Lancelot. Edgerton and I moved to opposite sides of the ring, brandishing our broadswords, and facing our counterparts at the other end of the ring. The trumpets sounded, piercing the general din of crowd noise. There was a hush, immediately broken by the thunder of hoof beats on the ground. The combatants raced at full gallop at one another, and all eyes turned to the center of the ring where these warriors would surely clash. Alas, on the first pass, neither made contact, but when they reached the opposite ends of the ring, they whirled on their massive steeds and raced toward each other again.

On the second pass, the evil Sir Donald managed a

glancing blow to Lancelot's breastplate but did not unhorse the champion of Christendom. Emboldened by his near victory, Sir Donald shouted as he turned his horse to make another pass. Again, the pounding of hoof beats assaulted the crowd and some shied away from the fence as clumps of dirt flew toward them, torn from the ground by the strides of the great beasts. The opponents met once again in the middle of the ring, this time with a loud crack as Lancelot's lance splintered against Sir Donald's chest. The crowd roared and King Henry shouted "Huzzah!" as Sir Donald fell to the ground.

This was our cue to join the battle. Edgerton and I raced to Sir Donald's side, protecting him as he got to his feet. Lancelot's men raced toward us—their broadswords raised defiantly. To my right, on the other side of the fallen Sir Donald, I heard the loud clash of Edgerton's broadsword against that of his opponent. As I glanced over at him, I saw Edgerton swing his sword, preparing to strike another blow. It occurred to me that I was supposed to be getting in a couple whacks here myself, and I looked up to find my opponent patiently waiting, his sword raised, a look of irritation on his face. I shrugged and raised my own sword.

My opponent tried to help me out by barely tapping my sword with his, but even so, he nearly knocked it from my hands. I stumbled to one side and was attempting to raise the sword again, when, thankfully, I heard the voice of the guy with the towel on his head ring out, ordering us to halt.

The ring announcer declared that combat would continue on the ground, and he ordered both men to arm themselves. Lancelot dismounted and walked slowly to his side of the ring to get his sword. Sir Donald wiped the dirt from the back of his trousers and picked up his sword as the crowd jeered.

We all moved to the middle of the ring—Sir Donald and Lancelot facing each other in the center, the rest of us flanking our lords. Hefting his broadsword with an overhand motion, Sir Donald was the first to strike. Sparks crackled, but Lancelot parried, pushing the smaller man back with a wince-inducing shriek of metal raking against metal. Again, the Black Knight swung his heavy iron blade, but again Lancelot was able to meet the blow with his own. It was now Lancelot's turn to strike, but Sir Donald deflected the blow and drove Lancelot's blade to the ground. He stepped quickly to the side and slashed Lancelot across his armored shoulder. Eckels fell to his knees and when he tried to raise his sword, Hess kicked him in the wrist, knocking the blade out of the bigger man's hand. Hess then brought the flat of his blade down hard against Eckels' helmet. I exchanged an anxious glance with Edgerton. This most definitely was not in the script.

Again, Hess cracked Eckels in the helmet with his broadsword. Gape-mouthed, I watched as Hess then kicked the kneeling Eckels in the chest, sending him over onto his back. Hess was dropping to the ground to deliver another headshot, this time with the pommel of the sword, when movement to my left caught my eye. I nearly didn't turn quick enough to see that the man I was supposed to be covering had decided to attack me.

I held my broadsword in front of me, head lowered, hoping my opponent would stick to the script and merely rake the blade of his sword against mine. Instead, he took a full swing, driving the tip of my blade to the ground. Although I was able to hold on to the hilt, the blow almost knocked me to the ground. I took a couple of steps back and motioning toward Hess and Eckels, I shrugged my shoulders hoping that my attacker would realize that I had nothing to do with Hess' deviation from the script. My attacker lunged at me again, this time bringing the blade down on my right arm, just below the shoulder. Despite the protection of the greaves, my arm went instantly numb, and I was unable to keep a hold on the broadsword. Grasping my right shoulder, I turned to my opponent, imploring him to show reason and to stop hitting me. Reason evidently wasn't one of his long suits. He came at me again, swinging his heavy blade at my head.

He was nearly on top of me when I dropped to my knees before him. His target suddenly gone, he stumbled forward off balance. I raised myself into a crouch and rammed my helmeted head into his midsection. Then I stood and tossed him over my shoulder to the ground. Going over, his helmet slipped off his head and he lay face up, one arm flailing for his dropped sword. There was still no feeling in my right arm, and I frantically looked to Edgerton for some help. He and the guy he was covering were standing in the middle of the ring looking completely dumbfounded. I turned back to find that my opponent had reached his sword and was rolling over to get to his feet.

Still clutching my injured arm, I dropped my left knee straight down on his head. The knee drop had all of my weight behind it, so even though I landed only a glancing blow, the guy was no longer a threat to hit me again. Unfortunately, I was left in a bit of a quandary. I didn't know whether to continue to hold on to my injured shoulder or to use my one good hand to grasp at my knee, which had exploded in pain. So, I just went limp. I fell to the ground beside the man whose head I had just tried to crush, and together we rolled on the ground moaning in painful dissonance.

Suddenly there were many footsteps around me. Someone mumbled, "Excuse me," when he kicked me while rushing past.

I turned toward the mumble and saw a crowd forming around Hess and Eckels, who were still having it out in the dirt. Hess had pulled Eckels' helmet off and was repeatedly punching the bigger man in the face. Strings of blood and saliva dangled from Eckels' nose and mouth. Finally, Hess was pulled off Eckels and dragged several feet away from the prostrate defender of Christendom.

Hands came to help me to my feet. It was Edgerton. I tried to take a step but the pain in my knee nearly sent me to the ground again. I leaned against Edgerton, breathing heavily.

"Wow!" was all he said.

Chapter Seven

Otis was really mad. As we sat on the ground,
watching the crowd thin out, he came over to us. Several
members of his court followed, Otis leading the way,
waddling with purpose. As always, his left hand was held
perpendicular to his body for Queen Anne to hold on to.
For her part, the Queen didn't seem quite as disinterested
as she had before. Something blazed behind her cool,
green eyes as she looked down at Hess.

"That was the most outrageous display that has ever
occurred in all the years of this festival," Otis blustered.
"If I have anything to say about it, you three will be
booted off these grounds forever. Of all the unmitigated
temerity. We are looking at breach of contract, reckless
endangerment, breach of contract—"

"You're repeating yourself," I interrupted.

"What?" Otis asked, giving his head an exasperated
shake.

"Quiet, Dahms," Hess said softly. "You're right,
Otis. I was way out of line and if the festival officials
want to punish me, then they should punish me."

"What on earth possessed you to attack him like
that?" Otis asked.

"I've got my reasons."

"Would you like to share those reasons?"

Hess shook his head. "I don't think so."

Otis puffed himself up. "Well, then I think we all

know what my recommendation to the festival board will be as regards your future. I have to do what I have to do."

"You're gonna buy us all ice cream?" I asked.

Otis got very red in the face. "Come, all of you. We're going."

He turned, and he and his entourage toddled away.

We sat there in the dirt for a few more minutes. I was very tired, my arm ached, my knee throbbed, and I felt as though I weighed a couple of tons. The sun was too bright, and the only thing that distracted me from my misery was watching the sweat drip from my face to my breastplate. The warm, shining metal was streaked with rivulets of perspiration, drying white with salt before my eyes. Both Edgerton and Hess were similarly engaged, studiously avoiding conversation.

"Can we get out of this damned armor?" I asked.

Hess nodded.

"Good. Now can someone help me to my feet?"

Both men stood and each took one of my arms and raised me to a standing position. They had to support me part of the way, but with each step the pain lessened, and I was able to limp back to the armory mostly under my own power.

Soaked with sweat, I crawled out of my armor and changed back into my street clothes. Edgerton and Hess reopened the armory, and it was then that I realized that I hadn't seen Julia since we had left for the joust. I assumed that she had been there, but she'd evidently not returned to the armory. But if Hess was worried about where his wife had gone off to, he didn't show it. He and Edgerton somewhat grimly set out all the displays, but when customers started stopping in, Hess seemed to regain his usual hearty demeanor. Edgerton too, seemed content to pretend that nothing odd had happened, though I thought it significant that he didn't ask his boss why he had decided to go after Eckels.

I decided to make my way over to the Cock and Bull. Getting beat up is thirsty work and I really needed a beer. I also wanted to find out what Naomi might have to say about the fight that had broken out at the jousting ring. The ache in my arm still bothered me, but it was really no more than a presence in the background unless I used my arm for anything more strenuous than wiping my nose. I stretched the arm slowly before me and felt oddly reassured when it responded in pain. Maybe Naomi would respond to my injuries with kindness, I thought.

Instead, when she saw me hobble into the Cock and Bull, she stared at me without expression and began clapping her hands together slowly with rhythmic sarcasm. "There he is," she said, "my brave knight come home from the crusades. How fare you, my lord? I caught your last battle. I'd have to say that your folks wasted their money on your fencing lessons."

"You can't fence with a broadsword," I muttered.

"You couldn't slice your way through a pat of warm butter with a broadsword," she replied, now smiling as she came out from behind the bar and kissed me on the cheek. "Honestly, how are you doing? You're limping a little."

"That's not true. I'm limping a lot. But my pride took the worst of it. I'll be okay."

"Take a seat. I'll get you a beer."

It was mid-afternoon and the place was crowded, but I spotted a small, unoccupied table in the center of the room. I zigzagged my way through the crowd and, with some difficulty, managed to reach the table. Seated, I watched as Naomi negotiated the crowd like a ballet dancer—darting and swirling in her great poofy skirt, picking up empty glasses as she went. She set my beer in front of me and waved me off when I reached for my wallet.

"Thanks," I said.

"You deserve it," she answered as she sat in the chair opposite me.

"What are you doing after this joint closes, cutie?" I asked.

She sighed. "Oh, Lyle. It's Sunday. I've got to work in the morning. I've got laundry to do. Tons of stuff. I'll have to go right home after closing."

"Oh. Uh, okay."

"You're disappointed."

"No. I'm just…Okay, yeah. I'm disappointed."

"Good." She smiled broadly. "That ought to bring you back here next weekend."

I gave it some thought.

"Naomi, seeing you is the only thing that could bring me back here next weekend. But to be frank, I think I'd rather man the buffalo dung concession at a fertilizer convention than come back out here again. Could we just see each other during the week? Away from here?"

"Really, Lyle, you haven't exactly had the most normal of festival experiences. If you come back out here next Saturday, and plan to stay the night, I promise that you will have a completely different experience than you had this weekend."

"Not completely different, I hope. I mean, last night with you is something I wouldn't mind repeating."

"Why sir!" she gasped. "Whatever do you mean?"

I smiled. "Okay, no promises. But I will try to come

back next Saturday. In the meantime…"

"In the meantime," she said, standing and digging into a pocket, "I admit I was confident enough that you would ask that I wrote out my phone number for you." She handed me a scrap of paper. "Call me."

"Count on it."

She got a couple of steps away before she stopped abruptly and came back. "I almost forgot. Did you run into LeGrand again today?"

"Yeah. He took a run at me with a baseball bat, but Eckels—you know, Lancelot—stopped him. Then he tried it again and I stopped him."

"You might want to steer clear of him."

"Why's that?"

"Eckels might want to steer clear of him, too. That is if he recovers from that pummeling he took from your buddy the Black Knight."

"Oh, Don didn't really hurt Eckels."

"Really, it took two guys to carry him off."

"It took two guys to carry me off, too. You don't see me whining about it."

"You're so tough," she sneered.

"Tough as boiled owl, baby. Now what's this about LeGrand?"

"He was in here earlier talking loud. Making a big show. Making sure that I could hear him, you know. Said he was going to take care of both the fat guy and Lancelot. He said he was going to kill both of you."

"You sure he wasn't talking about some other fat guy?"

Naomi shook her head. "He sounded serious."

"They always sound serious. But after he cools off, he'll see things differently."

"You think?"

"Yeah," I assured her. "Still, maybe next time I see him I'll try to make peace. Try and apologize or something."

"Maybe you should just stay away from him."

"Maybe you're right."

I took a deep draught of my beer and when I looked up, Naomi bent down and kissed me hard on the mouth. She stood and stared at me for a moment with rather a glazed expression.

"What's wrong?" I asked.

"I was just remembering. For the first couple of weekends of the festival, LeGrand and Jason were palling around. Then last weekend they were in here after hours. They got pretty wasted and got into some kind of argument. I didn't think too much of it at the time. You know how it is when guys get wasted. They say all sorts of stuff. But during their argument, LeGrand yelled something like, 'I'm gonna kill you, man.' "

"Do you know what they were arguing about?"

"I haven't a clue. But I'm starting to get worried. Do you think—"

"I think it's like you said. Guys say all sorts of stuff when they're drinking. LeGrand's a blowhard. I don't see him as a killer."

Naomi stared at me for a few more seconds. "That's crap, Lyle. You're just telling me what you think I want to hear."

"What makes you say that?"

"You just told me that LeGrand came at you with a baseball bat. I think we ought to go to the cops."

"Next time I see Dungstubble, I'll mention that LeGrand and Gilroy argued. But I don't think that's going to be enough to get him hauled off to jail. Besides, grabbing a bat and going after someone is different than stalking someone with a crossbow. One is an emotional, heat-of-the-moment kind of thing. The other is…Well, it takes some thought, some planning. I think LeGrand is apt to act only in passion. If he and Gilroy argued last week, I think he would have gotten over it long before the murder."

"But you'll admit that you don't really know the guy. I mean, you and LeGrand have never really even spoken."

"That's right."

"Then you don't really know shit."

"That's right."

"This is supposed to reassure me?"

"That's right."

"You stink at this, Lyle."

"You can't be good at everything."

She managed a tight little grin. "Watch out for LeGrand, okay? I just met you; I'm not ready to lose you."

"I may not be good at everything, but I'm real good at watching my back."

She nodded. "I wonder if Jason felt the same way."

Chapter Eight

As I left the Cock and Bull, I heard a great cheer arise from a crowd that was gathered near the Irish Cottage, where Clan Highland was encamped. I stared toward the cottage and directly into the late afternoon sun. Between the glare and the long shadow cast across the field by the cottage itself, I was unable to see exactly what the commotion was about, so I ambled over that way. I passed Dick Peterson sitting alone on a stool next to his Elephant Ride cart. The elephants were tethered to a pair of metal poles a few feet away.

"Business a little slow?" I asked when I got with earshot of Peterson.

"Always slacks off in the late afternoon," he said. "People start bringing their kiddies home. Folks got to work in the morning."

I walked up to Peterson and introduced myself.

"I've seen you around this weekend," Peterson said as he shook my hand. "Figured you for a friend of the Hesses."

"Friend of Stephen Edgerton's actually," I told him. "Stephen tells me that you got two great kids. Says the older one is a helluva video game player."

Peterson smiled and ran a hand through his prematurely graying dark hair. "I say that Jack spends way too much time playing them things. Hell, as much as he carries that Switch around with him, you'd think that somebody superglued it to his hand."

"Kids go through their phases," I said. "I guess everybody has their little obsessions."

"You're telling me." Peterson laughed. "Last year it was comic books, this year Nintendo. I can't wait to see what he comes up with for next year."

"Well, he's old enough to start asking if he can pierce various body parts and join a rock band."

Peterson nodded, "Yeah, and your pal Edgerton ain't helping things. The other day he brought his guitar and was showing Jack some chords. Just what I need, a little Eddie Van Halen."

We both laughed.

"Still," Peterson continued, "I guess any hobby that isn't dangerous, or criminal, is a blessing. It really does get awfully dull out here for the boys. And we've been doing three festivals every summer for the last six years. I don't worry so much about Simon, he's the younger one, the seven-year-old, but Jack is fourteen and being bored can cause even a good kid to act out."

"So I remember from when I was that age," I said.

Peterson nodded a couple of times. I was about to make my excuses and move on when he said, "I was really sorry to hear about poor Gilroy. Any word from the police? Do they know who killed him?"

"Not that I've heard."

"It's a terrible thing. Especially happening here. And nearly in front of my kids. Lucky thing they were out getting something to eat at the time."

I looked at Peterson closely, puzzled. "You know, I could be wrong." I told him. "But I was right over there when that arrow flew and I remember both kids being here, on the track, with the elephants." I ran the moment back through my mind a couple of times. "That's right. Jack was leading a rider and Simon was in his wheelchair watching. I remember it. Don't remember where you were though."

Peterson shrugged. "Oh yeah. I forgot. They were here. But I don't think they saw anything. At least I hope they didn't. They've had enough death to last them a while."

"How's that?"

Peterson turned away momentarily. "Their mother died. Been nearly a year now."

"I'm sorry. I didn't know."

"They seem to be handling it okay. Seem to have gotten over the shock. But it's hard to tell with kids. The other night I heard Simon sobbing in the middle of the night. I was going to go in to him, but I heard Jack in there trying to comfort him. Thought I'd let them have a moment. I'm really lucky that they get along so well. Jack's always been devoted to Simon. More so since his mom died."

"She die suddenly?"

"Yeah. Brain hemorrhage. Just left us one day."

"Hard to say if that's easier on the kids than a long illness. Maybe not. An illness gives you time to prepare."

Peterson looked at me with soft eyes. Not teary but softened with memory. "I don't think you can ever be prepared. Not really."

"I don't suppose."

Another loud cheer rose from the crowd around Clan Highland.

"I think they're doing the caber toss over there," Peterson said, forcing a smile. "My kids went over to watch. You want to go over with me?"

"What about the ride?"

"I can close down for a few minutes. Nobody here anyway. It's not as though I have to lock anything up. All I got is the cart, this stool, and the elephants. And I don't see anybody making off with the elephants. They're too big to fit in the back of a Subaru."

Peterson reached up into the cart and got out a sign that said, "Back in Five Minutes." After he hung it on the cart, I asked, "What if you're not back in five minutes?"

"Probably won't be. But we're not going far. I'll keep an eye out. The five-minute thing is a small lie. Really kind of an estimate."

As we walked over to join the crowd, I thought about his small lie. And about another, maybe not so small. Gilroy had been killed only the previous day. There was no doubt that the cops had questioned Peterson. He would have been asked to describe exactly where he and his kids had been at the time of the murder. He may have been asked more than once. There was just no way that he could have forgotten the murder happened within view of his children. Just no way.

Peterson spotted his kids in the crowd, but they were on the opposite side, too far away from the elephants, so he and I took a spot nearer to his rides. Over the heads of the spectators in front of us, I could see a man in a kilt walking toward a telephone pole that was lying on the ground in front of him. When he reached it, he picked up one end of the telephone pole, lifting it over his head. Another man, also wearing a kilt, joined him and together they walked the length of the pole, raising it as they went, until it was standing on its end. The first guy bent down, grasped the pole with both hands, and rested his shoulder against it.

The pole was about fifteen feet long and looked really, really heavy. It must have been, because the man grunted brutally as he hoisted it up off the ground and took a few steps forward. Suddenly, he stopped and swung both arms upward. The pole flipped over in the air, so that the end that the thrower had been holding crashed to the ground opposite him. It struck the ground very nearly straight across from where he had released it. The crowd cheered noisily, several partisans whooping with glee.

"That was a good one," Peterson told me.

"You've seen this done before?"

"Oh yes. Highland games have become a staple at Renaissance festivals. I've been to lots of them. You want to talk caber toss, stone put, throwing for weight, for height, or for distance, I'm your man."

Peterson laughed, but also searched my eyes for approval. Although I smiled, his laughter trailed off self-consciously and his eyes darted back to the competition.

A couple of Clan members went out on the field to reposition the pole for the next man.

"Doesn't the phone company get pissed that these guys are ripping out their poles for this kind of thing?" I asked Peterson.

"It's called a caber, Dahms. It's big, but not nearly as big as an actual telephone pole."

"You wouldn't say that if they made you toss the thing."

Peterson grunted.

The next guy to toss was my new pal, Max Wiseman. He was laughing heartily with his spotter as they walked the pole upright. His face became serious as he hoisted the caber off the ground and took his steps forward. Wiseman issued a great guttural roar as he flung the caber into the air and stood puffing as he watched it pitch away from him. It landed a bit to the right of where he had released it. He got applause, but it was mixed with sounds of disappointment. Wiseman smiled but shook his head as he did so.

"That wasn't as good as the last one?" I asked Peterson.

"No. But it wasn't bad. Picture the field as a big clock. When the thrower releases the caber, his feet are at six o'clock. If the small end, the end that was down at the start of the toss, flips completely over and lands directly in front of the thrower, that's twelve o'clock and that's perfect. But all scores from the nine o'clock to the three o'clock positions are good."

"Do they all use the same pole?"

"No. They start with lighter and shorter cabers and work their way up until all but one man is eliminated."

"So, Wiseman gets to go on to the next round?"

"Who's Wiseman?"

"The guy who threw last."

"Yes. He gets to go on to the next round."

We watched the competition together for quite a while. The throwers moved on to even longer cabers and one by one all were eliminated except Wiseman and this short, squat, no-neck guy with enormous upper body development who looked like he could be on the Bulgarian weightlifting team if only he didn't drink so damned much beer. He was hugely muscled, but so round that you expected him to simply roll rather than walk from place to place. The crowd roared with approval as he tossed what looked to me like a perfect score in the last round.

It was Wiseman's turn. He stood in front of the caber composing himself for a few seconds before getting into position. The crowd noise quieted to a murmur as Wiseman approached the caber. But off to Wiseman's left, someone began to shout wildly. Wiseman shook his head, then bent down to start raising the caber, but the shouting continued. Wiseman stood up and cast an angry glare toward the shouting man. It was LeGrand. I couldn't make out what he was shouting, but it sounded pretty ugly.

The people who had been standing next to LeGrand began to back away until LeGrand was standing alone, isolated within the throng. A ripple of confusion and fear radiated through the crowd. He pointed at Wiseman and red-faced, shouted at the top of his lungs. "I Want You!" over the noise of the crowd.

With one finger violently puncturing the air before him and his wild eyes blazing at Wiseman, LeGrand was like some deranged Uncle Sam. I began to elbow my way over toward LeGrand, wondering if I would be able to reach him before he made a move on Wiseman. Then a phalanx of blue uniforms moved in on him. Dunstable's men dragged the still shouting LeGrand from the scene and the crowd swirled back in to fill the gap left by LeGrand's removal. Wiseman made a poor toss to end the competition.

As the crowd thinned, Peterson was able to signal to his boys to rejoin him at the elephant ride. He shook my hand as we parted, and I went to look for Wiseman.

He stood with a few fellow Clan members, just outside their large tent. I stood a couple of feet distant until Wiseman saw me and parted from the others.

"Okay," he asked. "Who *is* this loony?"

"Don't you remember? He's the guy that tried to part my hair with a Louisville slugger earlier today. You really should pay more attention."

I didn't know Wiseman well enough to be able to read him. He didn't smile at my joke, but he didn't appear to have been overly frightened by LeGrand and did not appear angry with me. "Don't you ever give a straight answer to a question?" he asked.

"Not often."

"How about giving it a try now?"

"The guy's name is Dirk LeGrand. He runs the kinky sex chain mail concession out here. On the side he antagonizes people and picks fights. That's really all I know about him."

Wiseman sighed, then led me around to the back of the tent where we sat down on the ground in the shade of a maple tree. There was something vaguely rectangular on the ground next to him covered in burlap. Wiseman reached over and pulled back the burlap to reveal a cooler. He reached inside and pulled out two bottles of beer. He handed me one and opened the other for himself. I looked at the bottle of craft-brewed pale ale.

"Good beer," I said.

Wiseman nodded. "So," he said, drawing it out to multiple syllables. "Is this guy a threat or what?"

"I honestly don't know. My sense is that he is more bluster than bite, but I really don't know."

"What makes this really bothersome is that someone got killed yesterday," Wiseman said.

"Yeah."

"Is it possible that this Dirk did it?"

"I don't think it's likely. But it's possible."

"Do you know if Dirk and the dead guy knew each

other?"

"Turns out that they did."

"Do you know if they quarreled?"

"Yeah. Turns out that they quarreled."

Wiseman stared at me, then took a deep draught of beer. "What have you got me into, Dahms?"

"Sorry. I don't know what I could have done differently. You just happened to be with me when he took his last run at me. Now it looks like he's pissed at you just 'cause you were there. It doesn't really make a lot of sense."

"You're expecting this to make sense?"

"Most things generally do."

"Not if you're dealing with a madman," Wiseman said. "Not if the guy is nuts."

I couldn't really think of anything more to say.

"Sorry," I repeated.

"Me too."

We drank the beers in silence. Finally, Wiseman asked, "You really don't think LeGrand is the killer?"

The truth is that I knew of no other person that seemed even remotely likely to have killed Gilroy. LeGrand knew Gilroy, had quarreled with him, and had shown very violent tendencies.

"No," I lied, "I don't think he has it in him."

"You know what I think?"

"Tell me."

"I think that you are trying to convince me that this Dirk fellow hasn't got the chops to be a killer because you're afraid."

"It scares me that you think that," I deadpanned.

"Seriously, Dahms. Think about it. What if this Dirk is a killer? Who, right now, is number one on his hit parade? If he's going to kill again, who is he most likely going to kill?"

"Mostly likely me. I guess I'm number one. Number one with a bullet."

Wiseman stared at me. "Just try telling me that doesn't worry you. Just try."

Chapter Nine

Wiseman told me that the Clan had no plans to return to the festival the next weekend. We both agreed that this was probably for the best. I shook hands with him, thanked him for the beer, and wished him well, certain that I wouldn't see him again. Even if I did come out to the festival the next week to see Naomi, I was pretty sure that would be my last time. I had successfully avoided it for a number of years and there was no reason to believe that I would be unable to avoid it in the future.

As the sun neared the horizon and the crowds headed toward the exits, I approached the armory. Edgerton was beginning to pack things away, and I watched as he went over to the mannequin with the chain mail coat, put his arms around it, and lifted it momentarily off the ground. He must have changed his mind because he put it back down and stood for a moment fingering the woven metal work. A couple of last-minute customers still drifted around inside the armory and one of them went up to talk to him.

As I reached them, Edgerton put his hand on the chain mail coat. I heard him say, "About forty pounds."

The customer nodded his head a couple of times and walked away.

Edgerton glanced at me, and I gave him a little smirk. "Say, how much does that weigh?"

"Shut up and help me move it in back."

I picked up one side and together we moved it to the back of the building where it could be locked away. About halfway there, the barrel helmet that had been perched on the headless torso tumbled to the ground. We propped the torso against a wall in the back and Edgerton went out to get the helmet.

"Where's Hess?" I asked when he returned.

"He got called to the office."

"Is that like getting called to the principal's office in high school?"

"In this case, probably. Don hasn't been real talkative this afternoon. Not since he took after Eckels. He didn't tell me why they wanted to see him."

"You talk to him about the fight at the joust?"

"No. I didn't want to pry."

"Have you seen Julia?"

"She was here for a while. She and Don had some things to talk about, then she left."

"After they talked?"

"Yeah."

"How loud did it get?"

Edgerton shrugged. "Pretty loud, I guess."

"So, things aren't going so well between the two of them?"

"Not so well. No."

The cannon at the front gate fired and the sound rolled across the grounds like thunder, signaling the end of the festival.

Edgerton set the barrel helmet inside a weathered pine cabinet, then clapped shut the cabinet door. The latch didn't catch, and the door swung slightly open. I followed Edgerton out into the open part of the armory and leaned against the counter as he finished putting everything away. "What now?" I asked.

"We really can't leave until Don comes back. Besides, I'd like to know what the festival brass had to say to him."

I lit a cigarette with a crumbled match. "How much do you know about what's going on here?"

"I don't *know* anything," Edgerton said. "Nobody's talking to me, so I don't really know anything for a fact. But I think I have just about everything figured out."

"You figured out that Julia had an affair with Eckels and that's why Hess took after him rather than playing out the script?"

"Yeah."

"You didn't know before?"

"No."

"Would you say that you are as close to the Hesses as Gilroy was?"

"Closer. Why do you ask?"

"Gilroy knew about the affair."

"You think Don confided in Jason and left me in the dark?"

"It's possible. It's also possible that he found out from Julia or from someone else."

"What are you driving at?"

"Shit, Stephen. Don't be so defensive. I'm not driving at anything. I'm just trying to sort a few things out in my head."

"Well, quit being such a damned snoop. It's no business of yours anyway."

Edgerton turned and walked toward the fire pit. He sat down on the low stone wall, picked up an iron poker and stabbed at the cold ashes in the pit. I sat down next to him and wordlessly finished my smoke. Edgerton continued to poke at the fire pit. Flakes of ash wafted upward then fluttered like snowflakes back to the ground. Some fell against his pants leg, and he was brushing them away when Hess returned.

Hess smiled broadly at us. "Well. I have good news and bad news. Which do you want first?"

"The bad news," Edgerton replied. "That's all we've had for so long I don't think I could stand anything else."

"I'll give the good news first," Hess said, ignoring Edgerton. "The festival has decided that next year they will have daily jousts. They said the crowd response was tremendous."

"Really?" Edgerton asked.

"Now for the bad news," Hess continued. "We will not be involved. There's an outfit out of Racine, Wisconsin which, according to our fearless leaders, is professional, has experience at other festivals, and with them there is no risk of anything…shall we say anything *unexpected* happening during the competition."

"Great," Edgerton muttered, standing and tossing the poker to the ground.

"Cheer up," Hess said. "I got the impression that they had made this decision some time ago. I don't think what happened today changed their minds. They were going to go with these other guys all along."

"How did the meeting go?" I asked.

Hess grinned. "Not too bad, considering. The festival board wanted to know if I understood the difference between high-spirited fun and assault with intent to do bodily injury. I assured them that I did and that nothing like this would happen in the future. You know. I told them what they wanted to hear. Otis was there and he kept asking them what kind of disciplinary

107

action they were going to take. Finally, just to shut him up, the board told me that if I acted up again, they would have to consider revoking my license to operate on festival grounds. I acted the part of the penitent, and the meeting broke up. That was it."

"Was Eckels there?" I asked.

"Nope. And that is a bit strange because the meeting had been scheduled for some time. It was originally to be a follow-up to discuss how the jousting went this weekend, not just to call me on the carpet."

"Well," I said, "maybe he just didn't want to be in the same room with you."

"Yeah. I'm afraid Greg Eckels and me just aren't destined to be great pals. Not after today."

"Just what happened today?" Edgerton asked.

Hess didn't answer. Instead, still smiling, he reached into a shirt pocket and pulled out a nearly full pack of cigarettes. He lit one and was about to put the pack away when I stopped him. "Can I get one of those from you?"

"Sure," he said, tossing me the pack.

I took one and tossed it back to him. "I didn't know you smoked."

"Don't usually."

I nodded and rolled the cigarette gently between my thumb and forefinger. "Pall Mall" it said in a ring above the filter. I lit the cigarette and watched the smoke plume silently upward between the other two men and myself.

"What happened out there today, Don?" Edgerton repeated.

"I got a little carried away. Let's just say I was caught up in the moment."

"I heard you and Julia arguing," Edgerton told him. "I know about Eckels and her."

Hess' smile faded to a slightly bemused expression. "By now I expect everyone knows about that."

"Are you guys going to be all right?"

Hess lowered his head and stared at his boots for a few seconds. Then he walked over to Edgerton and gently set his hand on his shoulder. "I don't know, man. For now, she's left me. She didn't say that she was gone for good, but she said she needed some time to think things through."

"She's not in love with Eckels?"

Hess chuckled mirthlessly. "Oh no. At least she's not leaving me for Mr. Perfect. No, that's been over for a while. She had the thing with Eckels because she was lonely. I haven't spent much time with her the last couple of years. She says that she attends these festivals only to be with me and that I barely notice that she's here. She's right, I suppose. I do get swept up in other things. And I haven't exactly been always faithful myself."

"Does that mean you've been unfaithful?" I asked.

"Yes, Lyle. That's what it means. I'm only human."

"I hear that excuse a lot."

Hess didn't respond. Instead, he tossed his cigarette away, went to the door that led to the back of the armory. I heard his footfalls going up and down the stairs and when he emerged, he was holding the biggest jar of olives I had ever seen. He leaned against the counter and unscrewed the lid. The olives were big too. Huge, pitted green olives swimming in light green brine. Slowly he reached into the wide opening of the jar and pulled out an olive. He studied it for a moment, then popped it into his mouth.

When he finished chewing, he turned the jar so we could see the label and asked, "Anybody want an olive?"

I shook my head. "We're talking about your marriage, and you suddenly feel a need for olives?"

"I like olives. You sure you don't want one?"

I stared at him. He ate another olive.

"Sure, I'll have one," I told him.

"Me too," Edgerton said.

They were very good olives.

Finally, Hess screwed the lid back on the jar and he and Edgerton went upstairs to their bedrooms. Before long, both men came down carrying rucksacks stuffed with their belongings and we all went to the back of the armory. Hess closed and carefully latched the inner door blocking the rays of the setting sun, shrouding the narrow room in darkness. Then we exited the outer door, which Hess secured with a padlock.

I looked at the padlock and at the hinges of the rough wooden door. "A thief would take all of five seconds to get through that door,"

"We don't get thieves way out here, Lyle," Hess said with his usual smile.

Edgerton grunted. "No thieves. Just murderers."

He let his eyes wander toward the part of the armory where Gilroy had died. Then he threw his bag over his shoulder and said, "This weekend sucked. Let's get out of here."

Hess had parked his car just outside the festival wall. He offered to take Edgerton home, but Edgerton elected to ride with me. We nodded to Hess as he drove away and began to walk to my car. I looked out across the field where I had parked. In the gathering dusk, only a few cars remained and a few dark figures, most laden with purchases, plodded out toward them.

We got in my car and the engine started after some

prodding but conked out twice as we bounced over hill and ditch on our way to the road. Neither of us felt like talking, so I clicked on the radio, and we listened to Tony Bennett stepping out with his baby as my headlights swept the pavement and lit up a sign that warned of deer crossing the road. I got to wondering how they knew where to put the *Deer Crossing* signs. I mean, did they put the sign up and then instruct the deer to cross only at that spot or did they ask the deer where they liked to cross and then put the sign up? I was about to ask Edgerton if he knew, when he slapped himself on the forehead and informed me that we had to go back.

"Why's that?" I asked.

"I forgot my book."

"Ah. You got plenty of books."

He looked at me blankly. "But this is the one I'm reading."

"Read another."

"Turn the car around."

"This is stupid. It's late. I'm not going all the way back there just so you can get some book."

Edgerton kept looking at me. I turned and faced straight ahead, but I could still feel him looking. He didn't say anything. Not even when I turned the car around.

"What book is it?" I asked as we bounced back across the parking field to the door at the rear of the armory.

"*Green Mars* by Kim Stanley Robinson."

"Huh?"

"It's about humans settling Mars."

"You brought science fiction to a Renaissance festival?"

"Yeah," he said. "I like the contrast. It's good to contemplate the future as you explore the past. After all, the past is where the seeds of the future were sown."

"Wait a minute," I muttered, "let me get a pencil. I want to write that down."

"Whatever," he said.

I pulled up directly to the back door of the armory. Edgerton got out and pulled his key ring from his pocket. Although there couldn't have been fewer than fifteen keys on the thing, he didn't seem to have one to the padlock that fastened the door.

"You want I should break it down for ya?" I joked.

"I don't think so."

"Just get out of my way," I told him.

I had far fewer keys on my key ring—just the key to my room at the Bijou, the key to my car, the key to my office, and a nifty little gadget I picked up at a security convention that could be used for picking simple locks. I had the door open in seconds.

"You're welcome," I said as the door swung open.

"Whatever," Edgerton replied.

He pushed his way past me and began to inch his way up the stairs to his room in the dim light of the back hall. That struck me as odd. That there was dim light. I moved forward and saw that the door that led from the backroom to the open part of the armory was ajar. I distinctly remembered that it had been latched. I called to Edgerton who made grumbling noises as he came down the stairs.

"You guys closed this, right?" I asked, pointing to the open door.

"Yeah."

"Then somebody's been here."

"We should check it out."

I nodded and we went out together into the quiet. I turned to the right and slowly walked along the perimeter of the armory. There was no one there but something struck me as odd. The mannequin with the chain mail coat and barrel helmet was back outside in the armory's open-air market.

"Didn't we put this away?" I asked.

"We did."

I walked over to the mannequin and noticed something oily coating the service of the chain mail. I touched it, then rubbed my fingers together.

Edgerton turned and went into the back room, emerging with an electric lantern. He switched it on and walked toward me casting a halo of yellow light. A sick feeling stirred inside me. I took the lantern from Edgerton and motioned for him to stay where he was. I shone the lantern on the mannequin. A thick liquid was oozing from the helmet, dripping down the mail coat.

"Hold the lantern," I said, handing it back to Edgerton.

When he took it, I reached out with both hands and gently lifted the helmet off the torso. It was heavier than I'd expected, as though there was something inside. I shook the helmet and whatever it was slid out with a moist slurping sound.

"Jesus Christ!" Edgerton gasped.

As a wave of nausea rose within me, I dropped the helmet to the ground, swallowed hard, and took the lantern back from Edgerton. Gregory Eckels looked relaxed. His eyes were closed and there was something about the line of his mouth that suggested that he had simply drifted peacefully off to sleep.

But that was unlikely.

There was no sign of his body, just his head propped atop the mannequin, clotting blood slowly dripping from his severed neck.

I turned to Edgerton. He stood stock-still; his eyes were wide and unseeing as he stared at the dead thing. I stepped in front of him to block his view and called his name loudly. He remained motionless. I took him by the shoulders and shook him lightly. He still didn't move. Alarmed, I realized that he might be going into shock. I didn't know what to do, but knew I had to do something.

I moved in, put my mouth close to his ear and in a voice as gentle as a mother to her sleeping babe, I said, "Hey, Stephen. How much do you figure a thing like that weighs?"

His eyes snapped into focus. He stared at me, a look of absolute horror fixed upon his face. Then he lowered his eyes and finally lowered his head. His entire body began to draw into itself until he was standing before me stooped into a question mark. He shuddered once. Then a second time. He gulped, then gulped again. His body was soon racked by convulsions, and the eerie sound of his involuntary laughter shattered the deadly quiet around us.

Chapter Ten

About three o'clock the next afternoon, I found myself staring at my reflection in the bathroom mirror at the Bijou, the rooming house where I lived. Although I'd managed some five hours of sleep, after the exertions of the day before, and particularly, after the night I'd spent at the Little Crow police station, I was bone tired. My knee still hurt, my arm ached, and answering the same questions over and over to the same cops hour after hour had left me with one helluva headache. I filled the bathroom sink with cool water and splashed my face repeatedly. I buried my wet face in a towel, then smiled at the wan visage watching me from the mirror. After some coaxing, the weary reflection smiled back at me. I padded back to my room for some coffee.

I had to pass Edgerton's room on the way to my own, but I didn't hear him stirring so I didn't knock. I knew he had the day off. I wasn't sure if he had to work his night job at the copy shop, but his day job making armor was definitely on hold, what with Gilroy dead and Hess in the Little Crow jail house arrested for the murder of Gregory Eckels. I shook my head—glad to be out of it, glad to be going back to my regular life.

Then I got dressed, left the house, and walked the two blocks over to my office in the Minneapolis Technology Center. The last few years the former high school turned office building had housed only a handful of businesses and had seemed headed for foreclosure. But it was saved when the owners made a deal with the nearby University to provide space for their employment office. I should have been happy. I hadn't been anxious to move, but I'd gotten used to the quiet of the nearly deserted building and now had to share the hallways with throngs of jobseekers, all hoping for a civil service ticket to economic security. I contented myself with the thought that the University was rehabbing an older building on campus that was slated to house the employment office in a year or two. Then the quiet would return, no doubt to be followed soon after by the sound of an eviction notice being slid under my door and the pounding of windows being boarded up.

I unlocked the door to my small office—called a "suite" by the building management company—and picked my mail up off the floor. Then I made some coffee, fired up my PC, and was staring at a blank screen when Augie Tarkof came in.

Tarkof, an old-timer on the Minneapolis Homicide squad, had flecks of gray in his brown hair, and the strain that his belly placed on his suspenders both testified to his long years in on the job. He didn't greet me. In fact, he didn't say a word as he entered and took a seat in one of the client chairs that faced my desk. He wore a blank, almost sleepy expression on his face, but his cold blue eyes swept the room alertly.

We stared at each other for a moment. "Dunstable call you?" I asked at last.

"Yep," he said, absently straightening up the pile of mail that I had left on my desk.

"He ask you about me?"

"Yep."

"What did you say?"

"I told him what I tell everyone that asks me about you, Dahms. I told him that you're an irritating sonofabitch who has the bad sense to keep sticking your nose where it don't belong. I told him that you call yourself an investigator but wouldn't be able to find your own ass with both hands and a copy of *Gray's Anatomy*."

Tarkof reached into the inside pocket of his wrinkled gray suit coat and pulled out a stick of gum. He unwrapped it, slipped the gum into his mouth, and tossed the wrapper on the floor. "What the hell you doing down in Little Crow?" he asked.

I sighed. "I ain't doing shit down there, Augie. I went down there to visit a friend and people started getting killed. That's all I know."

"Dunstable tells me that this friend of yours, this Hess, is the killer. All he wants to know is—did you help?"

"Hess didn't kill anybody."

"Oh, and you would know. You being such a great investigator and everything."

"I don't *know* that Hess didn't do it, but I think it's pretty unlikely."

Tarkof groaned. "I'm know I'm gonna hate myself for asking, but you wanna explain to me why you don't think Hess is the killer?"

"For one thing, I know that Hess didn't kill Jason Gilroy. I was looking right at him when that murder took place. Lots of other people saw him, too. That's a fact."

"Hess wasn't arrested for killing Gilroy. He was arrested for killing the other guy."

"I don't think Hess killed Eckels either."

"Hess provoked a fight with the dead guy earlier that

day. Hess' wife had been sleeping with the dead guy. Hess has no verifiable alibi for the time of the murder. He sounds right to me."

"What do you mean Hess has no alibi for the time of the murder? According to the other guy that works at the armory, and I'm sure this can be verified by other witnesses, Hess was at the armory until he had to go a meeting with the festival brass. He left the meeting and returned to the armory just after the festival closed at seven o'clock. We talked for a few minutes, I walked out with him, saw him get in his car and drive away. And he sure as hell wasn't around when I returned to the armory only about fifteen or twenty minutes later. You telling me that he was able to double back, find Eckels, hack his head off, put the head on display in his own shop, and leave all in the space of twenty minutes?"

"He could have," Augie said. "But he didn't have to kill Eckels after you left that night. He could have done it earlier that afternoon."

"I just told you that Hess was at the armory until he left for the meeting. He didn't have the time."

Augie smirked. "That meeting got started around five o'clock. Hess left for it shortly after four. That's what your pal, Edgerton told the Little Crow cops, anyway. Hess had nearly an hour to find Eckels, kill him, hide the body, and still make the meeting. Remember, Eckels wasn't at the meeting. But he was supposed to be there. It was important to him."

"So, you're saying that Hess kills Eckels, decapitates him, and shows up at the meeting showing no sign of the crime, not one hair out of place, not one speck of blood on his clothes?"

"Could have happened that way, but in this case the

M.E. says that victim died from blunt force trauma to the head. The killer didn't actually cut off his head until after the guy had been dead a while. Of course, it don't matter to me. It ain't my case."

"If it don't matter to you, Augie, why are you here? Why want to talk to me about it? Dungstubble ask you to keep an eye on me?"

"I ain't got the time to do Dunstable's job for him."

"Then what?"

Tarkof's eyes wandered briefly around the room. "Fellow cop asks you to do something, you do something. I ain't gonna have one of my guys follow you around 'cause it would likely be a waste of time. So, I came here to talk to you. See if I think you're involved."

"And have you reached any conclusions?"

"Yeah," he said, rising from the chair. "I've concluded that you're too vacuous to have had anything to do with those killings."

I smiled. "*Vacuous?* What? Did you get one of those 'Word of the Day' books?'

Tarkof grunted.

"Tell me, Augie. Did Dunstable mention a guy named LeGrand to you?"

"Yeah. He said you spent most of last night trying to pin the killing on him."

"Did Dunstable say he was looking into it?"

Tarkof shrugged. "Dunstable's a cop. Cops look into things."

He started toward the door.

"What do you think of him?" I asked. "What kind of cop is he?"

Tarkof turned and eyed me narrowly.

"He's the kind of cop I used to be when I was just

119

starting out. Before I was actually any good at the job but was plenty mean enough that nobody really wanted to question me about it. Before age mellowed me, sensitivity classes got me in touch with my feminine side, and lawsuits for police brutality turned the entire force into a bunch of Oprah wannabes with guns. Little Crow likes to think of itself as one of them towns that time forgot. You know, they're far enough out of the city that they figure they're immune to big city problems, like crime and guns and gangs and drugs. Thing they don't realize is that those aren't just city problems. They're everybody's problems."

Tarkof sighed. "A few years ago, a fairly large drug operation gets busted. It's headquartered right there in Little Crow. The guys running it are adults, but a couple of high school kids working for them cop to selling dope and coke to other kids. The good people of Little Crow don't much like hearing that kind of thing about themselves. So, they appoint Dunstable Chief of Police. Dunstable promises to get tough on crime. To do it the old-fashioned way by scaring the drug dealers out of town. Little Crow eats this stuff up. They essentially tell Dunstable he can do what he wants as long as he keeps the bad guys away. Dunstable's not stupid. He knows he can't keep all the bad guys away. But he knows that his town hired him to be their tough guy, you know, to brutalize the bad guys. And he takes that very seriously."

"So, you're saying that Dunstable isn't all that devoted to due process?"

"You could say that. Dunstable likes the way he scares people. He likes to hurt bad guys. He likes to show he's badder than anybody else. Down in Little Crow, Dunstable can beat the crap out of a suspect and ain't nobody gonna say a word."

"Like the good old days, huh?"

"I get misty just thinking about it."

"So, what are you telling me?"

"You might want to steer clear of Dunstable. He don't like you. He gets the chance, he's gonna let you know it."

"I appreciate the warning."

"Yeah," Tarkof said, shaking his head. "Too bad you're too vacuous to heed it."

Chapter Eleven

After Tarkof left, I spent several minutes watching a fly walk across a large map of the greater Twin Cities metro area that I'd tacked to my office wall. The fly had started off in the south metro, down around Hastings, then went north to the confluence of the Mississippi and Minnesota rivers in Mendota Heights near the airport. He must have got spooked by the sound of an airplane taking off or something, because the fly itself took off, circling the room before returning to the map to land in the northernmost part of the metro, near East Bethel. He headed west and made it to Clearwater before I smacked him lightly with a rolled-up newspaper. The fly's body fell to the floor, but I had to get a tissue from the desk to wipe a little wet fly stuff off the map.

After that, I decided that I had worked enough for the day. I locked the office and walked one block over to McCauley's Pub.

McCauley's was a college bar located in Dinkytown—a neighborhood adjacent to the University of Minnesota. Most of the people who lived in Dinkytown were only there for a couple of years. They got their degrees and moved along. But there was a core of folks you could not imagine ever leaving. Some had set up small businesses there, like Tom the Tailor or Dave the Barber—people who formed the soul of the place, whom you could count on for a kind word and a smile, and without whom the neighborhood would lose something immeasurable. But other long-term residents were lost souls—people who came to get a degree but never made it onto any kind of career track. Some of these lost souls were genuine nutbars. And many of these nutbars hung out at McCauley's, interspersed among the regular clientele of students, staff, and faculty like fifth columnists at an embassy cocktail party.

When I arrived, Skip the bartender was down at the end of the bar clearing glasses from a group of students gathered in front of the TV. He slipped the glasses into the rack of the small dishwasher behind the bar, grabbed a red plastic basket and scooped it full of popcorn from the machine next to the dishwasher. He wiped the bar in front of the students with one hand and dropped the basket before them with the other. Skip never even looked in my direction; he just picked up a clean glass, pulled a Schell's dark from the tap and set the beer in front of me, a trickle of foam running down the glass just like in the commercials. I set a ten spot down on the bar. Skip picked up the money and rang the beer up on the cash register. He put my change in front of me, but a little closer to his side of the bar than mine.

"How's it going?" I asked.

"Same old," he said, with his curious half smile.

I didn't really know that much about Skip. I think he liked it that way. I didn't know where he was from, I didn't know exactly how old he was, and I didn't know if he had a family. I never got up the guts to ask him how half of his face had become paralyzed. I didn't know if his previous employment had been as a bartender, a prison trustee, or as the director of a day care center, but I knew that if I were ever in serious trouble, I would want

Skip by my side.

He was not a big man, only about medium height and spare, with long, brown arms that seemed longer than they were because of his tapered, clearly defined muscles and the refined, dignified way he carried himself. And he had quick hands. Most of the time this was evident only as he pulled beers or snatched up empty glasses, but he kept a baseball bat behind the bar, the barrel shortened a bit so he could get it out quickly. If there was trouble, you didn't even see him move, you just heard the loud snap of the bat on the bar and usually that was the end of it. If someone was too drunk or too stupid and gave Skip a hard time after the bat came out, there was the enormous .44 that he kept behind the bar.

I'd often wondered why McCauley's hired a guy like Skip to tend bar. I wondered if he scared off some of the customers. But then I figured that when he applied, the owner was probably too frightened not to give him the job.

I ordered a second beer, and when he brought it to me, Skip asked, "How's Stephen?"

"He's doing okay," I said.

"Hard to lose a buddy like that."

"How'd you hear?"

"Saw it on the TV," Skip replied. "Even saw you and Stephen in the background in a couple of shots."

"I wasn't in armor, was I?"

Skip raised an eyebrow. "No," he said, "I'm sure I would have remembered that." He wiped the bar in absent motions. "Stephen's a sensitive sort," he said. "Be a good idea for you to keep an eye on him for a while. Be around. That sort of thing."

"He seems okay. He seems to be handling it well."

"He'd seem that way," Skip said, looking at something at the other end of the room. "You being such a tough guy and all, Stephen would probably make sure you thought he was handing things."

"You think he might be hiding what was really going on?"

Skip shrugged. "What do I know? You want to look at the menu?"

"I could eat."

Skip flipped me a menu and went out to clear some tables. When he came back, I ordered a cheeseburger and onion rings and went to sit in a booth.

My burger came, I ordered another beer, and ate without much enthusiasm. I was nearly finished when Edgerton came in. He nodded to Skip, who then motioned him to come over to the bar. Skip held out his hand and when Edgerton went to shake it, Skip took the hand and pulled Edgerton close enough to say something to him quietly and privately. I didn't hear what it was, but watched Edgerton mouth the word "Thanks" to Skip. I don't think Skip ever once shook my hand in all the years I had known him.

Skip pointed at my table and Edgerton came over and sat down.

"You working tonight?" I asked him.

"No. I took the night off. I'm a little worried about Don."

"Yeah," I said, "it's pretty lousy, but I wouldn't worry too much. Dunstable had to arrest somebody, and Hess was the closest thing to a suspect that he's got. But Hess can prove that he didn't kill Gilroy, and if he didn't kill Eckels, eventually proof of that will turn up too. He won't spend too much time in jail."

"What do you mean *if* Don didn't kill Eckels?" Edgerton asked. "I know he didn't."

"Jeez, Stephen. Don't be so sensitive. And face it, you don't *know* that he didn't kill Eckels, you just don't believe that he did. And I didn't say I thought that Hess offed Sir Lancelot either. I got no idea who killed the guy. When they had me down there, I told the cops that I didn't think Hess did it. But he could have. He had motive and opportunity, but without evidence that he did the crime, the cops shouldn't be holding him. I doubt that they'll issue formal charges. His arrest is probably political. Makes it look like Dunstable is doing something. But if he didn't do it, he'll be released."

We sat in silence for a few minutes.

"I wonder how Julia's taking it?" Edgerton asked at last.

"Have you talked to her?"

"No. I called and left a message on their machine, but she hasn't called back. She's probably devastated. I'm probably more worried about her than about Don."

"Why?" I asked. "Is she liable to do something stupid?"

Edgerton glared at me.

"No. Why did you say something like that? I figure she's upset. That doesn't mean that I think we should start dragging the rivers for her."

"If you say so."

"You know," Edgerton began, his eyes flaring, "you're virtually a complete asshole. There's only a couple of minute particles left in your being that haven't metamorphosed into assholeness. Any day now the change will be complete and even I won't be able to stand you anymore."

"If you say so," I repeated. "You going to eat?"

He ate. I watched him eat. A fly buzzed around the room, finally perching on the back of the booth behind my left ear, and the fly watched him eat. I wondered if this fly was related to the one I'd killed back in the office. Perhaps he was. Perhaps he was the other fly's little brother and here he was unknowingly perched inches away from his brother's murderer watching someone eat. I wondered if flies felt anything when other flies died. I wondered if they looked into windowsills with horror when they spotted their dead brethren lying with their legs in the air, their delicate, parchment wings stilled. It was September. Winter would be here soon. Soon all the flies would disappear.

Edgerton finished his meal and we each got another beer. I left him nursing his and went to the bathroom. At McCauley's the bathrooms were located on opposite sides of a little alcove with a pay phone between them. A regular named Sylvia had dragged a barstool into the alcove and was talking on the phone. She was a big woman, well over six feet tall and built like a linebacker, with a loud voice and the social skills of an orangutan in heels. She wore her dark hair in an enormous and, I feared, unstable beehive.

As I entered the bathroom, her excited shrill voice followed me. "Oh, today was wonderful. I went shopping and oh…I had a good bowel movement."

When I rejoined him, Edgerton sighed. "It's just been bugging me is all."

"What's been bugging you?"

"I just can't stop thinking about it. I can't help wondering if it's more important to live or to have lived."

I shook my head. "You sort of lost me there."

He snorted. "Just let me get this out, will ya. I mean is the living of your life the thing that's important or is it what you leave behind after you're gone?"

"I'm still not following."

"We're all gonna die. That's a given. That's the one thing we're all going to do. And death raises a question. If we are going to die, then why are we here in the first place?"

"I don't think you're going to answer that one, man."

"But we have to," he replied, becoming animated. "We all have to. I'm not talking universal truths here. All I'm saying is that each of us, in order to live what we can call successful lives, has to decide why we are here. Are we here to simply live out our days as painlessly as possible while we wait for death? Or are we here to accomplish something? Do we need to leave something behind in order to consider our lives to have had meaning? And if so, what?"

I thought about that for a moment. "We all leave something behind," I said. "For some it's kids. For others it's…I don't know, a monument, or a piece of art, or some other work. Or maybe it's just a memory. A memory of us carried by someone we leave behind. Maybe it's just a story about us told around the family dinner table at the holidays. Whatever, it's something."

"Yeah," he nodded. "But is it enough? And how can you be sure?"

"Beats me," I told him.

"Do you ever wonder what it is that you will leave behind?"

I smiled. "Well, I had a really good bowel movement today."

Chapter Twelve

At about ten o'clock the next morning, Edgerton banged on my door. "Are you ready?"

"Ready for what?"

"The funeral," he replied. "Wear something nice. Some of these people are my friends."

I thought back over the night before and had no recollection whatsoever of Edgerton telling me about any funeral. I was about to argue with him when I realized that it must be Gilroy's funeral, and since Edgerton didn't drive, he was going to need me to get him there. I also thought about what Skip had said about Stephen not sharing his grief. I decided that his not telling me about the funeral until the last minute was probably another way of keeping his feelings to himself. So, I didn't say anything. I just went to my closet to look for something "nice."

What I came up with was a pair of charcoal gray Dockers, a white shirt, green paisley tie, and my favorite lime green sports coat. By this I do not mean to suggest that I had more than one lime green sports coat, only that it was my favorite sports coat. It also had the distinction of being my only sports coat.

When I stepped into the hall, Edgerton was there waiting for me. He was wearing a dark gray, double-breasted suit with a conservative pinstripe, a crisp white shirt, and a maroon tie. He had pulled his long red hair back into a ponytail and from the front looked like he could pass for an investment banker.

"How long have you had the suit?" I asked.

"Bought it yesterday. Got it over at Al Johnson's. They gave me a good deal on it. I told them it was for a friend's funeral."

"Nice," I said.

He pulled at the sleeves of his shirt so that the shirt cuffs peaked out from under the cuffs of his jacket. "Where did you get your outfit? You pick that up at a menswear store on the campus of Clown College?"

I ran a hand down the side of my jacket and posed provocatively. "My clown name is Dimples."

"Let's go, Dimples. We're running late."

The funeral was being held in the suburb of Bloomington, where Gilroy had been living with his mother. Edgerton told me that Gilroy had moved back home to take care of his mom after his dad died, and now the old girl was all alone. As I pulled into the church lot, I couldn't help but notice that there were plenty of empty parking spaces. Inside the church, an elderly woman was sitting in the narthex flanked by two slightly younger women. The woman in the middle was stoop-shouldered, with red-rimmed eyes, her hands in her lap, a wadded-up Kleenex in her right fist.

The other women scanned the faces of everyone entering the church and occasionally leaned in to say something to the woman between them. I figured it was Gilroy's mom. Her two companions didn't say anything to her when Edgerton and I walked in. Gilroy's mom just stared straight ahead the whole time.

There were three doors leading from the narthex to the nave of the church. Edgerton opened the middle door, and we paused a moment before entering. There were three distinct seating sections radiating upwards from an altar in the center. Behind the altar was a large pipe organ and some rows of additional seating evidently intended for a choir. In front of the altar was the open casket.

I followed Edgerton inside. When he reached the casket, he put one hand against it as if steadying himself, cocked his head and looked down at his dead friend. Stephen's face was as expressionless as Gilroy's. After a few seconds, he removed his hand from the casket and walked slowly away.

I glanced briefly at the corpse before following Edgerton to a pew. They had placed a small pillow under Gilroy's head so that his chin was angled down toward his chest. A buttoned collar and a full Windsor knot in the tie were all they had needed to hide the hole in his neck.

We took a seat about halfway up the middle section and waited for the funeral to begin. I soon spotted Donald and Julia Hess sitting together near the front. I wasn't surprised that Don had been released, only that Edgerton hadn't told me. But then, maybe he didn't know. The Hesses sat close to one another, holding hands. But they stared straight ahead at the casket in front of them. Julia let go of her husband's hand briefly to brush a hair from her face, and when she did, she turned and nearly faced us. Impulsively, I thought to wave to her, but fortunately caught myself in time. Julia retook her husband's hand and resumed staring at the casket. I stared at it too.

I have never looked at a corpse without fully expecting that, at any moment, the dead person would suddenly move. I looked at Gilroy stretched out against the white lining of the casket and waited for him to stir. It was as if my mind could not grasp the fact that a person could be stilled. Every day we see hundreds of people—businesspeople hurrying to appointments, young mothers pushing squirming children in strollers across busy intersections, a drunk passed out along the side of a building, groaning as he turns in heavy slumber—all moving; sometimes imperceptibly, but all moving. It is awful to see a person stilled. Awful and so alien as to be nearly unbelievable.

As I was staring, I became vaguely aware that someone had joined us in the pew. Whoever it was had moved in beside me and was sitting close, close enough that I involuntarily tightened up, finally becoming uncomfortable enough that, grimacing, I turned to face the intruder. My grimace softened to a smile when Naomi reached out to take my hand.

Edgerton turned to look at us with an eyebrow cocked. I pulled Naomi a little closer to me and shrugged slightly as if to say, "Okay, so I brought a date. What's it to you?"

The funeral service was simple but consoling. Even Edgerton—an avowed, at times militant, atheist—seemed to derive some measure of comfort from the rite. The pastor got to say some things about how our lives touch the lives of those around us. An uncle of Gilroy's got to tell a story about how when Jason was six, he climbed up into a tree house that some neighbor kids had built and was too scared to come down. Every kid on the block, Jason's mom and dad, and even a policeman all stood at the base of the tree and hollered up at Jason, trying to get him to climb down. But Jason was just too scared. Finally, everyone decided to leave and let him come down on his own. Within a few minutes of the crowd clearing, Jason was walking in his kitchen door asking for something to eat. The uncle said that this showed that Jason liked to do things his own way and in his own time. I thought it showed that the six-year-old Gilroy just didn't want everyone to watch his knees wobble as he climbed down the tree. Uncontrollable fear is a thing most of us like to keep private. But it wasn't my place to argue with the choice of anecdote. Besides, the things that we fear the most are pain and death, and Jason Gilroy was beyond both.

When the funeral service ended with the pastor saying a few words about eternal life, how we would be joined together for all eternity in a great heavenly banquet, and how after a brief service at the gravesite everyone was welcome to return to the church where ham sandwiches were to be served in the church basement.

As we stood to leave, I took Naomi's arm, and Edgerton followed us out to the narthex. I nearly bumped into Otis McInerny coming out the door. When his eyes met mine, he paused and fuddled about as if he wanted to say something to me. Then his eyes traveled from me to Naomi and Edgerton, and Otis simply turned away. I watched him walk out the door and thought I saw Dick Peterson climbing into a car across the street.

Don and Julia joined us, and we all walked out together. A large ash stood in front of the church spreading its leaves against the cloudless sky. A light breeze was blowing as we gathered beneath the tree and above us the leaves quaked, filtering the bright sun and sending splinters of light dancing across the ground like a school of tiny fish darting nervously in the sea.

"You guys going to the cemetery?" Edgerton asked.

"You want to?" I asked him.

"Not really."

I glanced at Don and Julia. Julia lowered her eyes and Don shook his head. "No," he said. "I think it would be better to celebrate his life, rather than mourn his passing. A cemetery is no place for a celebration."

"Where to then?" asked Edgerton.

"A bar," Hess said.

"Which bar?"

"How 'bout the Thunderbird out on the strip?" Hess said. "It's nice and we're dressed for it."

"Okay," Edgerton said.

Naomi was standing next to me, impatiently shifting her weight from one leg to another. Julia mostly looked at the ground, but occasionally glanced up at Naomi. Finally, Naomi reached up, took my arm, and pinched it.

"Oh. Sorry," I started. "You've not all been introduced. This is Naomi Miller. Naomi works out at the festival. At the Cock and Bull. She, ah…She knew Jason."

Julia looked up at Naomi and with a sad, sweet smile said, "It's wonderful to meet you. The circumstances are not the best, but…It's wonderful."

Edgerton and Hess both smiled tightlipped smiles and nodded their heads as they glanced from Naomi to me.

"You want to ride with us, Stephen?" Hess asked.

"Well, I came with Lyle, but…" He squinted over at me. "Sure, I'd love to. That all right, Lyle?"

"Okay by me."

We were still standing there, shuffling our feet when I heard someone from the street yell out, "Hey, Fat Boy!"

I turned.

Dirk LeGrand drove a white Firebird. He had pulled up across from the church and stuck his head out the open window. "Hope you like walking, Tubby!" he called out. Then he raced his engine and laughed like a madman as he spun away.

Although there were several mourners still gathered in front of the church, my guess was that he had not been addressing another overweight funeral-goer. I walked slowly around the church to the parking lot where I had left the Ford. It was shorter than usual. LeGrand had slashed all four tires. I didn't say anything for a long time. I just stood there looking at the rims of the wheels resting on the dark asphalt and counted silently to myself.

I think I was in the seventies when Edgerton said, "I'm guessin' that guy don't like you."

"I guess not," I murmured.

Naomi took my arm and pulled herself close to me. "I like you."

I smiled. "I need to make a phone call," I said. "You guys head over to the bar. I don't know how long I'm going to be."

They all stared at me.

"No, really. I'll join you as soon as I can."

"I'll get him there," Naomi said. "He'll ride with me."

Edgerton and the Hesses got in Don's car and drove away while Naomi waited for me in the sunshine just outside the doorway of the church. I used my cellphone to call a nearby service station and the truck showed up about fifteen minutes later. A guy with the name "Ed" embroidered on his grease-stained shirt set my car on a flatbed, took my credit card number, and wrote me a receipt. He said they would get to work on the car right away and I could ride over to the station with him if I wanted. I told him that I had something I needed to do, and that I would be by to pick up the car in a couple of hours. He gave me the thumbs up sign and drove away.

I couldn't help feeling a little proud of myself. From the moment I had seen what he had done to my tires, I had been having a vivid vision of my tearing open LeGrand's chest with my fingernails and ripping out his heart. But I had smiled at Ed, had put my arm around Naomi, and had patted her shoulder reassuringly. All the while, however, I was imagining LeGrand, a gaping hole in his chest, staring wide-eyed as I bit into the still pulsating organ.

When we got to Naomi's car, I asked her if she had a pen and some paper. She popped open the glove box and rummaged around inside for a few moments. She then opened her purse and soon emerged with a stubby pencil and an old dry-cleaning ticket. As we pulled out of the church parking lot, I jotted down the license number that I had gotten off LeGrand's car.

It's amazing the kind of personal data you can get on someone if you have their license number. Go to a computer and in seconds you can have a guy's address and phone number, his marital status, the make and model of his vehicle, and a record of any moving violations he's had. It's a great place to start if you've decided to stalk someone.

The Thunderbird was a hotel located on Interstate 494 along a stretch known as the "Strip," which consisted of a row of hotels near the airport, where the old Met stadium and Met Sports Center used to be.

Naomi pulled the car off the interstate, down the frontage road, and turned into the Thunderbird's parking lot. We passed through the shadow of the huge faux totem pole that stood in majestic tackiness before the front entrance. We parked in the side parking lot and left the bright sunlight for the dim lighting, deep browns, and polished brass of the hotel bar.

Edgerton, Don and Julia were at table in the back of the bar. Hess raised a beer glass in salute as we approached. A glass of white wine nearly three-quarters full sat in front of Julia, but the boys were draining their beer glasses as we sat down to join them. A waitress wearing black slacks, a tuxedo shirt, and a black bow tie arrived to take our order. Naomi glanced over at Julia and ordered a glass of white wine. Edgerton and Hess each ordered a Summit Great Northern Porter and I, remembering how little cash I had in my wallet, ordered a Schmidt.

"Did ya get the tires fixed?" Edgerton asked.

"They're being fixed."

"What did you do to that guy to get him so pissed?"

"I hit him a couple of times. No big deal."

"He looked kinda familiar."

"He works out at the festival. He's the kinky sex chain mail guy."

"Oh," Edgerton said, nodding. "What did you do, stiff him on a pair of mail bikini briefs?"

"He was defending my honor," Naomi said, giving my arm a squeeze. "That's really how Lyle and I got to know each other. He acted with chivalry when Dirk pressed me with unwanted advances. Lyle is my champion, my knight in shining armor."

Edgerton smiled. "His armor didn't do all that much

shining during the joust on Sunday. Did you see it?"

"Yes. And I thought he was magnificent."

"She's lying," I said. "But you got to love her for it."

Edgerton nodded.

"I've met LeGrand a couple of times," Hess said. "He's always struck me as harmless enough. But I've heard he's got a bit of a temper."

I grunted.

"Do you think he's dangerous, Lyle?" Julia asked with genuine concern.

"He may be. In fact, he may have killed Gilroy and Eckels."

Julia gasped. "Do you really think so?"

I took a deep draught of my beer. "He had a bit of a run-in with Eckels on the day he was killed. And Naomi here saw him arguing with Gilroy the weekend before he was murdered. I've seen him threaten others, and he came at me with a baseball bat the other day. If he isn't a murderer, it's at least safe to say that he's more than a little apt to fly off the handle. Slashing someone's tires isn't the act of someone well-adjusted."

Edgerton looked narrowly at me. "I've been wondering about that. How did he know which car was yours?"

"He must have staked out the church parking lot hoping that I would show up at the funeral."

"And you didn't spot him? I thought that you P.I. types could spot that sort of thing in the dark with sunglasses on."

"I had no reason to be looking for him. It's not like I'm working a case or anything. Remember, I'm not trying to solve Gilroy's murder."

My ears burned a little when I said that. I

remembered that Julia had asked me to try to bring Gilroy's killer to justice. I glanced at her. She didn't return my look.

"Does that cop, Dungstubble, suspect LeGrand?" Hess asked. "I mean, it would be nice if I'm not the only one he suspects is the killer."

"I told him about it," I said, "but I get the impression that Dunstable isn't much for taking advice."

"He isn't much for listening to the truth either," Hess said. "Those guys questioned me relentlessly. I told them everything I know inside of the first five minutes. I spent the next day and a half repeating myself and listening to the same questions over and over. Then, all of a sudden, a cop walks in and says I can leave. Just like that. No apology. No smiley face. No 'Have a Nice Day.' Nothing. Maybe they let me go because they got something on LeGrand."

"Maybe," I said. "Or maybe they didn't have enough evidence to formally charge you for the murder. They can only hold you for 48 hours without bringing charges against you. My guess is they haven't managed to build a case against anybody. But they likely consider you their number one suspect. Did they ask you where you went before your meeting with the festival brass?"

"Sure."

"What did you tell them?"

"The truth," Hess said, more than a trace of defiance in his voice.

"Well?" I asked, raising both eyebrows.

"I told them that I was walking the festival grounds. I was thinking about how best to approach the festival board about letting us continue doing the jousts. At the time, I thought we still had a shot at being signed on as the festival's resident paladins."

"Anybody see you?"

"I'm sure lots of people saw me."

"Anyone in particular that you recall?"

Hess raised his hands and shrugged. "I was thinking. I really wasn't paying attention to anything else."

I nodded. "And Julia? Where were you at that time?"

Julia turned to me and smiled a sweet, sad smile. Then she looked over at her husband, then glanced at both Edgerton and Naomi. "I guess it's pretty obvious that Don and I have been having some troubles lately," she said. "We'd had an argument and I didn't feel like I could stay at the armory, so I took off. I went out the back gate and drove my car into Little Crow. I had coffee at a Perkins, went to the grocery store to pick up a frozen dinner, then went home. I was pretty out of it. I wasn't sure if Don was even planning to come home that night, but when I heard his key in the lock, I had the feeling that everything was going to be all right. Later the police came and arrested him."

She sipped delicately from her wineglass. Her eyes had moistened and there had been a catch in her voice as she spoke. "I guess you could say this has been a pretty hard couple of days for us," she continued, managing another smile. "I just want it all to be over so we can go on with our lives."

"Why are you asking us all of this, anyway, Dahms?" Hess asked.

"Just curious."

"You sure you're not working the case?"

"No," I said. "But I'm involved. I had to answer the cops' questions on Sunday night too. Dunstable asked a

Minneapolis homicide detective named Tarkof to keep an eye on me, and the guy I think of as the prime suspect in both murders tried to brain me the other day, and today slashed my tires at a church. These kinds of things can make a guy curious."

"Sound's logical," Naomi said, forcing a smile and apparently wanting to change the subject. "And I need another glass of wine. Anybody else?"

"Beer here," I said.

Naomi signaled for the waitress, and we ordered another round. Everyone but Julia, who still had better than half a glass of wine in front of her.

"Naomi," Julia said softly. "If you'll excuse me for asking, I was wondering…um, how long did you know Jason? I mean, he worked with Don and didn't have many friends besides us, and he didn't mention you to me. Please don't take this the wrong way. Like Lyle, I guess I'm just curious."

Naomi smiled at Julia, but there was something brittle about the smile. "I don't mind your asking. Frankly, Jason and I hadn't known each other long. We met at the festival just a few weeks ago. He used to come to the after-hours parties over at the Cock and Bull. I first noticed him kind of looking my way, maybe trying to get up the nerve to come over and talk, you know. He would come to the parties alone and sort of sit off by himself, smiling and wanting to join in. I thought he looked sweet and lonely. I introduced myself and we talked a couple of times."

"Well," Julia began, "it certainly says a lot about you that you were moved enough to come to the funeral. I mean, you barely knew him and yet felt the loss enough to come to say good-bye."

"I didn't say I barely knew him," Naomi said, her brow furrowing. "I said I hadn't known him long. I would have liked to have known him better, but in some ways, I knew him very well indeed."

"Oh," Julia nodded. "So, you and Jason were…um, you were intimate?"

Naomi looked at Julia narrowly as she lifted her glass to sip her wine. Replacing the glass on the table, she said, "Yes."

Julia smiled.

"It didn't last long," Naomi said. "In fact, the very next weekend we were at the Saturday night party and Jason seemed a little different. He drank too much and started hanging out with LeGrand and some other people that I wanted nothing to do with. When I asked Jason if he wanted to leave, he snapped at me. Told me that he didn't want to walk out on his *friends*. He had just met them, for god's sake. That was really the end of it for us."

"So, after you ended it, he continued to hang out with LeGrand?" Julia asked.

"Yeah, for the next two weekends. But then, they had a huge argument. It may have even been about me. LeGrand had been trying to put the moves on me. It may have bothered Jason."

"You didn't want anything to do with LeGrand?"

"Not really."

Julia cocked her head. "He is a pretty good-looking guy."

"Yeah," Naomi replied. "I admit I thought about it. About going out with LeGrand, I mean. But he's just too creepy."

Julia took another sip of her wine and nodded her head as if in thought.

"So, you were with Jason" she said. "And now you're with Lyle." Julia nodded slowly. "At Jason's funeral."

Naomi's eyes glinted fiercely. "Yes," she said.

"Oh," Julia said.

An edgy silence clamped down around us. First, I stared at Julia, trying to figure out what had just happened. Then I looked over at Naomi, trying to gauge her reaction. Both women wore virtually blank expressions except for a sharpness flashing in their eyes. No one said anything for some time.

Finally, thankfully, Edgerton looked at his watch. "Sorry everyone, but I got to work this evening. I'd better be getting along. Lyle?"

I looked at my watch too.

"Yeah," I said, "my car should be ready about now. Could you give me ride to the gas station, Naomi?"

"Certainly," she said.

"Damn," Edgerton said, "I forgot you don't have your car." He looked at the Hesses, then at Naomi. "I don't suppose I could catch a ride with you. Over to Lyle's car, I mean."

"We'd be happy to have you with us," she said, emphasizing the "you" slightly, but noticeably.

As we stood, Naomi added, leveling a clear gaze at Julia, "It certainly has been a pleasure getting to know you two better."

"Oh, the pleasure has been ours, I assure you," Julia said told her.

Hess stood and bowed slightly to Naomi but said nothing.

As we were leaving, I sneaked a look back to the table. Donald Hess was leaning in close to his wife, saying something to her, his eyes crinkled with confusion.

Naomi was not confused. "The bitch!" she loudly exclaimed the instant we had exited the bar.

Edgerton and I both stared at the ground in silence. Then I looked up at Naomi and started to say something, but words failed me. I was about to try again when a jet taking off from the nearby airport crossed the sky above us, filling the silence with its roar.

Chapter Thirteen

The next morning early, I was sitting in my car parked across from Dirk LeGrand's apartment on Dupont in South Minneapolis, sipping convenience store coffee and nursing my anger against the guy who'd slashed my tires. I didn't have a plan exactly. I just figured that if I kept my eyes open and waited long enough, something that I could use against LeGrand would present itself. Either that or I'd get tired, forget subtlety, and just beat the crap out of him.

Some clouds had moved in the night before, and although it had not rained, the overcast made it seem more like twilight than morning. The unwelcome heat and humidity of the previous weekend had lifted, the temperature dipping into the low fifties. In the unheated vehicle, my fingers tingled with cold, and I had to breathe on them from time to time to keep them warm. I was parked under an elm tree, and I watched as a brown leaf floated down and landed on my windshield. I looked over at the trees in front of the apartment building. They too were beginning to turn color and the ground beneath them was spattered with dead leaves. This was the first time that year that I had noticed the approach of autumn.

I was reaching for a cigarette when LeGrand's white Firebird came down the driveway from the rear parking lot. He headed south toward Uptown. I followed him, making sure I stayed well behind him so he wouldn't spot my car.

LeGrand had a small storefront in the Uptown neighborhood from which he sold his chain link undergarments. His "studio" was on Hennepin Avenue, sandwiched between a chiropractor's office and a place called the Condom Collection. LeGrand pulled into the alley behind his shop, and I parked on a side street with a pretty clear view of both his front door and the alley. I watched the lights go on in the store and after a few minutes LeGrand unlocked the door. Unfortunately, that was the most exciting thing that I saw for the rest of the morning. I sat and stared at the door. Occasionally I glanced over to where the alley emptied into the street. Then back to the door. Nothing happened. LeGrand stayed in the store, very few customers stopped by, buses rolled down the street, cars honked at each other, and people walked past.

After a couple of hours, I really needed to go to the bathroom. As luck would have it, there was a coffee shop across the street from LeGrand's store. This one was called "Here's Mud in Your Eye," a spacious place with wobbly tables, not enough chairs, and a few paintings on the wall—all with price tags affixed to the frames.

I bypassed the counter, instead heading down a rear hallway to the men's room. It was locked, but a young barista gave me no trouble when I asked for the key. When I came out, I surveyed the menu and ordered an uncharacteristic double tall cappuccino with a dusting of powdered chocolate. I didn't want look like a tourist.

I brought my coffee over to a table near the window and resumed my watch. By mid-afternoon I had downed three coffees and two pretty good chocolate macadamia nut scones before I went back to my car to continue my surveillance.

The gray overcast day had changed to a gray dusk when the lights went off in LeGrand's store. By then, I had to go to the bathroom again, but instead followed LeGrand back to his apartment. From my car I watched uncomfortably as the lights went on in LeGrand's apartment and the gray of the day faded into night. It was well after ten o'clock when I decided to go home.

He repeated the pattern the next day, as did I, sitting in my car or in the coffee shop waiting for something to happen. I didn't mind the waiting. It's a major part of what I do. But it's easier when I'm working for a client. Easier when I'm getting paid for it.

The next day was Friday and I resolved that it would be my last day of watching LeGrand. I almost gave up early. I spent the entire morning and afternoon following the pattern I had established for myself the previous two days. The coffee shop didn't have any chocolate macadamia scones, so I had to settle for a lemon poppy seed muffin. Then I got adventurous. I ordered the turkey chili. Let's just say I don't think I'd order it again.

I'd become pretty demoralized sitting in front of LeGrand's apartment as the darkness of the third night enveloped me. It was Friday night, I reminded myself. Edgerton and Hess would be going out to the festival site to prepare for the weekend. Couples would be going to restaurants, and single guys would be going to bars in the hopes of becoming coupled. At least I could be at McCauley's trying to wash away the heartburn I had from the turkey chili. Then the lights clicked off in LeGrand's apartment.

I followed his Firebird downtown and watched him pull into a parking ramp. I followed him into the ramp, and he headed up to one of the upper levels, while I was able to nab a spot on the second level being vacated by a guy in a Lexus talking on a cell phone. I hustled out of my car and down the stairs to the street. About halfway down the block, a group of people was waiting for a bus, and I managed to hide myself among them before LeGrand came out onto the sidewalk. I stayed about a half a block behind him as he walked down the street.

Legrand's step was lively, and his head bobbed jauntily from side to side as he made his way to a club near the corner of 6th and Marquette.

The place was called "Prime," and I knew it by reputation. It was one of those impossibly trendy places that becomes suddenly famous for being difficult to get into. The club took no reservations. Instead, patrons were expected to line up at the door and were either allowed in or turned away based either on the number of people already inside or, more often, on whether they looked like the right type of people to let in. Local celebrities avoided the line at the door and just breezed in. Others stood in the line, sometimes for hours, hoping to gain admittance through that portal and to cross into this Minneapolitan Elysium where only a select few were allowed to cavort. Or so I had read in the newspaper story about it.

To my surprise, LeGrand walked to the front of the line and was ushered right through. I also made my way to the front of the line. The people waiting made no sign of protest. They simply waited, some talking, even laughing, but most just staring with glazed expressions at the man who worked the door.

He was tall, well over six feet, and clearly spent many of his off hours at the gym. He wore black denim pants and a tight-fitting black T-shirt. He had ebony skin, a clean-shaven square jaw, and close-cropped curly black hair. He scanned the crowd in front of him with alert brown eyes framed discretely by eye liner and when he blinked, I caught a glimpse of what appeared to be chartreuse eye shadow. When I approached him, his mouth was set in a grim little smile.

I reached into my jeans pocket and pulled out my set of keys. "Excuse me," I said. "You know that guy that just went in. LeGrand. Well, we were having dinner earlier and he left his car keys on the table. You mind if I run these in to him? Won't be a minute."

The gatekeeper chuckled lightly. "Nice try," he said in a soft voice that managed to convey both superiority and compassion.

"Pardon me."

"You don't really expect me to believe that he had dinner with you. Do you?"

"Yeah, we had dinner. We had some business to conduct. What's not to believe?"

The gatekeeper shook his head and looked me directly in the eyes. "If you are in business with him, then you are not the kind of person that would care if he lost an arm, let alone his car keys."

"Just trying to get on his good side," I said.

"Candyman don't have a good side."

"Candyman? Is that what they call him here."

"That's what I call him," the gatekeeper said. "People inside probably just think of him as the man who can get them what they want."

I arched an eyebrow. "Are you saying that the gentleman with whom I just dined is involved in some kind of criminal activity?"

The gatekeeper cracked a smile. "I'm sorry to have to be the one that breaks it to you."

Still dangling the set of keys in front of him. I said, "You're not going to let me in, are you?"

He waited a moment before responding. "If you want to leave those keys with me. I'll see that they get to him. But I'm guessing that if you do, you'll be walking home."

I nodded as if in thought. "I could always take the bus."

He smiled again "Like I said, nice try. Now, why don't you just run along?"

I put the keys back in my jeans pocket then pulled out my wallet and drew out a couple of twenties. Folding them, I asked, "You sure you can't find a way to let me in? I won't cause any trouble, I promise."

The man's expression hardened. "You gotta be shittin' me if you think a couple of Jacksons is all it takes. Just look behind you, man."

Behind me the line of would-be patrons had grown even longer.

"What your name, man?" the gatekeeper asked.

"Lyle. What's yours?"

The man smiled. "Clarence."

"Pleased to meet you, Clarence."

"Well, the pleasure is all yours, Lyle. Do me a favor. Look over there." He pointed to a man in a cheap suit, maybe thirty-five with his hand on the arm of slender young woman in her early twenties. "That couple there. He probably told her about how he comes here all the time. About how maybe it's hard for some people to get in, but not for him. No, he's special, I'll bet he told her. But there ain't nothing special 'bout him. He just wants to get laid. Just like the rest of us. And I'll tell you, I want him to get laid. I want all of us to get laid. But I can't let him in."

Clarence surveyed the crowd. "Look over there." He pointed to two young women standing close to one another, both in revealingly cut, simple, short, black dresses, shivering visibly in the cool, evening breeze.

"Those two ladies been here every weekend night for a month. I keep telling them not to waste their time. I tell them they just ain't getting in. But they keep coming. They keep looking at me and I can see in their eyes how much it means to them. But they ain't getting in. Not ever."

"Why not?"

"'Cause they ain't right."

"How are they not right?"

"They just ain't," Clarence said. "It's not something you can explain. It's something that you feel."

"And I ain't right?" I asked.

A huge grin broke across his face, "Shit, man. You ain't never gonna be right."

"But that guy that you let in a minute ago. That 'Candyman.' He's right?"

"Long as they buying what he's selling. Yeah. He's right enough. Now, go on with you."

I gave him a two-fingered salute. "Be seeing you, Clarence."

"I doubt that, Lyle. I doubt that very much."

I put the twenties back in my wallet and started walking down the street toward the ramp where I'd parked my car. It wasn't a total loss, I told myself. Three days' work and I'd learned at least a couple of things. I'd found out that LeGrand was dealing drugs, and since he was serving an elite demographic, I could assume that he was doing fairly well with it. I could speculate that perhaps LeGrand's sideline was something that he practiced out at the festival as well. I hoped that he was. It would be great fun to feed him to Dunstable.

I was grinning at the thought and turned to take one more look at the line outside the club just in time to see someone else I knew walk up to the door. It was Dick Peterson, the elephant, guy, and Clarence let him right on through.

Chapter Fourteen

I didn't make it out to the festival until late in the afternoon the next day. When I arrived, I was even happier for having stayed away the greater part of the day. The armory swarmed with customers, many simply gawking, but a surprising number looked to be buying. When I emerged through the back entrance, I found Edgerton behind the counter, totaling up a sale using a very un-Renaissance pocket calculator. He pushed a small dagger across the counter toward a paunchy guy about fifty; the guy handed back some wrinkled currency. As the man walked away, Edgerton said, not really even looking up at me, "Man, it's been crazy around here today."

Several other customers waited in a line in the front of the counter. Edgerton didn't really look at them either. He just focused on the item they were buying, then at the calculator, and finally at the money. "I can't believe this," he said. "These people are buying everything. Not only are we gonna sell everything we got out here, but we've been taking special orders all damn day. We got enough work to keep us busy for the next couple of years. It's just nuts."

I spotted both Donald and Julia Hess taking various items off the wall and showing them to customers. They replaced most of these things on their pegs next to little signs that said, "Floor demo only. Not for sale."

I pulled a stool out from behind the counter and set it next to Edgerton. "People want to take a little bit of death home with them," I said, sitting down. "Maybe mount it on the wall like a trophy. Say they conquered it, or something."

Edgerton cast me a quizzical glance but kept making transactions.

"People are buying stuff from you because of the murders," I told him. "They want a souvenir. They want to bring home something touched by death."

Edgerton grunted. "You're probably right. Earlier, some guy offered me ten thousand dollars for the mail coat that we found Eckels' head propped up on. That is, after the cops give it back."

"What did you tell him?"

"I told him to bring me a cashier's check."

"You sentimental fool."

Hess finished up with an older couple who had been studying the display of broadswords and then approached us with an exuberant smile. "Business is so good I might even be able to pay your salary, Stephen," he said.

Edgerton, still busy with customers, said, "Oh, joy. Now I can get that villa I've often dreamt of."

Hess laughed, then turned to me. "You know, Lyle, it's amazing how many people today have walked right up to me and asked if I killed Eckels. No hesitation or anything. They've just been walking up and asking."

"What have you been telling them?"

Hess laughed again. "I've been telling them no, but I would have if I'd have known what effect it would have on business."

"Either of you see LeGrand around today?" I asked.

"Oh, Tire Boy!" Hess chuckled. "Not today."

"Nope," Edgerton said. "Now why don't you guys get lost. Go look for him or something. Just get out of here and let me work."

Hess laughed again, clapped Edgerton on the back, and went to work the crowd. I stood and kicked the stool back out of the way.

"Where you going?" Edgerton asked. "You're not really going to look for LeGrand, are you?"

"No. I'm going to go see my sweetie."

"Well, bully for you," Edgerton said as I left for the Cock and Bull.

Naomi was navigating the narrow space between some tables when I arrived, picking up glasses and trying to avoid being goosed by men who had had too much to drink and were rather too taken up by the lusty atmosphere the festival tried so hard to create. And it's possible I was rather taken up by it myself because as I watched her, I didn't even bother to hide the lascivious nature of my thoughts. Naomi saw me ogling her. As she began to wend her way toward me, I thought I noted a little extra action in her hips, a little something extra designed to appeal to me. My breath seemed a little too loud as it escaped my open mouth.

"Would you like me to get you a bib, sir?" Naomi asked me when she got close. "I do believe you're drooling."

"I heard chicks love that."

"You heard wrong."

She put the empty glasses on the bar and a bartender immediately scooped them up, tossing them into a huge plastic garbage can behind him. "I really can't talk now," she said. "Will I see you later?"

"Oh God yes!"

"Men are so easy," she said, returning the smile. "Come by around seven thirty."

"Neither the sting of the sword nor sweet siren's song could keep me from our appointed rendezvous, my lady."

Naomi smirked. "This place is getting to you. Next thing I know you'll be wearing panty hose and stuffing hankies up your sleeves."

"The hankies, maybe," I said.

Naomi chuckled. "See you at seven thirty."

I had a few hours to kill and I could think of nothing better to do than to just keep on doing what I had been doing for the last few days. I went to go watch LeGrand. I tried to be inconspicuous as I took up a position across from his chain mail concession. I stood in a glassblower's stall and handled a few bottles—some intricate and delicate, made up of tubes that writhed like snakes, others simple and rustic, slight imperfections evident in the colored glass.

LeGrand didn't appear to be around. The blonde he had working for him was sitting on a stool behind the counter, looking rather bored and biting at a cuticle. Whenever a potential customer approached, she smiled and if it was a man, she leaned over so that he could see the way the chain mail pressed against the flesh of her bosom. I watched for several minutes. No sign of LeGrand but lots of bosom.

After a while, I left to take a stroll around the festival grounds. I told myself that I was looking for LeGrand, but actually I just enjoyed the sunshine and the cool breeze that had replaced the moist heat of the previous weekend. I treated myself to a deep-fried shrimp kabob, and having finished it, hoped that my breath didn't smell too much of onions. I walked some more. There were a lot of uniformed cops around—two-way radios squawking, service revolvers riding in holsters on their hips. A roar of approval rose from a crowd that surrounded a nearby stage, but I couldn't see what it was that they approved of. The soft sounds of harp music floated by.

I rounded a clump of buildings and saw Joyous Guard sitting apart in a small clearing in front of me. The two guys that had accompanied Eckels to the joust the previous weekend both sat in armor on rough-hewn wooden chairs by the front door. I slipped by unnoticed. I didn't know how they would react to seeing me so soon after their leader had been slain. They would want to blame someone. I didn't want it to be me.

I was about to return to the armory when Otis spotted me. He was walking alone, in full kingly regalia, waving and smiling to anyone who took notice of him. At first, he gave me the same standard wave and smile, but then he turned on his heel and approached me with purpose. "Can we go somewhere and talk?" he asked in a hushed, conspiratorial tone. "Privately."

I shrugged and Otis led me over to a building I hadn't noticed before. It stood along the perimeter fence, which probably meant that it had a back door that led beyond the walls of the ersatz kingdom. But unlike buildings such as Don Hess' armory, this was not designed to display or sell wares. It was a simple, windowless structure with a door in the middle of a broad expanse of roughhewn planks.

Otis' hands disappeared beneath his robe and emerged with a key ring. He unlocked the door and ushered me inside. As he closed the door behind him, he switched on an electric light. Inside was an office filled with a couple of standard issue metal desks with big desk calendars serving as blotters, calculators, cups filled with pencils, and the like. On one of the desks sat a laptop computer. Beyond the office was another room and in its darkened interior I could see a rather large, round table and several well-padded chairs. Otis switched on the light in this room and bade me take a seat.

"This your office?" I asked.

"Well, no. This is the on-site office that the festival organizers use when they are here. Frankly, they are not usually here, and this place is rarely used. But the brass is kind enough to let me have a key. We should not be interrupted here."

"And what it is that we want to discuss without interruption?"

"I have a small problem."

"Yes."

"I, um...I understand that you are a private investigator."

"I don't recall mentioning it."

"Are you saying that you are not an investigator?"

"No. I just don't recall mentioning it to you."

Otis smiled knowingly, placed his fingertips together and leaned back in his chair. "I checked you out. As titular head of this realm, I thought it my duty to find out a little about you after our first meeting. It wasn't hard."

"It's not something that I try to hide, Otis. I even print up little cards with my name on them saying that I'm an investigator. Would you like to see one? My mom thinks they're really effective."

"Be that as it may, since you are an investigator, I was wondering if you would—"

"I once ran an ad in City Pages. It had a little drawing of an eye looking through a magnifying glass. My name was on that, too."

"Do you always interrupt your clients when they are trying to talk to you?"

"Only the pompous windbags."

Otis got red. "I think this interview is at an end," he said, rising.

"Oh, come on, your highness," I cooed. "Just having a little fun with you. If we can't laugh at ourselves, who can we laugh at?"

"But we are not laughing at ourselves," he said with surprising dignity. "You are laughing at me."

"Forgive me for choosing such an easy target."

Otis shook his head and pointed toward the door. "I'll just see you out then."

"Come on, Otis. You just referred to yourself as a client. What is it that I'm going to do for you?"

He sat back down and stared at me for a couple of seconds. "I've decided to trust you. I have a problem and despite the levity with which you have treated me thus far, I do believe that you are the best person to help me. You are, after all, acquainted with the individual involved and have, I've heard, demonstrated an ability to look out for yourself in situations that could be described as hazardous."

"Huh?"

"You know Dirk LeGrand and have, I am informed, bested him in two confrontations to date."

"Yeah. I busted him up real good. Now, what do the two of you have in common?"

Otis shook his head. "Nothing. And I want nothing to do with the man. In fact, I've come to believe that he is…How do you say it in the vernacular? That he is up to no good."

"And just what is this no good that you believe that LeGrand is up to?"

Otis slumped deeper in his chair. He stopped looking at me and began to study his right thumbnail. Something about the thumbnail must have been pretty interesting because he looked at it a long time before saying anything further.

"LeGrand has asked me to meet with him. This evening. He says that he wants to discuss something 'mutually beneficial.' I don't trust him. I've heard rumors. And then there is the way he has been acting. The yelling. Accosting fairgoers such as yourself. Frankly, he scares me."

"He should," I said.

Otis' smile was paper thin. "I'm so glad you understand. So, we are agreed. You will meet with LeGrand in my stead?"

"I don't remember agreeing to anything."

"But you must!" Otis exclaimed. "You must find out what he is up to and tell me so that I can relay it to the authorities."

"Why don't you just share your suspicions with the festival management? Better yet, tell the cops. Why get further involved?"

Otis shook his head rapidly several times. "But don't you see, I am involved. I have…" He sighed. "I have on several occasions…Unfortunately, I have allowed myself to be used by this individual and should that come to light it would create…It would create difficulties."

"What kind of difficulties?"

Otis waved a dismissive hand. "It's nothing really. I mean, it could prove embarrassing but only if seen in a particular light."

"What light are we talking about?"

"As part of my duties as King, I meet frequently with both the festival management and those providing security here on site."

"The festival has its own security force?"

"Not exactly. Security here at the festival site, like it is in the town of Little Crow, is provided by the police."

I grunted. "Chief Dunstable and company."

"Precisely. And I admit there have been occasions when I became privy to certain information that Mr. LeGrand asked me to share with him. For a price."

I raised my eyebrows. "What kind of information?"

"Reports of what they termed suspicious activity. That sort of thing. In retrospect, I see that this was incautious on my part. But at the time I saw no harm. Now, I simply want to sever all ties with LeGrand. To be done with him for once and for all."

"Skip the meeting," I told him. "Instead, go and do whatever you kings do in your downtime. Beat a few serfs. Steal a maidenhead or two. Leave LeGrand alone."

"But I can't. You see, because I have acquiesced to his requests in the past, I have left myself vulnerable. Suppose he tells the festival heads? Suppose he tells Chief Dunstable? What would that mean for me? Really, I need you to meet with LeGrand and explain that our relationship, insignificant though it was, is at an end."

I thought about Otis' story. Several things bothered me. While I could believe that LeGrand would approach Otis for information that would help him avoid impediments to the successful conduct of his drug operation and that Otis would be fool enough to provide such information for a fee, I couldn't think of a reason why he would choose me to meet with LeGrand in his stead. It felt like a trap.

The more I thought about it, the more I decided that the whole story stank pretty good. But I was now more than a little curious as to how Otis figured into things, and I'd been watching LeGrand anyway. It would be better if someone was paying me to do it. Besides, given the principals—pompous, ineffectual Otis and overconfident LeGrand—I figured I could more than handle any surprises they may have planned for me.

"I get two hundred dollars a day plus expenses," I told him. "First day's payment in advance." I held out my hand.

Otis' smile faded quickly. "That seems a bit steep," he said, patting at his robes. "I don't think I have that much cash on me. I could write you a check."

"No checks. Get the cash. We'll settle up later. What time is the meeting?"

"The meeting?"

"Your meeting with LeGrand. When and where?"

"Tonight. Seven o'clock. The Irish Cottage."

I nodded. "I'll be in touch. Make sure you get the money."

I left Otis and began walking back to the armory. I knew he hadn't told me the truth. That he was hiding something behind that smile, that wave, and his hardy huzzah. Maybe by meeting with LeGrand I'd find out what. But it's like the man from Stratford said, "Through tattered clothes small vices do appear. Robes and furred gowns hide all."

Chapter Fifteen

The festival had just closed up for the night when I slipped into the Irish Cottage to wait for LeGrand's appointment with Otis. I moved into a corner where the slanting rays of the early evening sun couldn't find me, and for the next hour I sat in the quiet and listened.

As I waited, I occasionally heard a person walk by and once a man and a woman stepped inside the cottage, looked around and giggled. The man had his hand inside the woman's blouse, and he kissed her sloppily and noisily on the mouth. As the man sought to draw her further inside the cottage, the woman snorted loudly and pulled him back outside. They didn't see me.

Sitting in the shadows, I once again cautioned myself to show some restraint with LeGrand. After all, every time I had met him face to face, I'd popped him. And even though he clearly deserved it, I resolved that this time would be different. I would simply confront him, explain that I was working for Otis, and the king was not interested in continuing any relationship that existed between them.

And even if Otis' story was bogus and LeGrand was using him to get at me, I had an edge. I knew that LeGrand was dealing drugs. All I had to do was threaten to turn him in to the redoubtable Chief Dunstable if he didn't play nice. Of course, I had every intention of turning him in anyway, but that could wait until I had a clearer idea of what LeGrand and Otis were up to.

The more I thought about it, the prouder I was of myself for resolving to handle the matter as a civilized adult. I wasn't a kid anymore and my first reaction to adversaries shouldn't always involve fisticuffs. My attitude was maturing. I was evolved.

Evolved, but a trifle impatient. I had been waiting a long time and while sitting on the ground inside the cottage my underwear had been creeping up on me badly. I pressed the button for the little light on my watch and saw that it was nearly ten minutes after seven.

A couple of minutes later I was about to check my watch again when LeGrand entered the cottage. "Otis, you son of a bitch. Are you here?"

I let the silence answer him.

LeGrand stepped outside, looking around with a whispered curse. Then he stepped back into the cottage. By that time, I was on my feet and had maneuvered to within his reach.

"God damn him," LeGrand said as he turned to survey the interior of the cottage again.

I cleared my throat, and when he turned toward me, I smiled. Then I hit him. I caught him hard on the side of his head and he spun around about a quarter turn before he fell to the ground. His hands clawed at the dirt, and as he got to his knees, I stepped around behind him, planted a foot in the small of his back, and sent him sprawling, face first, back to the ground.

"What the…" LeGrand began as he rolled over onto his back.

I didn't let him finish his question. I reached down, and wrapping my right hand around his throat, pulled him to his feet. When our eyes met, I drove a hard left into his abdomen. As the breath left his lungs, I noticed that he, too, had been eating onions.

"I'm kinda upset with you, Dirk," I said, still holding him by the throat. "You're going to have to pay for that tire slashing thing."

LeGrand tried to catch his breath, but I hit him again in the belly, tightening my grip on his neck. His eyes got wild, as it dawned on him that there was a possibility that I wouldn't let him take another breath. A croaking noise like a massive door moving slowly on rusty hinges issued forth from his upper airway. He struggled to break my hold on his throat. I hit him in the gut one more time and watched him go limp and the fight go out of his eyes. As I stared into his vacant eyes, I let out a little chuckle. Then my head exploded.

Suddenly, I was on the ground, and although my eyes were open, I couldn't see. Everything had simply dissolved into nothingness. Everything, except a thick cocoon of pain that muffled all sound. My vision gone, I strained to hear what was going on. I could hear a voice. Then more than one. I couldn't tell how many voices, only that LeGrand and I weren't alone.

Then I heard my own voice. Only it wasn't really a voice, it was a yowl. It took a while, but I finally realized that someone had hit me. Someone had come up behind me and hit me with something hard, and now my head had exploded, and my brains had spilled out all over the ground. All over the dirty ground. It's a good thing I couldn't see, I thought. I didn't want to look at my brains lying there in the dirt.

LeGrand said something, then someone kicked me in the side. He said something else, and then someone kicked me in the head. Then I couldn't hear anything, but

I saw a sliver of bright light crack through the nothingness. I reached out toward the light, but got kicked in the side again, and the light was gone. But I could hear again.

A new voice rang out, "No! I told you no!"

I was kicked in the side again, but the new voice shouted for that someone to stop. I took another boot to my side, then heard something that sounded like a ratchet. No, not a ratchet. It was something else, something familiar. It was the sound of a bullet being chambered. The kicking stopped. I felt a smile break involuntarily across my face. It was a handgun. Sounded like a semi-automatic. They weren't going to kick me anymore, I thought. They were going to shoot me.

I heard the voices again, then some footsteps. Then I heard nothing.

I don't know how long I lay there on the ground. I know I wasn't conscious the whole time. After a while my vision returned, and when I looked around, I didn't find my brains in the dirt. I managed to sit up, ran a palm across the back of my head, examined it, and I found I wasn't even bleeding. There was a bump. Well, *bump* doesn't quite cover it. It was more like a whole new rear lobe had appeared. Like I had mutated, and my skull had expanded to accommodate some additional gray matter. I sat in the dirt and held my hand against the back of my skull hoping that this new broadening of my cranium would bring with it the sense never to let myself get suckered like that again.

I struggled to my feet. I tried to take a step, but my legs were one big quiver. A wave of cold ran through me. I backed against the wall of the cottage and let the shivers overtake me. I hugged myself until the shivering subsided. Before long I was able to walk, and when I could, I made my way slowly back to the armory.

It was dark. I looked at my watch and it was nearly ten. There was a campfire burning outside the armory. It looked warm. I stumbled toward it.

I heard Edgerton's voice. I was surprised at the distance it carried in the cool, quiet night. Then I heard laughing—two, three other voices. No, just two other voices. Edgerton was laughing with them. Then I could see them, sitting around the fire. Edgerton and Hess and someone else. Someone big. Someone my size. I touched the back of my head again, then stared at the figure of the big guy sitting with Edgerton and Hess by the fire. I was confused. I seemed to be sitting there by the fire with the other guys. Maybe no one had hit me. Maybe I hadn't gone to meet LeGrand after all. Maybe I had stayed at the armory. I gave my head a painful, little shake. No, I decided. It wasn't me. It must be someone else.

"Where the hell have you been?" Edgerton asked, his laughter turning to sudden irritation as I approached.

I didn't respond. The fire was burning brightly, and I studied each of their faces. Edgerton looked ticked off, Hess appeared concerned, and Max Wiseman was searching the ground next to him, trying to remember where he had set his beer.

I took a seat on the ground next to Wiseman and stared into the fire.

"Where have you been?" Edgerton repeated.

When I didn't say anything, Hess asked quietly, "Are you all right, Dahms?"

"I will be," I told him. "Someone hit me with something. In the back of my head. I think I've been unconscious awhile."

There was a pause. Finally, Wiseman asked, "Should we get you to a doctor?"

"Nah. I've been hit in the head before."

"Let me take a look at it," Wiseman said.

"Why? You a doctor?"

"Shut up and let me take a look at it."

I didn't say anything, but I turned so that the light of the fire shown against the back of my head. All three men stood and moved around in back of me to take a look. One of them flipped on a flashlight.

"You're not bleeding, but you got a helluva bump there," Wiseman said. "Looks really nasty, Dahms. We should get you to a doctor."

"I gotta think he's right," Hess agreed. "I can drive."

Edgerton looked but said nothing.

"No," I told them. "I'm fine. I'm feeling much better now. Besides, I don't like doctors."

Wiseman smiled sympathetically at me. "You probably have a concussion."

"That would be my guess," I said, careful to make my reply sound casual.

"Why don't we take you to the hospital then?"

I shook my head. "No. I'll be fine."

"Listen, Dahms," Wiseman began, "you can't really be—"

"Don't waste your breath, Max," Edgerton finally spoke up. "You can't talk any sense to Lyle once his fool mind is made up. He'd rather just sit there and die than admit he needed our help."

"But he could be seriously injured," Wiseman said to Edgerton. "His judgment may be impaired. We can't just let him—"

"The blow on the head isn't what impaired his

judgment," Edgerton interrupted. "His judgment's always been impaired. A couple more blows to the head and maybe his judgment will improve."

"Thanks for taking my side in this, Stephen," I said. "It's great to have friends to look out for you."

Edgerton gave me a crooked, borderline malevolent smile. "Oh, hell, Lyle. You know I'll look out for you. You say you don't want to go see a doctor, I say we should let you have your way. Tell you what. If you keel over unconscious, we'll go ahead and haul your sorry ass off to the hospital. If you don't die before we get you there, you can later say that there was no reason for us to have taken you in. That should work. That way you would get the treatment you need, without having to admit that you ever needed it."

"What the hell did I do to you? Why are you so damned pissed at me?"

Edgerton waved a hand at me. "I don't have the time to waste being pissed at you. Jeez, just try and help some people."

"You're a fucking saint, Stephen."

We sat in silence for several minutes, Edgerton and I staring resolutely into the fire, Hess and Wiseman alternatively staring at us and then looking at each other. The silence lasted long enough to go from being awkward to ridiculous, and I was thinking about getting up and leaving them, when a figure came out of the darkness toward us.

Dick Peterson was smiling broadly, carrying a small cooler in one hand and a can of beer in the other. "Hi, guys," he said. "Mind if I join you?"

The fact was that I wouldn't have minded if Lucifer had asked to join us, as long as it held out some promise of breaking the silence. I wasn't the only one. We each loudly hailed Peterson's arrival. "Anybody want a beer?" he asked as he took a seat on the ground.

"Sure," I said, reaching toward him.

"It's a Lite," Peterson said as he handed it to me.

My disappointment must have been pretty obvious, because just as Peterson's smile began to fade away, Wiseman said, "I've got a brown ale if you prefer."

"I do like something with a little bit more body," I told Peterson, then turned toward Wiseman.

Edgerton said something to Hess that I couldn't quite make out, but I suspected it had something to do with my weight. Hess laughed as quietly as he could.

Handing me the beer, Wiseman said, "I'm not sure that someone whose just been injured should be drinking."

I took the beer from him. "I appreciate the concern. But I think I'll be all right."

"Did you hurt yourself, Lyle?" Peterson asked.

"A little. But I'm feeling much better."

Edgerton grunted but said nothing.

I sipped at the beer gingerly. There was a painful thrumming that swelled inside my head, and when I closed my eyes arcs of light crackled like lighting against a night sky. I knew that I shouldn't be drinking, but after a couple of sips it didn't appear that the sky was gonna fall on me or anything, so I convinced myself that it would be okay.

I turned to look at Wiseman. Something still confused me. "I thought you told me that you weren't coming out here this weekend," I said.

"I wasn't going to, but I couldn't help myself. I just had to know if you had found out anything about the murders. I mean, you know, about our friend in the chain mail."

I glared at Wiseman. He clammed up, but I figured the damage was already done. I hadn't wanted Peterson to know that I was interested in LeGrand. I knew from my stakeout of Prime that they knew each other, and I didn't know how well, or what exactly their relationship was. I tried to appear nonchalant as I glanced over at Peterson. If Peterson was particularly interested in what Wiseman had said about LeGrand, it didn't show in his expression. He was just staring at the beer in his hand.

Then Peterson smiled, rose suddenly, and walked over to Wiseman. "I don't believe we've been formally introduced. I'm Dick Peterson. I run the elephant rides."

"Max Wiseman," he said, shaking Peterson's hand. "I'm with Clan Highland."

"I know, I know. Lyle and I watched you compete in the caber toss last week. Sorry about how that ended for you. That guy that yelled at you when you were trying to make your last toss, he…Well, some people just shouldn't be allowed to live, if you know what I mean."

"*I* damn sure know what you mean," I said with rather more animosity than I intended.

Peterson looked at me curiously but didn't question me further.

We all fell silent again. Peterson kept looking at us, his glance darting from face to face, a quizzical little frown furrowing his brow. Snatches of song drifted across the festival site from other gatherings around other fires. When "Earth Angel" by the Penguins began to play somewhere not too far away, Peterson cracked a wide grin. "I love that song. We played it at our wedding. When I close my eyes, I can still see her in that dress. So beautiful." He paused. "Old songs are time machines really. They take you back where you want to be."

Wiseman smiled softly "And where would you like to be, Dick?"

"You mean, if I had a time machine?"

"Yeah."

Peterson gulped at his beer. "I'd go back to the births of both my sons. Proudest moments of my life. I'd hold my wife's hand again and see the joy in her eyes when she held them in her arms. When she held them and looked into my eyes. That's where I'd go."

"You really miss her," I said.

"I really miss her."

Peterson searched the faces around him. We all wore the same impassive, though vaguely sympathetic expression.

After a short silence, Peterson looked up at me and said, "What about you, Lyle? If you had a time machine, where would you go?"

I thought for a moment, then it hit me. "Shit," I said.

"What is it?"

"Damn, damn, damn. If I had that time machine, I think I'd head back to seven thirty this evening."

"What happened then?" Edgerton asked.

"That's when I was supposed to meet Naomi."

"Why didn't you?"

"I was unconscious at the time."

Edgerton shook his head. "Not good enough, pal."

"She didn't come by here looking for me, did she?"

"I didn't see her," Edgerton said.

"I saw her," Hess said. "She came by here about eight o'clock. Didn't stay long. Stephen here had gone to the privy."

"What did she say? Was she ticked?"

"I didn't talk to her, Lyle," Hess replied. "Julia talked to her and all she told me was that she was looking for you. Didn't seem like she thought it was any big deal."

"I'll bet she was ticked," I said. "Where is Julia? Maybe she could tell me more. Maybe Naomi left a message."

Hess shrugged. "She didn't say anything to me about a message. And she took off shortly after Wiseman here showed up."

"I have that effect on a lot of women," Wiseman said, smiling.

Hess chuckled. "Julia said she wanted to go into town. She didn't mention that she wanted to escape you, Max. But then, she doesn't tell me everything."

I sighed. "Screw it," I said, rising. "Not much I can do about it tonight. I'm gonna go take a leak."

"You want a flashlight?" Hess offered. "It gets pretty dark out there."

"Sure."

Hess picked up a flashlight and lobbed it to me. I fumbled at it and the flashlight fell to the ground. When I bent down to pick it up, I was nearly blinded by pain as the contents of my head immediately swelled, straining against the inside of my skull. I paused to let the pressure subside, switching the flashlight on to be certain that it still worked.

"Thanks," I murmured, turning to leave.

"Onward, Christian solider!" Hess exclaimed.

As I headed away from them toward the bathrooms, they began humming the old hymn.

About halfway to the bathroom, I stopped to look

over at the lights shining brightly from the Cock and Bull across the festival site. I thought about going over there and trying to find Naomi. It was late, I thought. Screw it.

On my way back to the armory from the bathroom, I thought about it again. It was late and I was tired, but I had a choice. I could try to find some corner of the armory to curl up in to get some sleep, or I could try to find Naomi. Maybe curl up next to her. I'd missed our date, but I had a good excuse. She'd probably feel sorry for me. She might want to take care of me.

I turned toward the tavern. There was a dip in the terrain between the tavern and me. I was going up the rise when my foot caught something. I stumbled, pitching forward to the ground. I managed to break my fall with my hands, but the impact jarred me. My head throbbed with pain. Screw it, I thought.

As I was getting to my feet, I swept the beam of the flashlight across the ground hoping to see what I had stumbled upon. It was a shoe. A bone-colored running shoe. There was still a foot in it. Then I realized there was a whole person lying there on the ground. I moved the flashlight to get a good look and something shiny reflected the beam back into my eyes. Chain mail. The guy was wearing chain mail.

In the light of the flashlight, I took a long look at Dirk LeGrand's blackened eyes, and the bruise marks I'd left on his neck. I knelt next to the body. There was a hole about the size of a half-dollar in his bare chest, with a circle burned into his flesh around the hole. Unlike Gilroy, it wasn't an arrow that had killed LeGrand. It was a bullet. Someone had shot him at close range.

And I knew that everyone was gonna think that it was me.

Chapter Sixteen

Before long, every cop in Little Crow converged on the festival site. Dunstable wasn't taking any chances. It looked like everyone on the city payroll had been called in. There were patrol cars everywhere, circling and sweeping the festival site with search lights, and when the rear gate was opened, I spotted a fire truck inexplicably stationed in the parking lot.

We were asked to sit quietly around the fire and wait to be interviewed. The cops guarding us evidently had orders not to speak because it got awfully quiet. At one point the fire began to burn down, and Hess asked if he could throw some more wood on. A cop held up a beefy hand in response but said nothing. Instead, he eyed Hess carefully before tossing a couple pieces into the fire.

The silence surrounding our fire was invaded by the voices of the cops examining the corpse that drifted across the field toward us. I winced at the loud and, I thought, forced laughter of the men at the crime scene. They had set up bright arc lights around the body that glowed with an otherworldly intensity.

Flashes of even brighter light intermittently pulsed beyond the perimeter of this halo as the crime scene photographer took pictures of the corpse. I winced. Each pulse was a little finger of pain probing the inside of my battered cranium.

When I closed my eyes, I clearly saw LeGrand's

body on the ground, his head cocked at an odd angle, mouth open, a deceptively small hole in his chest, and a pool of blood spread wide beneath him. With each distant flash I imagined the police photos—the final portraits of a man whose appearance meant so much to him in life—the still pictures of a sullied, now stilled soul. Maybe these flashes would capture some secret, I thought. Some secret as to why he ended up shot dead in the grass. And who had shot him. Maybe the flashes, like the moment of death itself, could stop time and give me answers to the questions that, like the gnats that swirled in the firelight, nagged at me.

I looked across at Dick Peterson. I needed something, I thought, something that would help shed light on Peterson and his involvement with LeGrand. They had some business together. That much I knew. But was Peterson involved in LeGrand's drug business? His status as a loving family man seemed to preclude this, but still, you never know. Lots of pushers, pimps, and murderers have what pass for good family lives.

I was thinking about Peterson's kids when Dunstable approached, trailed by my old pal Officer Thompson.

"Well, now the gang's all here," I noted with mock cheerfulness as they approached.

Thompson stroked his goatee and glared at me. "We're taking you back to the station with us, fella. We'll see how funny you think all this is after you've been with us awhile."

"Okay, everybody on your feet!" Dunstable ordered.

We all stood up and a policeman moved over to each of us. Officer Thompson moved in next to me.

"Cuff 'em!" Dunstable snapped. And the cops

produced a pair of handcuffs for each of us. Once we'd been handcuffed, Dunstable said, "Okay, take 'em in," The cops began to prod us toward the parking lot.

"Is it all right for me to ask why you're taking us away like this?" Wiseman asked. "I mean, are we under arrest?"

Dunstable didn't even look at Wiseman. He just nodded to the cop who was escorting him. The cop slugged Wiseman in the gut. Wiseman doubled up and his knees buckled, but the cop who slugged him steadied Wiseman before he fell to the ground. Dunstable waited so that we could all get a good look at what had happened to Wiseman. Then he nodded again, and the cops prodded us forward.

Thompson pulled his truncheon from his belt and pressed it lightly against me. I glanced back to check on Wiseman, and Thompson gave me a tap. "Eyes front, fella!" As I turned, I wondered why, when I'd looked, Wiseman had been smiling.

The cops ushered Edgerton and Hess into the back of one patrol car and Peterson and Wiseman into the back of another. Thompson and a chubby officer I had not seen before directed me into the back of yet another car.

"Not that I'm complaining or anything," I said as we pulled away, "but is there any special reason why I get to ride by myself?"

"Not a special reason," Thompson said.

I didn't much like the look in his eyes.

When we reached the highway the other two cars turned left toward Little Crow. The car I was riding in turned right. We went down the dark county road about two miles and made another right down an unmarked dirt road that was lined on both sides by birch and ash. About a quarter mile down the dirt road, we came to a deeply rutted driveway that led into the woods. We turned into the driveway and soon reached a clearing hidden behind the trees. The patrol car rolled slowly to a stop. There was no way anybody was going to see us from the road.

Thompson came around and held the door open for me so I could get out the car. I wasn't in much of a hurry, and the other cop had to come around and tug me out into the clearing. No one offered to take my cuffs off.

"You're lucky, fella," Thompson said as he took his jacket off.

"That so?"

"Oh, you probably don't realize it, but yeah, today's your lucky day."

"You're from Publishers Clearing House and I've won a thousand a day for life?"

"No, even better," Thompson said, running his palm repeatedly over his pointy beard. "You get to have a life. We ain't gonna kill ya."

"That's gratifying, officer."

"Hell, fella, let me tell ya, you were near death," Thompson told me. "Yes sir. Our Chief was going bring you out here himself. But you know, the Chief's got a temper. Told me he was afraid that if he brought you out here things might get out of hand. You might not make it back to the station to sign your confession. The Chief's a...whatchamacallit? A very prudent man. He asked me to handle the interrogation for him. Me? I can probably keep my temper under control. Don't get me wrong. I'm gonna enjoy shutting up that smart mouth of yours. When I'm done, the only thing you're gonna use that mouth for is to confess to these here murders. I hope you don't lose too many teeth. I want to make sure you look good enough to have your picture on the TV news as we cart you off to prison."

"Officer Thompson," I said, watching him stroke the ragged clump of hair that clung to his chin. "I feel like I need to share something with you. Something important."

"What's that, Dahms?"

"That beard of yours? That weird ass tuft on your chin? Makes you look like the result of an unnatural coupling with a billy goat."

Thompson shrugged. "I might just kill you after all."

"Do what you gotta do, Goat Boy."

I didn't say anything else. At least not that I remember. I do remember Thompson driving a hard left into my abdomen. I was still tender from the beating I had taken earlier in the evening, and I folded like a cheap card table. After that, he probably hit me in the head. That I don't remember. I don't really remember anything else until I woke up the next afternoon.

****

I opened my eyes and struggled to see through the film that, like petroleum jelly, seemed to coat my eyeballs. My head throbbed, and every time I breathed it felt like my sides were going to split open and my guts were going to spill out. I was lying in a bed and there was some movement around me. It turned out to be a woman dressed in blue scrubs with a stethoscope around her neck. She fiddled with some tubing that sagged in a lazy loop down to my arm where a needle was fixed with white tape. When she saw that my eyes were open, she nodded, but didn't seem to be nodding at me.

In the distance, a voice called out, "Looks like he's awake."

With difficulty, I turned and saw a uniformed officer standing in the doorway, staring down a hall. The nurse smiled, first at the officer, then at me. "Someone will be in shortly to speak with you," she said.

"Where am I?"

"You're in St. Joseph's Hospital in Little Crow."

"How am I doing?"

"Excuse me?"

"Am I seriously injured? Were last rites administered? Did they harvest any of my organs while I was out? That sort of thing."

"The doctor will be in shortly to speak with you."

"Can't you just—"

She shook her head. "Better to wait for the doctor."

So, I waited. The nurse was kind enough to raise the head of my hospital bed, and even showed me how to work the TV controls. Since no one would talk to me, I flipped channels until I hit pay dirt, a rerun of *Petticoat Junction*. As the program began, I closed my eyes, and softly sang the theme song to myself. As the nurse checked my IV, I thought I heard her murmuring the words of the song along with me. The cop at the door turned sideways in the doorway and looked in at the TV. I thought I saw him smile when we reached the part about Uncle Joe "movin' kinda slow." Everybody loves Uncle Joe.

Finally, the doctor came in and told me that I had been roughed up pretty good, had a mild concussion and some badly bruised ribs, but the x-rays hadn't shown any broken bones, and I was going to be just fine if I took it easy for a couple of weeks. I asked the doctor if he knew if I would be taking it easy at home or in jail, but he told me that wasn't his department. He suggested I ask the cop guarding the door. When I did, the cop said he couldn't talk to me until my lawyer got there.

"I don't have a lawyer," I told him.

"That's not what I heard."

The nurse had to leave, but the cop came inside and together we watched the TV in silence. The program was nearly over when a man entered the room.

He was only about five foot five and had a slight build, except for the requisite paunch of a successful, older man. I figured him for about sixty. He had a full head of gray hair—styled perfectly. He was wearing a blue pinstriped suit that likely cost more than everything I owned. But it wasn't his hair or the suit that suggested that he was not to be trifled with. There was a glint in his eyes. The glint of high carbon steel.

He strode directly into the room, not looking around as he walked, but rather staring directly at me as he approached. It was as if it was accepted that anyone or anything that stood between him and his goal had damn well better get out of the way. Even the cop shrank away as he passed by.

"Who are you?" I asked.

He didn't answer. Instead, he turned to the cop and said, "You can leave now."

The cop left. The short man looked down at me and winced. "Christ, you look like hell," he said.

I hadn't had seen myself in a mirror, so I took his word for it. "Are you my lawyer?"

"Gustav Pendergast," he said. "Now, I don't know you and you may not know me. What I do know is that you are in a heap of trouble. You have been arrested pending charges of murder. You were spotted stalking the deceased, and you've had repeated altercations with him. You've been uncooperative with the police, and they will do everything within their power to see you go to prison for the murder. You have made a particular enemy of Chief Dunstable of the Little Crow Police Department and he is not a man you want as your enemy. But…" he paused, "you have a powerful ally. You have me. You should know that I am one of the few people in this state that can get you out of this trouble. I'm not bragging. I'm just stating facts."

"Okay," I said.

By then I had remembered who this guy was. Gustav Pendergast was a high profile, highly paid attorney, the kind of guy the media builds into a local legend so they have something to cover every time he walks into a courtroom. He was probably a pretty good attorney, but I suspected his real value was his reputation and the sway he had with the authorities.

"Now I don't want you to worry about my fee," he continued. "You can't afford me and I'm not going to charge you. I'm here as a favor to an old friend and because I cannot abide police corruption. Now, what you need to do is sit tight. As soon as these idiots charge you—if they charge you—I'll arrange for your bail. The next thing I want you to do is…nothing. Don't do a damn thing. I'm going to take care of this, and I don't need you prowling around making things difficult for me. Do you understand?"

"Not really," I said.

Pendergast arched an eyebrow at me. "What part of that do you want me to go over?"

"You said you were doing someone a favor. Who?"

"I can't tell you."

"Why not?"

"I can't tell you that either."

I sighed. "Am I the only one that has been arrested?"

"Yes," Pendergast said. "Your friends from the festival were questioned but have all been released."

"How do you know that they're my friends?"

"Let's not play games, Mr. Dahms."

I closed my eyes and slowly opened them again. "What did you mean about police corruption?"

He arched that eyebrow at me again. "They beat you up, didn't they?"

"Yeah."

"They're not supposed to do that."

I stared intently into Pendergast's cold, blue-gray eyes. My mouth was dry. There was a pitcher of ice water and a throwaway cup on a table next to my bed. I filled the cup and took a long drink, rattling the ice a little as I finished. When I turned back to face Pendergast, his eyes met mine with a gaze that gave nothing away. They were expressionless—no impatience, no concern, nothing.

"What do you really want from me?" I asked.

"As I stated, I don't want anything from you. I'm doing a favor for a friend. He asked me to see if I could help you. I think I can. That's all."

"You didn't ask me if I killed anyone."

"No," he said. "I didn't."

"Were you planning to?"

"No."

"Does it matter if I killed anyone?"

"No."

"Do you think you can get me off?"

"Oh my, yes," he said, as if the question astonished him.

"But it doesn't matter if I killed anyone?"

Pendergast leaned back slightly in his chair. "No," he repeated. "As I see it, this is not about that young man's death at all. Tragic though that may be. No. This is about the pervasive corruption of the Little Crow police force. I intend to shine the light of public scrutiny on Dunstable and his entire department. To spotlight the Gestapo tactics that are employed to rob citizens of their constitutionally guaranteed civil liberties. Further, I intend to show that the police department itself is involved in criminal activities—activities carried out behind the safety of the very badges they wear to shield the citizenry from such harm. I intend to show that corruption is so pervasive in the department that the results of any investigation run by that department are suspect and not to be trusted."

I smirked. "In other words, I may be guilty, but because I was arrested in Little Crow, by Little Crow cops, I should go free?"

Pendergast nodded. "That is an oversimplification, but essentially, that is correct."

"Uh huh," I nodded back. "You said that the Little Crow cops are crooked. What is it that you claim they are doing? It can't just be that they beat up some P.I. That's not what got you interested."

"You weren't the only person assaulted by the police that night," he reminded me.

I thought back and finally remembered Wiseman taking one in the gut before they led him away.

"No one else ended up in here, did they?" I asked. "I mean, no one else had to be hospitalized, did they?"

"No. You were the only one with whom they allowed themselves to get so carried away,"

With that Pendergast abruptly stood up and took a

couple of steps toward the door. "I think that's all that we need to cover at present. I do have other appointments this afternoon. I probably won't see you again until they arraign you. If it comes to that. They may see the light and simply release you. God knows they haven't enough evidence to proceed to trial. As long as you don't do anything completely stupid, like confess, I think they will simply let you go."

Pendergast turned to the door, but I called after him. He turned to face me. "Yes, Dahms."

"I didn't do it."

"You didn't do what?"

"I didn't kill LeGrand. I didn't kill anybody."

"You didn't need to tell me that."

"Yes, I did."

"Well," he said shaking his head, "if it makes you feel better."

After he'd gone, I asked the nurse for a mirror and looked at myself. My left eye was surrounded by a swollen mass of discolored flesh—the eyeball floating amid pink and purple swells, bobbing upon a raw and painful sea. There was a good-sized abrasion at the line of my jaw, and although I couldn't see it, the back of my head throbbed with such pain that I imagined it bulging with my every heartbeat. I cringed at what I saw in the mirror, but only with effort could I turn away, I was so fascinated by the ruins of my face. Finally, I closed my eyes, let my fatigue wash over me, and waited for sleep to come and take some of the pain away

Chapter Seventeen

They kept me in the hospital one more night for observation. The next day they came in, pulled out the IV, and said I could be released. What they couldn't tell me was if I'd be going home or to jail. The doctor did tell me that I needed several additional days' rest, and that I should schedule an appointment with my regular physician for the middle of the next week.

I didn't tell him that I didn't have a regular physician, and in fact didn't even have the money to pay for his services, let alone for some follow-up appointment. I wondered if the City of Little Crow would maybe cover it. After all, their cops put me in the hospital. I made a mental note to ask Pendergast the next time I saw him. At about that time, Dunstable appeared at the doorway.

The doctor nodded silently at Dunstable, then turned and left the room. I worked the controls on the hospital bed until I was sitting most of the way up, my head resting on a couple of pillows. Dunstable took up a position just inside the door, leaning against the wall and staring down at me coldly. Although I'm sure he wanted it to appear completely natural, he began to flex the muscles of his upper body in the most affected manner possible. Doubtless, he hoped that the sight of his rippling forearms and pulsating pecs would fill me with dread. I smiled at him and began to pick my nose.

"Don't this hospital air just dry your nose out something fierce?" I asked, looking down to examine the end of my finger. "You haven't got any nasal spray on you, do you?"

"Who killed LeGrand?"

"I sort of figured you thought I'd done that, Chief."

"I did."

"Something change your mind?"

"Well," he said moving out of the doorway and toward the bed, "we've been looking into it, and we just don't think you pulled the trigger. We found your .38 in your car out at the festival site. We tested it. It wasn't the gun that killed LeGrand who got capped with a 9mm. Now, you could have used another gun. You could have ditched it someplace before we picked you up, but I don't think so. The doctors here were kind enough to let us test your hands for powder residue while they fixed you up following that accident you had after your arrest. You tested clean. You could have been wearing gloves, but…Anyway, we can't prove that you'd fired a weapon. Things are looking up for you, but we still need a couple of things. I'd like to hear your version of what happened that night."

"Well," I said, scratching my head, "the thing that stands out most is when you had your boys play knick knack paddy whack on me. After that I imagine that they panicked and brought me to the hospital instead of doing the wise thing and just leaving me in the brush to die."

Dunstable smiled his thin smile. "I'm sure that our investigation will help us piece together exactly how it was you sustained your injuries, but I'm equally sure that none of my men were involved in any violation of your civil liberties, Mr. Dahms."

"Ain't you polite all of a sudden, Chief. This Pendergast got you a little scared, does he?"

"Who's Pendergast?" Dunstable asked.

I grunted.

"Besides," the Chief continued, "the events that occurred after your arrest don't interest me. I'd like to know what you were doing before your arrest. Specifically, what were you doing between the hours of six and ten o'clock that night?"

"Just the traditional medieval merrymaking that makes the Renaissance Festival such a delightful family attraction."

Dunstable shrugged. "Whatever you say, Dahms. But it might be a good idea for you to let us know what you're really doing out there at the festival. It might help you get out from under a murder charge."

"I thought you said you didn't think I did it?"

"I said we don't think you pulled the trigger. That doesn't mean you didn't have it done. It's the same thing really. You see, we may be a small town and have a small-town police force, but we can find out some things just like the big boys. For example, we know you were involved with LeGrand. You want to comment on what kind of business you had with the dead man?"

"I'll tell you the truth, Chief," I said. "And this is a trifle embarrassing, but I was actually looking to recruit him for the Big Brothers/Big Sisters program. A boy like me just needs a role model. Someone to look up to."

"You're a funny guy, Dahms," Dunstable said with a nod. "They're gonna love that in the pen down in Stillwater. They're gonna love that quick wit of yours when they stick it to you. At least you won't be lonely. It's nice to be popular with the other inmates."

"Keep your fantasies to yourself, Chief."

Dunstable grunted, walked around the bed and started fiddling with the empty IV bag that still hung on its pole beside my bed.

"Just what do you figure you can lock me up for, Chief?"

He chuckled and gave the IV bag a little tap with his finger. "Drugs, pal. You're a dealer, aren't you?"

I sat all the way up in bed and stared at Dunstable. "Just where did you come up with this little gem?"

"It's like this, Dahms. We know you had a beef with LeGrand. We know that he was a dealer. The way I got it figured, you and LeGrand were working together. Maybe he held out on you or tried to cut you out of the operation. Whatever. It doesn't matter. But I figure you had those run-ins with LeGrand over drugs. You may not have killed him, but with him gone, you're the one who stands to profit. You probably figure you can take over the operation. But you figure wrong."

"You're an audacious sonofabitch, Chief. I'll give you that."

"How so?"

"You know goddamn well I got nothing to do with LeGrand's drug operation. You haven't one shred of evidence against me, and it defies logic. You're just trying the theory on for size. Seeing if it'll be something you can sell to the district attorney."

"Defies logic?" Dunstable asked. "How do you figure that? We have you on record admitting that on two occasions prior to the day that he died you assaulted the deceased. In addition, we have a witness that will testify that he saw you attack the deceased in the Irish Cottage only a few hours before he was shot. We know that

LeGrand was a drug dealer and most drug dealers who meet violent ends do so in squabbles over drugs. Or money. Just because we can't prove that you pulled the trigger doesn't mean that you didn't want him dead. Maybe you just had someone else do it. Maybe you figured that way it wouldn't be traced back to you."

"I'm not like you, Dunstable. I don't have other people do my dirty work for me.

Dunstable squinted at me in mock bewilderment. "What are talking about, Dahms? What *dirty work*?"

"I figure it's because you're a pussy," I continued. "I figure you work out all the time hoping that no one will know that under all those engorged muscles beats the heart of a little girl."

"Keep talking, fat boy."

"You didn't have the guts to take me on yourself, limp dick. You had to get Thompson to do it. And you weren't man enough to shut up Wiseman at his arrest either. You had one of your boys hit him for you."

Dunstable flushed a surprisingly vivid shade of red and a bubble of saliva formed at the corner of his mouth. "Nobody hit Wiseman, goddammit. And I'm not going to let any slimy, drug dealer say otherwise."

"Why are you so scared of Wiseman, Chief?"

Dunstable balled up his right hand and moved to within inches of me. "Before this is over, I'm going to knock every goddamned tooth out of your goddamned mouth."

"You know what I'm wondering, Chief," I said. "If you knew that LeGrand was a drug dealer, why didn't you arrest him? I thought they made you Chief because you were going to keep drug dealers out of town. And here you are telling me that you knew about this

LeGrand, and you didn't do anything. How are the good people of Little Crow supposed to react to that?"

Dunstable backed away from me, desperately trying to rein in his anger. It took him a while, but eventually he managed it. "I know what you're doing," he said after his normal color had returned. "You figure if you can goad me into hitting you, you can sue the city. Good idea. Make a pile of money and garner a bunch of sympathy at the same time. Well, Dahms, that's not going to happen. Not today anyway. I came here to tell you that I'm letting you go, but you're anything but free. We're going to be keeping an eye on you. We're going to be watching your every move. You're not going to able to take a shit without us knowing how much it stinks. And you're going to screw up. We're going to nail you and we're going to throw your ass in prison. This, I promise you."

I stared into his eyes. "You're scared of something."

"Not of you."

"Maybe not. But something."

He started to make one last comment, but checked himself, turned, and left the room.

With Dunstable gone, I got up, got dressed, and went about getting myself discharged from the hospital. It wasn't until I stepped out of the front doors that I realized that I was miles from home and had no way to get there. I had left my car at the festival site, but I figured the cops had it in their impound lot. I could go pay them a visit, but given my conversation with the Chief, I decided that might be unwise. I'd have to ask Pendergast to get me the car back. I could take a bus to Minneapolis, but that would be a real drag. There aren't many buses that run from the city to the outer suburbs, and I really wasn't feeling up to the wait. I tried to think of someone I could call for a ride. Edgerton didn't drive. Skip would be at work. Naomi? Well, I'd inadvertently stood up Naomi on Saturday night and I didn't want the next time we spoke to be my asking her for a favor.

I had resigned myself to the bus when I heard Wiseman call my name. He was parked close by in a red Subaru Forester, the windows rolled down. "I figured you'd be looking for a way home," he said as he leaned across and opened the passenger side door for me. "Hop in." He smiled as I climbed in the seat next to him. His smile became strained as he studied me my face. "Christ," he said, "you look like hell."

"Thanks, Max. How'd you know when I'd be released?"

"I didn't really. I just happened to call a little while ago and they told me that you were about to leave. My office is just up in Bloomington, so I hightailed it down here."

"Thanks."

"Don't mention it."

"I'm not sure this is a real good idea though.

"What?"

"You picking me up."

"Why not?"

"It's not a good idea for you to get any more involved in this thing. I mean, Dunstable just told me that he'd be having me watched. He figures me for a criminal. He sees you picking me up, he might suspect you as well. Might not be too healthy."

"In for a penny, in for a pound," Wiseman said.

"Let's try and make sure it's not a pound of flesh. Your flesh."

"Ah," he smirked, "I'm trying to lose some weight anyway. Besides, I'm pissed at Dunstable. I'd like to do what I can to make him uncomfortable. You know, 'if you prick us do we not bleed? If you wrong us, shall we not revenge?' and all that."

Wiseman cuffed me lightly on the shoulder, then asked me where I lived. I told him, and we pulled away, driving for several minutes without further conversation. The drive gave me time to think, and after I'd thought long enough, I just had to ask.

"How'd you swing the high buck lawyer, Max? You don't look as though you're rolling in dough?"

Wiseman smiled. "Pendergast tell you?"

"No. He told me he was doing a favor for a friend. Wouldn't give me the friend's name."

"Well, I'm not going to pretend to be a friend of Gustav Pendergast's," Wiseman said. "But my old man knows him pretty well."

"Your dad?"

"Yeah. He's district court judge, Samuel Wiseman. This is the first time I've ever had to ask Dad for this kind of favor. I hope it works out."

I let that sink in for a moment. "It'll work out, Max. I didn't do anything."

"Didn't figure you did."

Wiseman clicked on the car radio and dialed up one of those stations that claims to play the greatest hits of the '80s, '90s and today. I wouldn't know. All we heard were commercials.

After a while I got tired of hearing about all the wonderful new services that were available from my local cable company and asked Wiseman how he managed to convince his dad to go to bat for some P.I.

he'd never met.

"He didn't really do it for you. Or even for me. I think he did it because he doesn't like Dunstable."

"Golly, you mean he doesn't like cops that arrest and punch his son for no reason?"

"Well, there is that," Wiseman said. "But there's something more. I got the impression that it's not just Dunstable's lack of respect for suspect's rights that bothering him. I got the impression that my dad thinks Dunstable's crooked. You know, into something really criminal."

"More criminal than having us beat up?"

"Yeah."

"Did he say what?"

"No," Wiseman said. "I asked, but Dad just told me to wait and see."

"That's why he set that pit bull Pendergast on him. He's going to try and bring down Dunstable."

"So I gathered," Wiseman said.

I bit my lip. "I don't know how much I can help."

"What do you mean?"

I stared out the windshield for a moment. "I just hope they don't need me to testify against Dunstable or anything."

"Why? Would that be a problem?"

I rubbed my chin a couple of times. "I just don't think I could testify against a cop. Any cop."

Wiseman tried to catch my eye, but I kept staring straight ahead. "The guy had you beat up. He put you in the hospital."

"I know."

"But you don't want to see him lose his job for that? You'd rather let him go right on doing that to others?"

"Of course not. It's just that I can't testify against cops, that's all."

"Why the hell not?"

"Look, Max. I appreciate everything you and your old man have done for me. And I'm going to do all I can to help clean this mess up. But the fact is that I can't go on doing what I do without the cooperation of the police. In my line of work, you are constantly bumping up against cops. If they don't want you to work, you don't work. If I rat out one of their own, I'm looking for a new job."

"Even if the cop's a criminal?" Wiseman asked. "Even if he's crooked?"

"Even then."

The car got very quiet. "You don't show much gratitude," Wiseman said at last.

I gave him a doleful smile. "I show as much as I can."

Chapter Eighteen

Wiseman dropped me off at the Bijou, and as I walked down the hall, I heard the tapping of keystrokes coming from Edgerton's room. Edgerton had recently updated his PC and had immersed himself in a world of adventure games, computer-based animation, web surfing, and HTML coding. It was all geek to me, but I pretended to be interested when he talked about it, as long as he plied me with beer and didn't get too technical. And to be fair, he'd produced some really interesting stuff using something called "ray tracing." That day, however, I wanted none of it. I wasn't feeling very well and just wanted to crawl into bed and sleep, but since I hadn't seen him since we were arrested, I decided I'd better look in on him.

I knocked and Edgerton shouted, "Come in!"

He didn't even turn around; he just kept typing.

"Stephen," I said.

"Just a minute," he said, his eyes fixed on the computer screen.

"I only wanted to—"

"I said just a minute!" he snapped, still not looking in my direction.

I wasn't happy, but I waited. There was a slight musty smell to Edgerton's room. I sniffed and let my eyes wander about the room. Shelves on every wall were crammed with books and stacks of paper that threatened to topple at any moment. There weren't enough shelves to hold it all, so the floor along each wall was also lined with books—both hard and soft-covered, a jumble of different sizes and different subjects. Piles of comic books, each sealed from the elements in its own protective plastic sleeve, leaned precariously against one of the walls. Against another wall, crates full of LPs, CDs, and tapes were stacked on either side of a boom box and turntable that sat on a low table made of bricks and boards. A solid body electric guitar was standing in a corner. Two completed Viking helmets sat in another corner and scattered before them were scraps of sheet metal and leather. The bed was mostly clear, except for the rumpled bedding and two open books—one having something to do with the computer, the other a biography of the adventurer Sir Richard Burton. Tacked to the wall at the foot of the bed was a large map of the solar system, and on the wall at the head of the bed, Edgerton had hung a hand-lettered syllogism that read:

Fear God

God is Love

Fear Love

I shuffled around for something like five minutes before Edgerton stopped typing. "Hey, Lyle," he said, evidently forgetting that I'd been waiting. "Christ, you look like hell. When did you get out of the hospital? Wait a minute? Why aren't you in jail?"

"I just got out of the hospital. And I'm not in jail because I didn't commit a crime."

"Yeah." Edgerton nodded. "Hey, you want to see what I've been working on?"

"Not really."

"Oh, come on, this is really cool."

"No, really, Stephen," I said, turning for the door. "I just wanted to be sure you had made out all right and I wanted you to know that I was back. It's not like you would have known my condition from all those visits you made me in the hospital."

Edgerton shrugged, "I figured there'd be cops around, and you know it's not easy for me to get out there. Besides, I called, and they told me you weren't so bad off."

"I appreciate that. You're the freakin' wind beneath my wings."

Edgerton chuckled. "So, do you want to see what I'm working on?"

"No."

"Okay, then. I'll just tell you about it. I had this great idea for a website."

I turned around. "Huh?"

"A website," he said. "You *have* heard of the Internet?"

I showed him my middle finger.

"Good. Well, this would be a virtual gravesite. A cemetery that you can visit from the comfort of your computer terminal. Sort of a no mess way of interring folks."

"Interesting," I offered.

"See, I got the idea from an article I read in a sci-fi magazine. It turns out that a California company offers a service where they can fire lipstick-sized containers containing cremated human remains—they call them *cremains*—into space. The capsule containing the cremains is supposed to remain in orbit around the earth for anywhere from one to ten years.

"The nifty thing is that when it does re-enter the

earth's atmosphere and begins to burn up, the occupants are already ash. I find that kind of economy really appealing. But it doesn't go far enough. It's too expensive and places too much emphasis on the deceased's physical remains. I figured there's got to be a better way."

"Go on."

"So, I thought, why be shot into space when there's cyberspace? Why not create a website where, for a fee, you can be laid to rest in cyberspace? Visitors would type in your name and maybe some other biographical information, like place of birth or year of death, or something, and then when they hit enter...voila, they're standing at your grave. Click on the grave and they get a picture of you, a brief bio listing your vital statistics and accomplishments. There could be testimonials from surviving friends and relatives. Perhaps a video message from you—taped, of course, prior to your demise. The grave plot itself would be situated in the environment of your choice. Wherever you want. Beside a stream; on the beach; under the Eiffel Tower; on one of the moons of Jupiter. Wherever.

"Visitors could leave virtual bouquets of flowers, little notes, whatever they want. Heck, for an extra fee, you could get a perpetual, virtual mourner—wailing and beating his chest. Guaranteed to grieve for all eternity. Or at least until the system goes down. What do you think, Lyle?"

I thought for a moment. "Okay. Let's say you opt for this cyber-cemetery thing. What's going to happen with your body once you're sleeping the sleep that knows no waking? You can't just some your loved one into the floppy drive?"

"They don't have floppy drives anymore, Lyle.

"Okay, but it's gotta go somewhere."

"I don't know," Edgerton replied. "Medical research. Organ donations. Landfill. Who cares?"

"Then what are you burying exactly?"

"I prefer the term *interring*. And we'd be interring a person's essence."

"Who's *we*?"

"Me and my investors. You want in?"

I shook my head. "What's this essence?"

"The bio, man. The testimonials. Statements of who you were and the mark that you made before shuffling off this mortal coil." He smiled. "The person with the best bio wins," he said, turning back to the flickering screen.

"Uh huh. You know for a moment there I thought you were going to admit to some other kind of essence."

"You mean like a soul?" he asked, chuckling. "You know better. But that won't stop me from adding an option to the site where you can view your loved one having tea with the Almighty surrounded by winged angels strumming golden-stringed lutes. Should be a real hit with the churchgoing crowd."

I grunted.

He went on typing, and I briefly stood and listened to the clicking of his keystrokes. "Stephen," I asked at last, "are you okay?"

He turned around. "Why wouldn't I be okay?"

"I don't know, just seems like you're a little preoccupied lately."

"What are you talking about? Preoccupied with what?"

"It's just that…you know, the other night at

McCauley's you were talking about…well, death. Then there was the funeral. Then another dead guy out at the festival. Now you're designing cyber-cemeteries."

"Got to fill up the days with something, Lyle."

He chuckled as he said it, but there really wasn't any mirth in his eyes.

"You didn't even bother to ask me about my hospital stay, or the cops, or anything."

"You're here. You're upright. I figured you're good to go."

"So, you're not still pissed at me?"

"When was I pissed at you?"

"The other night. At the fire. Before I found LeGrand. You were on my case something awful."

His eyes glinted with sudden anger. "You're pretty hard to please, Lyle. First, you're ticked because I don't fawn all over you now that you're out of the hospital, then you get on my case because I was a little concerned about you showing up late at the armory with your head nearly stove in."

We stared at each for a moment. "Forget I mentioned it," I told him.

"I will."

It was hard not slamming the door behind me, but I managed it. Then I went to my room and, after pacing around for a few minutes, I lay down on my bed and slept until the next day when I awoke to the sound of my phone ringing. I looked at my alarm clock. It was nearly one in the afternoon. "Lyle?"

"Yeah."

"Lyle, are you alright?"

"Yeah…um, yeah."

"I was starting to get worried about you. I'd heard

that you had been arrested, so I called the Little Crow police, and they told me that you were in the hospital, but the hospital said that you had gone home."

"Yeah...I...um," I muttered. It took a while, but finally I realized that it was Naomi. I held the phone in front of me and stared at it for a moment. I put the receiver back to my ear and said, "Yeah, I...um..."

"What happened? Were you hurt badly? I'm coming right over."

For some reason I asked, "Are you at work?"

"No. Why?"

"Oh, I don't know. I just woke up. I don't—"

"Oh shit, Lyle, I'm sorry," she interrupted. "I didn't mean to wake you up. Maybe you should go back to sleep. I can call later."

"No, it's all right. I've got to get up now anyway. I'd like to see you."

"You stay in bed. I'll come right over."

I chuckled. "As tempting as that offer is, I think that sort of thing will have to wait until I feel just a little bit better."

"I didn't mean..." She gulped, then laughing added, "You bastard."

"Yeah, yeah. You still coming over?"

"I don't know, if you can't service me, what's the point?"

"We can have coffee and snuggle."

"Okay. But just coffee. I don't want to overly excite a man in your condition. Should I stop and get some? You probably don't feel like making any at your place."

"No. I'm perfectly capable of making coffee," I assured her, "but let's meet at my office. I need to check my mail and my messages anyway. Besides, you've never been to my place and it's really kinda messy right now. I wouldn't want you to get the idea that I'm a slob."

"Lyle, I've seen the way you dress. You *are* a slob. Now, give me directions to your office."

After giving Naomi the directions, I took a quick shower, put on a clean pair of jeans and a clean T-shirt, and hoofed it over to my office. I made one detour. I stopped at nearby George's Bakery for some raised glazed and a couple of cream cheese kolaches. By the time Naomi reached my office, I had the pastries arranged on the desk and the coffee was hot.

She came in the door, looked at me, and for an instant, didn't seem to know what to say. "Christ," she said finally, "you look like hell."

"So everyone tells me."

She squinted at me and pointed toward the left side of my face. "That must really hurt."

"Nah. It looks worse than it is."

Naomi nodded uncertainly. "You're lying, of course."

"Yeah," I admitted, "it hurts a bit. But on the bright side, I expect that it makes you want to nurse me back to health. I might enjoy that."

"Do you want me to go out and rent some little nurse's uniform? With a short skirt and white hose with seams running up the back of my legs."

"Oh God! It would be a fantasy come true."

"Maybe later. Right now, I'm hungry."

I swept my arm dramatically in the direction of my desk and the pastries that I had laid out.

"Jeez! You didn't have to cook," she said. Then she kissed me, grabbed a donut, and looked around the room.

"What do you think?" I asked.

"About the donut?"

"No. About the office."

"Is *grotty* a word?"

"Yep. It's in the dictionary and everything."

"And this dictionary, you mentioned? Does it have a picture of your office next to the word *grotty*?"

"I'd have to check and get back to you on that."

"Never mind."

I ushered her toward one of the client chairs, poured us both a cup of coffee, and took a seat behind my desk. As I was leaning back in my chair, Naomi asked me, "How did you end up in the hospital?"

"I got beat up."

"Who beat you up?"

"Which time?"

Naomi reached over and picked up another donut without taking her eyes off me. "Maybe you should just start at the beginning."

"This gets a bit complicated. The cops beat me up the second time. But they just wanted me to confess to killing Dirk LeGrand. Only, I didn't kill LeGrand. I just beat him up. This was early Saturday evening. Long before he got killed, you understand. This was also well before I was supposed to meet you. I want you to know that I had every intention of being on time for our date."

"You just had an appointment to beat someone up before you picked me up?"

"It's not that I planned to beat the guy up. It's just something that happened."

"And it wasn't a date," Naomi said, sipping her coffee.

"What wasn't a date?"

"Saturday night. You said we had a date. We made

no date."

"No date?"

"No date. More of a…a rendezvous."

"Does that mean we were gonna…?"

"Yep," she said with a leer. "We were gonna."

"Damn."

"That's what you get for beating people up. You lose other opportunities."

"Never does one door open, but another closes," I said.

"Anyway, you were telling me how you got hurt."

"A guy hired me to talk to LeGrand on his behalf. LeGrand had set up a meeting with my client for early Saturday evening. I went to the meeting instead. When LeGrand got there, I was thinking about what he did to my tires and how maybe he killed Gilroy and about the drug dealing and I just kind of…I just kind of took out my frustrations on him. I just sort of jumped him."

"Oh!" Naomi exclaimed. "That was something I was going to tell you. About the drug dealing. I knew about that. LeGrand told me about that. He was trying to impress me."

"Well, thanks anyway," I told her. "But I managed to find out about that all by myself."

"Ooh," Naomi cooed. "You're getting to be such a big boy."

"Be that as it may," I said, "while I was taking my frustrations out on LeGrand—"

"After you jumped him, you mean."

"I didn't say I jumped him."

"Yes, you did."

"Okay, after I jumped him, someone jumped me."

"They sucker punched you, after you sucker

"Probably not."

Naomi nodded and set her cup down on the desk. Then she got up and came around to stand close to me.

When I stood, she smiled and wrapped her arms around me. I felt a little clumsy as I slipped my arms around her waist, closed my eyes, and was tugged gently into the warmth and safety of her embrace.

Chapter Nineteen

Naomi and I had dinner together at a nice little
Italian place in Dinkytown. I debated taking her down to
McCauley's for a nightcap, but decided it probably
wasn't a very good idea. I told myself that I should
probably lay off the alcohol until I felt a little better. But
the truth is, I just wasn't ready to take her down there and
introduce her to everyone. I was a little afraid that if she
saw me in my regular haunt, my loser status might be so
glaringly obvious as to be impossible for her to ignore.
So, after dinner she went home, and I went back to the
Bijou to watch TV and drink beer until it was time to go
to sleep.

In the morning I considered my next move. I knew
that Dick Peterson had been involved with LeGrand, but
I still didn't have the details. Because Otis had arranged
the ambush at the Irish Cottage, I now suspected that he
was also involved with LeGrand. But I didn't find Otis
as intriguing as Peterson. When Peterson had come by
the armory on Saturday night, LeGrand had already been
killed. Maybe Peterson knew, maybe he didn't, but he
came and sat with us and had given away nothing. If he
knew that LeGrand was dead, that took resolve. Otis
didn't have resolve. I needed to find out a lot more about
the man with the elephants.

Edgerton had told me that Peterson worked out at
the festival site full-time during the week doing grounds

work and maintenance, so I decided to head back out to Little Crow. I only had the one problem. I didn't have my car.

I called the Little Crow Police department and pretended to be one of Pendergast's underlings. I was told that the vehicle in question had not been impounded and that no further information was available regarding its whereabouts. I figured that meant the thing was still parked at the festival site. Since the site was not on a regular bus route and I just couldn't be without the car, I bit the bullet and called an Uber.

About forty minutes later I was pulling up next to my own car at the back entrance to the armory. I checked to make sure that the cops had not damaged the Ford when they searched it and finding it pretty much the way I'd left it, I proceeded to the back door of the armory. Since I hadn't thought to ask Hess for a key, I had to pick the lock.

I walked slowly through the darkened armory and passed into the sun-drenched field beyond. Soon I found myself standing alone in the middle of the track for the elephant ride. There was no one else in sight. I stood there for a few minutes with my hands in my pockets, until a short, well-built, older fellow wearing overalls and a plaid shirt with the sleeves rolled up almost to his armpits came out of one of the buildings and stared at me. I stared back.

"Well," he shouted. "What do you think you're doing here?"

"I'm looking for Dick Peterson. You seen him?"

The man approached me slowly, his eyes downcast, watching the little clouds of dust raised by his work boots as he walked. When he reached me, he looked up and studied my bruised face. He must have found what he was looking for, because he didn't ask who I was or what I wanted. "Peterson's over there," he said, pointing to the east. "He's out there clearing some brush. Over that way. Just head out through that gate over yonder and north. You'll see him working out there."

I nodded. "Thanks, I—"

He grunted, turned, and walked away keeping his head down as he went.

I headed across the festival grounds and through the gate that the guy in the overalls had indicated. A few moments later I spied Pederson.

He had a long-handled scythe, swinging the blade easily as he moved through a clump of tall grass growing close to the festival walls. Next to him was a pickup truck, the bed piled high with vegetation.

It was a beautiful fall day. The sun shone high and bright in the sky and a slightly cool breeze wafted through the tall plants that remained beyond the area that Peterson had cleared. Despite the breeze, Peterson's T-shirt was ringed with perspiration, his hair a wet tangle that clung to his forehead. When he paused to wipe the sweat from his brow, he spotted me approaching. "Jeez, Lyle," he said when I reached him. "You look like hell."

"People keep saying that."

Pederson shrugged. "That's because it's true." He paused. "What brings you out here, anyway?"

"I was looking for you."

"You found me."

"Of course," I said, smiling. "I'm a trained detective."

Peterson chuckled, but I thought I saw something in eyes when I said "detective" that looked a little like alarm. "So, what can I help you with?"

"Oh, I've just got a few questions. You know so much more about what goes on around here than I do. I thought maybe you could clear some things up for me."

"Okay. But I'm busy, so if you don't mind, I'm going to go right on working while we talk." He swung the scythe. "What do you need to know?"

I paused before asking, "Did you know that LeGrand was a drug dealer?"

Peterson stopped and turned back to me, his eyes clouded with confusion. I knew he was in a tough spot. He didn't want to tell me anything I didn't already know, but he didn't want to appear as though he was hiding anything from me either. "Yeah," he said, at last. "I knew."

"How long have you been working with him?"

"Huh?"

"How long have you been part of LeGrand's drug dealing operation?" I pressed.

Peterson turned away with an exaggerated flourish. "What the heck are you talking about? How the heck am I supposed to answer a question like that?"

"You could tell me the truth. It's not like I care. I mean, I'm no cop. I'm not going to turn you in if that's what you're worried about."

Peterson turned back to face me. Shaking his head dramatically, he said, "I can't believe that you are accusing me of this."

"Look," I said, "it's no great shakes as far as I'm concerned. My guess is that LeGrand somehow pressured you into helping him and once you were in, you couldn't get out. You're a good guy. I don't think that drugs were your first choice as a career. Not with having to raise your kids and all."

Anger flared in his eyes. "You keep my kids out of this!"

"That's just it," I said, careful to keep my tone calm and amicable. "It's gotta be getting harder to keep them out of it. Especially if you killed LeGrand."

"Jesus, Lyle!" Peterson shouted. "I didn't kill nobody! Heck, I was the one that kept them from killing you."

The instant the words left his mouth he realized his mistake. A look of real fear broke wide in his eyes. He held his breath and stared at me.

"I appreciate that," I said. "I truly do."

Peterson turned away and began mowing down more brush. Watching him work, I reached into my pocket and pulled out a pack of cigarettes. I lit a one, leaned against the trailer and thought about how best to play it. "So, just how deeply is Otis involved?" I asked after a while.

"He isn't involved," Peterson said, continuing to take his swipes at the tall plants.

"Bullshit."

"Believe what you want."

"It's hard to stop lying, isn't it, Dick?"

Peterson stopped working, but still hadn't turned around. "What makes you think that I'm lying?"

"Come on," I urged. "You can't expect me to believe that Otis isn't involved. Otis set up the meeting at the Irish cottage on the night that LeGrand was killed. He is the one that made sure that I would be there. He lured me there so that LeGrand and you could get rid of me. Isn't that it?"

Peterson turned and shook his head. "Aren't you

listening, man. I told you that I kept them from killing you."

"LeGrand and Otis?"

Peterson hesitated. "Yeah," he said finally. "LeGrand and Otis."

"You pulled a gun when LeGrand was beating on me," I said, guessing. "A 9mm, wasn't it?"

"Yeah. A 9mm."

"Same type of gun that killed LeGrand."

"I didn't kill the son-of-a-bitch!"

"Okay, okay. Where's the gun now?"

"Gone, man. Gone."

"You ditched it?"

"No. No, I didn't ditch it. I gave it to somebody. I hope I never see that damn thing again."

"If you really didn't kill LeGrand, you'd better hope that you see it again. It may be the only thing that could prove your innocence."

His eyes flooded with confusion. "What do you mean?"

I sat down on the ground and motioned for Peterson to join me. He eyed me warily for a moment, then sat facing me. "Let's just say, for a moment, that LeGrand was killed with your gun," I said. "And let's just say that you are arrested and tried for LeGrand's murder. Did you buy the gun legally?"

"Yes."

"Then the prosecuting attorney puts the medical examiner on the stand, and he testifies that LeGrand was killed with a 9mm slug. He then presents evidence that you, the defendant, owned a 9mm handgun. A handgun that you are unable to produce. He then points out that it would be a simple thing to test the gun to show whether it killed LeGrand, but the gun has mysteriously disappeared. Now, an innocent man would be eager for his gun to be tested, since it would prove his innocence. But a guilty man might hide the gun. He might toss it somewhere it might never be found, because the test would prove that his gun was the murder weapon. The prosecutor might be able to get the jury thinking that the missing gun is proof of your guilt."

Peterson looked down at his hands. He swallowed hard a couple of times, then asked, "What if LeGrand was killed with my gun? But what if I wasn't the one who used it to kill him? What then?"

"Who did you give the gun to, Dick?"

Peterson just looked at me, his mouth slightly open, a bubble of saliva hanging precariously in one corner. Then he swallowed hard, closed his eyes, and put his head in his hands. "I'm screwed," he moaned. "I'm totally screwed."

"Maybe not. Let's talk this thing out. Now, who did you give the gun to?"

"I can't tell you, man."

"Okay. Okay," I assured him. "Well, then, what *can* you tell me?"

"Maybe I better not tell you anything."

"How long have you been working with LeGrand?"

"What makes you think that I worked for him at all?" Peterson asked, raising his head defiantly.

"Because I've been following you guys. That's what I do, remember?"

"Oh," he said. Then he nodded and stared at his shoes awhile. "Just a couple of weeks. I've only been working for him a couple of weeks."

"Why?"

"Why have I been working with him? For the money, man. Why else?"

"Things been tough since your wife died?"

"Shit." Peterson sighed. "Goddamned insurance policy we had on her didn't even pay for the funeral. She'd always made more money than me. She did word processing, general clerical work. Worked temp jobs mostly so we could all travel together to the different festivals. She could always find work. Me? I've been scratchin' for a livin' my whole life. Couldn't hold on to a dollar if someone sewed the damn thing to my fingers. Since she died, the kids haven't had decent clothes, decent meals, nothing. Both kids got medical expenses like you wouldn't believe. My kids are running around here on the weekends taking handouts from some of the food vendors. You know how that makes me feel? It's not right. A man's got to take care of his family. Goddamned LeGrand kept bragging about all the money he was making. Kept asking me if I wanted in. He kept on asking. Finally, I just said yes."

I gave him my best forgiving smile. "Yeah, but you're no criminal. Not really. No jury's gonna put you away for trying to do right by your family. LeGrand's dead. Hell, there's not even anyone around that would be able to tie you into the drug dealing. Except Otis, maybe. Did Otis work for LeGrand. too?"

"Otis is a dipshit," Peterson said. "He didn't have anything to do with the actual drug business. LeGrand just kinda used him to keep an eye on the festival organizers. Otis was supposed to tip LeGrand off if they got wise to the drug thing, 'Course when it looked like the shit was gonna hit the fan, LeGrand told Otis that if he didn't help cover his ass, he was gonna feed him to the cops."

"You play, you pay," I said. "Why did it look like the shit was gonna hit the fan?"

"You know, the murders, cops everywhere. LeGrand mouthing off all the time. It just didn't look too good, you know."

"So, what did LeGrand need you for?"

"Oh hell, not much. He's got a bunch of other guys that do the real work for him. I sold a little bit for him. Stashed a little bit in my storage closet over by the Irish Cottage. He really never let me know that much about the organization. He told me he wanted to see if he could trust me before letting me really go to work. I didn't get the impression that he really needed me. Maybe he just wanted Otis and me in because we worked at the festival. Maybe he was playing us for patsies, or something. It sure didn't work out real well for either of us."

"Gilroy have anything to do with the drugs?"

"Jason Gilroy? From the armory?" Peterson asked, as if the thought had never occurred to him. "Not that I know of."

"But Gilroy knew about LeGrand and the drug business?"

"Lots of people knew. We were selling drugs for God's sake. We didn't take out an ad in the paper, but we sure as hell got the word out. Ain't no business without customers."

"You think Gilroy was using?"

"No. I don't think so. Big drinker though. And he loved to hang around with LeGrand. I think he thought it made him look dangerous."

"I heard that LeGrand and Gilroy had a fight. About a week before Gilroy was killed. You know what they were fighting about?"

"No. I don't know anything about that."

"Got any idea who killed Gilroy?"

"No idea at all."

"You sure you didn't see anything?"

"See anything?" Peterson said, screwing his face up with incredulity. "What are you talking about?"

"Well, it's just that the other day when we talked about Gilroy's murder, you were a little iffy on where you and the kids were when he got killed. I thought maybe you were trying to protect them or something."

"No. None of us saw anything," Peterson said.

I detected a strain in his voice, but I let it go.

"Why did you and Otis want me to meet LeGrand at the Irish Cottage?"

"What?"

"Why did you set me up to meet LeGrand?"

"I didn't. That was all LeGrand's idea."

"No, it wasn't."

"It sure was," Peterson insisted.

"No way. LeGrand didn't know I was in that cottage. If he had, I couldn't have surprised him."

"Then it must have been Otis' idea."

"So, it was Otis who hit me from behind?"

"Yeah. Otis hit you."

"No way. Otis ain't got it in him."

Peterson went back to looking at his shoes. Finally, he grunted and said, "I guess that is stretching it a bit. No, Otis didn't hit you. It was…"

Peterson stopped in mid-sentence. He leveled a stare at me, but I wasn't sure he could see past the fogginess in his eyes. Slowly, at first almost imperceptibly, he began to shake his head. "I'm screwed," he said quietly.

"I'm totally screwed."

"The person that hit me," I said, "you pulled a gun on him. You pulled a gun on both him and LeGrand. You kept them from beating me to death. Who was it?"

Peterson kept shaking his head, staring, unseeing.

"Who else was in that cottage with us?"

Peterson let his head drop.

"What happened to the gun?" I said. "You said that your gun killed LeGrand. Who'd you give the gun to?"

Peterson looked back up at me. At first his expression was as blank as an eggshell, but then his brow furrowed and the uncertainty that had clouded his eyes marshaled into focus, then crystallized into stern resolve. Dick Peterson was done talking to me.

He got up, picked up the scythe and tossed it into the bed of the pickup. Then he got in and drove back into the festival grounds.

Chapter Twenty

I returned to my car and, although it grumbled, I managed to get it started. I drove toward the county road that linked the festival with the real world. About one hundred yards back from the county road was a driveway that led behind some trees to a small, flat-roofed building that a sign indicated belonged to the railroad. I parked the car beneath the sign and waited for nearly an hour before Peterson drove by in his pickup. He turned toward downtown Little Crow. I gave him a head start before I followed.

I had to hang way back since there wasn't much traffic out there in the middle of the week and I didn't want Peterson to spot me. I narrowed the distance between us a bit as we turned onto the highway and neared Little Crow. I had no trouble keeping Peterson in view as he pulled into a restaurant just off the highway. The sign read, "Little Crow Grill."

I drove past the restaurant and into the parking lot of an appliance store in the middle of the next block. I gave Peterson plenty of time to get inside the restaurant before driving over to it and choosing a parking spot that afforded me an unobscured view of Peterson's car. When I figured that I had given Peterson enough time to sit down and order, but not so much time that he would be ready to leave, I climbed out of my car and walked toward the restaurant.

The restaurant had an outdoor seating area in front. Petersen was sitting at a table with a woman who had her back to me. He had his head on a swivel, glancing around nervously as though either waiting for someone else to join them or afraid that someone would. I turned abruptly and hightailed it around to the back of the restaurant.

There was a rear entrance, and I pulled the door open and walked down a short hallway where the bathrooms were hidden out of view of the main dining area. When I reached the end of the hallway, I peeked into the dining room. Through the front windows I could see Peterson's table outside. Unfortunately, I still couldn't see the face of the woman he was sitting with.

I took a seat in a booth in the main dining room, ordered coffee, and stared out at Peterson and the back of the head of his woman companion. I waited, sipping coffee until finally a waiter brought Peterson his check. He stood, took out his wallet, and placed several bills on the table. The woman also stood and took his hand as they stepped out into the front parking lot. I had a good view of them as they stopped for a moment before going to their cars.

Julia Hess lit a cigarette. Peterson spread his arms and Julia walked into them, embraced him, and kissed his cheek. I thought I could make out tearstains on her cheeks. They separated and Julia tossed the cigarette to the ground before getting into her car.

I followed them, watching as Peterson's truck turned toward the festival site and Julia drove away in the other direction. I reached down and picked up Julia's discarded cigarette. A Pall Mall. The same brand that her husband, Don, smoked. The same brand I found snuffed out at the spot where I figured Jason Gilroy's murderer stood as he took the fatal shot. *He*? I don't know why I assumed Gilroy's killer was a man. Just chauvinistic, I guess.

My car started without protest, and it wasn't until I pulled up in front of the Bijou that I realized just how hungry I was. I'd skipped breakfast, it was well past lunchtime, and I knew that the cupboard was bare at home. Since McCauley's was only a couple of blocks away, my first thought was to just walk over there, but then I thought about Stephen. Things hadn't been quite right with us ever since Gilroy's murder. Although I hadn't had much time to think about it—what with getting beat up so much and falling for Naomi and everything—I knew this was something that I'd have to tend to soon. Maybe Stephen would like to join me for a little dinner, I thought.

Inside, I knocked briefly before entering Edgerton's room. He was still typing away on into his computer. "Putting the finishing touches on that cemetery of yours?" I asked.

"No," he said without turning around. "I'm just trying to get the perspective right on this image I'm working on. I want the reflection of the Stonehenge monument to be distorted just the right amount by the curvature of the outer hull of the alien craft."

"Say what?"

"I'll show you when I'm done," he said with a sigh.

"What about the virtual cemetery?"

"Oh," he said, waving his hand dismissively. "I gave up on that idea. There are already some web sites out there that are doing pretty much the same thing."

"Surely not with the same panache that you would bring to the fore."

Edgerton just grunted, but he stopped typing.

"You want to grab something to eat?" I asked as he shut down the computer.

"Yeah, I guess."

"Well, shit, Stephen, try to contain your enthusiasm."

"Well, it *is* just dinner."

"You got me there."

We were about to leave when I noticed a stack of photographs on a small table near the door. On top was a picture of Don Hess in full renaissance garb.

"Where'd ya get the pictures?" I asked.

"Julia took them. I asked her for copies."

I picked up the stack and found a photograph of Julia. "She didn't take this one," I said, showing it to Edgerton.

"Don must have snapped that one. Pretty nice picture."

"She is beautiful."

"Yeah."

I set the photo of Julia aside as I looked through the others. I smiled when I found one of Edgerton in full armor, his sword raised, glowering at the camera. In the background stood Dick Peterson. I set that one on top of the picture of Julia. "Do you think I could borrow these?"

"Why?"

"Just for a day or two."

Edgerton looked at me closely. "I suppose. But you should look through the rest of those pictures. There's one of you in there."

I slipped the two pictures I wanted into my pocket and leafed through the rest quickly, stopping when I found the picture of me. It had been taken just before the ill-fated joust. In it I was trying on armor, desperately attempting to get the breastplate to fasten properly around my ample girth. My face was red and puffy with exertion and a roll of fat protruded indelicately under the belt I was using to cinch the thing around me. It was not what I would call a flattering pose. "I'll be needing this one, too."

Edgerton snapped the picture out of my hand. "Not on your life, pal," he said, smiling. "That baby stays with me. I'm thinking of having a poster made of it."

"Really, Stephen, let me have that one."

He ignored me. "Better yet. I could sell the thing to an ad agency that handles one of those diet plans. How about—*is your weight getting in the way of your success on the battlefield? Try a luscious shake in the morning, another in the afternoon, and sensible victuals at eventide. Your horse will thank you for it.*"

"Really, Stephen. Let me have the picture."

The smile faded from his face. "No. It's mine. You can't have it."

"Come on, Stephen. It's embarrassing. Just let me have it."

"No way."

"Why not?"

"Because I said no."

I looked at him closely for a moment before turning for the door. "That's great, pal. Thanks a heap."

"What about dinner?"

"Eat this," I said, as I walked down the hall, shaking my booty behind me.

Chapter Twenty-one

I spent Thursday morning in my office, drinking coffee and trying to explain to a couple of clients why I didn't seem to be spending any time on their cases. The fact that I had been hospitalized just days before didn't seem to hold much sway with them. I knew that if I didn't get back to working paying jobs, I was going to be in real trouble come the first of the month, so I spread the files of my open cases on the desk and got up to make another pot of coffee. I stared at them for a while, but after I'd consumed roughly half of the new pot, I gathered up the files, put them back in the file cabinet, then drove down to Little Crow.

At the Little Crow Grill, I showed the pictures of Julia Hess and Dick Peterson to every employee who would look at them. Two of the waitresses recognized Julia, but neither could tell me if she'd been in the restaurant on the nights that Gilroy, Eckels, and LeGrand were killed. All they remembered was that she'd been there more than once, and both remembered her only coming in alone. When I mentioned that she had been in there the previous day with the other man pictured, they both made clicky noises with their tongues and looked at me like I was simply wasting their time, asking questions to which I obviously already knew the answers.

Officer Thompson was leaning against my car when I got back out to the parking lot. "You got some kind of death wish, fella?" he asked as I approached him. "I mean, I'm just stopping by, and I see you here, in my town, big as life. You're just asking for it."

"Since when did this become your town, Officer?" I asked, hoping he wouldn't notice the slight tremor in my voice. "Did that boss of yours finally just burst while pumping himself up on the weight machine? That would be a damn shame. I never got a chance to ask him if it was true that steroid use shrinks your testicles."

"Save your funny stuff for later, fella. You're gonna need it. Right now, you can just get into my patrol car." Thompson pointed at his car, which he'd parked in back of mine, blocking me in. Then he rubbed his goatee and smiled.

It was a rigid smile that strained his face and narrowed his eyes to slits where no mirth could dance, where no emotion is betrayed. The back of my head throbbed, my bruised ribs ached deeply, and the battered side of my face felt numb and heavy. I made up my mind that there was no way I'd be getting into his car.

I glanced around and was dismayed to find that there was no one else in the parking lot with us. I turned back to face Thompson. The fear he probably saw in my eyes made his smile broaden. I knew I had to do something. "Get the hell off my car, asshole!" I shouted.

His face flushed indignantly, but his smile only flickered slightly. "What did you say?"

"You heard me, shithead. Get the hell off my car!"

Thompson put a hand on my shoulder. "That's it, fella. You're coming with me."

I shrugged the hand off. "No, I'm not. Now, out of my way. I've got places to go."

"This is beautiful," he cooed. "I can't believe my

luck. You're actually resisting arrest."

"I'm not resisting arrest, you moron. In order for me to be resisting arrest, you'd have to be arresting me. And in order for you to be arresting me, I'd have had to do something illegal. And since I haven't, you're going to move along. I'm sure you've got something better to do. I mean, isn't there some brownie troop that you need to harass?"

Thompson unsnapped the holster on his belt and rested his hand on the butt of his service revolver. "Get in the car!"

Just then, I heard the door to the restaurant open behind me, and a young couple stepped into the parking lot. The instant I spotted them, I dropped to my knees before Thompson. "Please, Officer!" I screamed piteously. "Please! Don't beat me again!"

The smile dropped off Thompson's face. He rocked back on his heels as his eyes darted to the couple who had come out of the restaurant. Then he looked back down at me. "Just come along quietly," he whispered, reaching out a hand to me.

Still on my knees, I wheeled around to face the couple who had stopped and were staring, stony-faced, at us. "Dear God! Dear God!" I shrieked. "He's not going to arrest me. He's going to kill me! Please don't let him kill me!"

The young man reached into his pocket, pulled out a cell phone, and started recording.

"Please!" I pleaded. "I've done nothing wrong. Please help me. He'll kill me this time. He told me so. Look at me! He's beaten me before! Don't let him kill me! Please!"

The young woman stepped back to the restaurant

door, opened it and hollered inside, "Hey! We need some help out here!"

It took a few seconds, but soon several people emerged from the restaurant. By that time, I had covered my face with my arms and had curled up into a ball on the asphalt, moaning and praying.

I heard Thompson trying to explain to the crowd. "I didn't touch him. I didn't lay a hand on him, I promise."

I sobbed even louder.

"I don't even want to take him in," Thompson insisted. "He's uh…he's uh…he's sick. I just wanted to make sure he's okay. I uh…I uh…Maybe I just better let him be. Until he calms down. You know."

I peeked my head out from under my arms and surveyed the crowd. "Please don't let him hurt me anymore," I implored. "Please help me."

An older woman with thin reddish-gray hair stepped toward me. She reached down and placed a bony hand on my shoulder. "We won't let him hurt you," she said. A couple of people in the crowd nodded their heads.

"What's your name, Officer?" a male voice from the crowd asked.

Immediately a chorus of voices joined in. "Yeah. What is your name? Why are you picking on this man?"

I glanced up at Thompson. He was shaken. He kept looking at the crowd, then at me, then at the relative sanctuary of his patrol car. "Shit!" he exclaimed at last. Then he walked over to his car, got in, and drove away.

I let the older woman mother over me for a couple of minutes. Then I thanked her and nodded somewhat vacantly to the crowd. After I had assured them all that I was all right, they let me drive away.

After I had driven out of sight, I tried to laugh, but

could only force up a strained cackle. I tried to congratulate myself on how clever I was, on how I had managed to outmaneuver Thompson, but felt utterly phony. I turned on the radio and tried to tap on the steering wheel in time with the music, but I kept messing up. My heart was pounding much faster than the beat of the tune that was playing.

When I finally reached the Bijou, I parked my car, but didn't much feel like facing myself, alone in my room. Instead, I decided to walk over to McCauley's.

The sun was high and warm and by the time I'd reached the pub it seemed to have baked some of the tension from me, leaving me feeling slightly sedated. Inside, I took a seat at the bar. Skip nodded at me, poured me a cold one, and dropped a menu in front of me. "Christ, Dahms," he said, "you look like hell."

"I've been hearing that a lot lately."

"Long as you know," Skip said without even a hint of a smile.

A chorus of unrestrained laughter erupted from off to my right and I looked painfully across the bar at Skip. He offered a half smile and nodded toward two young and very pretty ladies who were sitting at the corner of the bar. They were giggling loudly over a pitcher of beer, then leaned their heads together and stage-whispered behind cupped hands. Then they glanced with bright, even salacious eyes at Skip. When he returned their glance, they collapsed anew into paroxysms of laughter.

"You got plans for tonight?" I asked Skip.

"Not yet," he said, looking over at his admirers and setting off another hyena squeal. "But it looks like something might turn up."

I ordered a steak sandwich with fried onions and a

side of breaded mushrooms before heading for a booth along the wall. I chose one where the bulb had burned out in the hanging lamp above the table. It was dim and inviting. When I finished my first beer, Skip wordlessly came by with another. I barely looked up. Shrill peals of laughter sounded from ladies at the bar cutting through the darkness like the flash of a scalpel.

Skip came by with my order and along with it, he dropped most of that day's newspaper on the table in front of me. I roused myself and spread out the Variety section of the paper as I ate the sandwich. I read a review of a new barbecue place that had just opened up in Frogtown and the few comics that I still followed, then turned to the Metro section as I tucked into the deep-fried mushrooms. I was nearly finished eating when I spotted an article headlined, *Little Crow Chief under Attack.*

According to the article, an investigation had been launched by the State Attorney General's office, looking into reports that, on numerous occasions, members of the Little Crow Police Department, including Chief Robert M. Dunstable himself, had willfully violated the civil rights of suspects either arrested or questioned by them. It went on to say that in addition to the allegation of civil rights violations, the investigation would also target persistent rumors that members of the Little Crow Police Department had allowed certain criminal elements to thrive under their protection. It was charged that officers were taking payoffs from drug dealers in return for safeguards against arrest and prosecution. Chief Dunstable had declined to comment on these allegations. The Attorney General, however, had commented plenty. He told reporters that he would not rest until the truth was dragged from the shadows and subjected to the bright spotlight of public scrutiny. He was quoted as saying that "the people of Little Crow deserve to know that the faith that they bestow on those entrusted to protect and to serve is not being trampled on by the hobnailed boots of self-interest."

Pretty flowery stuff, but there was an election slated for November and the Attorney General had his eye on the Governor's office. Heading up a juicy investigation wasn't gonna hurt his chances any. And along with possibly raising the would-be Governor's numbers in the opinion polls, it occurred to me that this investigation was likely responsible for something else. It was probably the reason Thompson had backed away from me when the crowd gathered. He didn't want to get caught placing one of those *boots of self-interest* across my throat.

I folded the paper and laid it opposite me on the table. I couldn't help but admire Pendergast—I figured this was his work. He must have put out some feelers, and when he had something that looked bad enough, he likely called the media, his good friend the Attorney General, or both. Very slick. Maybe the neatest thing about it was that it didn't matter if they could actually prove any of it. It was now in the hands of the politicians and the press. And in their impartial, we-just-report-the-facts way, they had already found the Little Crow cops guilty. No way they'd come out of this smelling good.

I thought about the allegations that the Little Crow cops were protecting drug dealers. Even in a town the size of Little Crow you couldn't spit without hitting somebody who could score you a little weed, some coke, some meth, or something even more deadly. With that many people dealing drugs, even if the cops had an arrangement with some of them, it didn't necessarily follow that they were protecting LeGrand. But it was a damn good bet. I wondered if Dunstable himself was involved. Another good bet, I thought.

My impression was that the Little Crow Police Department was a very "top down" organization. If the cops out there were taking payoffs, my guess was that Dunstable not only knew about it, but controlled it, and got the biggest cut. So, if any of this were true, LeGrand and Dunstable likely had a financial relationship. It would also mean that Dunstable knew damn well that I wasn't part of LeGrand's operation. It would mean the Chief floated the idea to see if he could use me to keep the press from finding out about him. He could arrest me and parade me in front of the cameras where I could play the role of the main bad guy. Especially if he or Thompson could persuade me to sign a statement that put them in the clear.

But none of that made any sense. If Dunstable was working with LeGrand, then he'd know about Otis and Peterson. If he was going to arrest someone, why not arrest one of them? Maybe he was trying to protect them too. Maybe when casting about for a patsy, he figured I was the biggest sucker in the net.

I stopped thinking about it. Maybe the press and the politicians didn't have to prove anything, but I figured if I was going to be able to stay clear of this thing, I'd need to prove that I wasn't involved. And that meant I'd have to be able to prove who was. I could've gone on all night concocting theories about Dunstable and Thompson, not to mention whatever was going on with Dick Peterson and Julia Hess, but it wouldn't have done any good. Theories aren't the same as proof. Instead, I resolved to do something that I knew would do some good. I resolved to have a couple more beers. I got Skip's attention and gestured to him to bring me another cold one.

"How's Stephen?" Skip asked when he brought the beer over.

I shrugged. "I don't know. I haven't seen him today."

"He stopped in here earlier. Didn't seem real talkative. I got the impression that something is bothering him."

"I got the same impression yesterday," I said. "To tell the truth, he's been a real prick lately."

"Understandable," Skip said.

"You think so?

"Don't you?"

I sipped at my beer. "Hell, no."

Skip stared at me.

I set down my beer. "You figure Edgerton's still bothered by his friend at the armory getting whacked?" I asked.

Skip nodded. "No reason to think otherwise. And I think maybe Stephen's been a little hard on you lately because he's having a whole lot of trouble dealing with recent events. I'm guessing that seeing his friend get killed like that got him all stirred up inside. He might be dealing with it by lashing out at the people he cares most about. Maybe you've been bearing the brunt of all of this because he cares most about you."

I grunted and picked up my beer.

Skip turned and went back behind the bar. Only one of the ladies that had been sitting there remained. She had an empty glass in her hand, and she leaned forward to say something to Skip.

He held her gaze for a moment, shook his head, took the glass from her, then brought her some coffee. She accepted the cup from him with a sad smile. A sad and vulnerable smile.

Chapter Twenty-two

Things did not start off well the next morning. First thing out of the rack, I discovered I was out of coffee. Since a morning without caffeine is simply out of the question, I reluctantly resigned myself to a drive to the grocery store to replenish my supply. I dressed quickly and padded out to my car, but predictably, when I turned the key in the ignition, the car greeted me with a mournful groan, refusing to spark to life. I tried a few more times, listening as the engine turned more slowly each time, until finally there was no sound at all.

I really can't do my job without my car, but I can't do *anything* without coffee, so before doing anything else, I hiked to a coffee shop a few blocks away and forked over all of my available cash for a tiny bag of dark-roast Guatemalan.

I returned to the Bijou and after re-caffeinating myself, I felt able to face the car problem. I called a nearby service station that had a mechanic who had worked on the vehicle before. I arranged for them to come by and tow it to their garage. I then read them my credit card number, mentally picturing my card balance ballooning like a spooked blowfish. I left the key in the glove box and walked over to my office.

There, I checked my answering machine and found that Pendergast's office had called both the afternoon before and again that morning. I made a note to call him later then spent about an hour on the internet tracking down a deadbeat dad for a lawyer that threw work my way occasionally. After phoning the lawyer, I called the service station. The mechanic came on and told me that some part—I believe he said it had something to do with the engine—was broken and would have to be replaced. Oh, and it was going to be really expensive. That was the good news.

The bad news was that he didn't have the part and couldn't get it until Monday. When I asked if he had a loaner car available for me, he laughed so hard I could hear stuff blowing out his nose. I told him to do whatever was necessary and that I would make do until Monday.

Then I called the copy shop where Edgerton worked and asked him how he was getting out to the festival that evening. He told me that Donald and Julia were going to swing by and pick him up. When I asked him if he thought they would mind my hitching a ride with them, Edgerton paused, sighed deeply, and cleared his throat several times as if he were trying to dislodge something furry that was stuck in there. Finally, he said he supposed it would be all right, but he would have to check with the Hesses first. I asked him to let me know if there was a problem, and then I called Naomi.

The phone rang several times before she picked up. "Hello," she mumbled sleepily.

"Did I wake you?"

"I worked late last night," she said. "Got to work early tomorrow. I'm still in bed." She groaned quietly. "Still in bed," she repeated. "Naked."

"Hmm," I hummed. "Paint me a picture."

"Picture's good. Real thing's better."

"Will I get to see the real thing this evening?"

"That depends," she said. "How are you feeling?"

"Fit as a fiddle and ready for love."

"You going out to the festival site tonight?"

"If you are. I go where my love awaits me."

Naomi didn't respond right away. Finally, she asked, "Are you sure that you should go to Little Crow this weekend? Have you seen the papers? The cops down there are being investigated. Sounds like they're in hot water for beating you up. Might be wiser to stay away."

"Yeah," I agreed, "but my wisdom is clouded by a fever of desire. Desire to be with you, beloved."

"You're addled, all right," she said. "I guess that's something I'll have to learn to live with."

"Meet me at the armory at seven o'clock. Okay?"

"Hell no." she said. "Why should I have to come chasing after you?"

"If you do, I'll let you catch me."

"Oh, joy. Oh, rapture."

"The armory? At seven o'clock?"

"The Cock and Bull," she said. "At seven thirty."

"The minutes will seem like an eternity twixt now and then."

She chuckled. "Get me a break, Lyle. I got to get some sleep. I'll see you tonight."

"I really am looking forward to seeing you," I added.

"Me too. Now, go."

I hung up and quit work for the afternoon. As hokey as it sounds, I really didn't want to do anything but count the minutes until I was with her.

Chapter Twenty-three

The ride down to the Little Crow with Edgerton and
Donald and Julia Hess was a bit strained. Initially, all
three tried to joke around and get excited about the last
weekend of the festival, but it didn't really work. Then
Don talked about how much more money they had made
that year compared to the last, and Julia commented on
how beautiful the trees were as the crispness of fall
approached and they slipped on their multi-colored
raiment.

Edgerton whined that the coming of fall probably
meant that they would freeze their butts off that night,
sleeping in the unheated armory, but he did allow that
fall was his favorite time of year. It all *seemed* normal,
but there were a lot of dead spots in the conversation. I
got the impression they were really just repeating things
they had said to each other in the past. By the time we
reached the festival site, all had fallen silent, except for
Don who hummed softly to himself as he drove.

Once inside the gate, I glanced at my watch and
noted that I had nearly an hour before I was to meet
Naomi at the pub. I considered staying at the armory but
didn't think that the conversation would get more
stimulating any time soon, so I opted to go for a walk
instead. Some part of my mind must have been fixated
on Naomi, because even though I had set off planning to
meander about the grounds, I actually headed straight

over to the Cock and Bull.

There were only a few people there and, unfortunately, none of them was Naomi. I was able to somewhat assuage my disappointment by staring at a pretty young thing sitting at the bar. Her long, fair hair was caught up at the back of her head by a clip, but blonde tendrils fell delicately about her face. Despite a nip to the air, she wore a white, sleeveless blouse and a pair of denim shorts.

I spent several pleasant minutes watching her cross and uncross her long legs, and I was particularly happy every time she arched her back and her pert boobs turned up expectantly—like the face of a first date waiting for a goodnight kiss. After a few minutes she rose and made her exit. I was watching her walk away when something tickled my ear.

"See something you like?" a voice whispered to me from behind.

I turned to find Naomi grinning mysteriously at me.

"Oh good!" I exclaimed, rubbing my hands together. "Jealousy. That means you really do care."

"It just means that I might have to find other plans for this evening. That's all."

"And tell me, dear lady, just what exactly were your plans for this evening?"

"That, sir, is no longer your concern, now that your fickle attentions have turned elsewhere."

"I only have eyes for you, fair lady."

Naomi let out a clipped chuckle. "That, sir, is transparently false."

I shrugged and smiled. "Okay, you caught me. Want to get something to eat?"

Naomi crinkled up her eyes at me and started to say

something. But instead, she kissed me gently and laid her head against my shoulder. "Not around here. We could go to town."

"You drive," I said.

Naomi and I drove toward Little Crow for dinner at place a couple of miles outside of town called the Sagebrush Saloon and Grill. The burgers were pretty good and they had Leinenkugel Red on tap, but they also had some guy dressed up like Wyatt Earp walking around doing card tricks and making balloon animals. I didn't think I'd be back.

I really didn't feel much like sleeping on the ground that night, so after dinner, instead of returning to the festival, I suggested to Naomi that we seek more comfortable accommodations in Little Crow. Naomi said that there were at least two motels in town, and I took it as a good sign that she barely protested the leer that I gave her.

She drove, her high beams cutting a wide swath through the comforting darkness of the nearly deserted highway. We were almost to town when the interior of the car lit up suddenly. A vehicle was coming up on us fast from the rear. I wheeled around to see the swirling lights of a Little Crow patrol car right behind us. I gripped the armrest beside me tightly, closed my eyes, and said a silent prayer that the car would pass. When I opened my eyes, the taillights of the patrol car were already some three car-lengths ahead and speeding away.

Naomi gave me a moment before saying, "I don't think that one was for you."

"Sorry," I said, unable to hold back a sigh. "I guess I'm a little more worried than I'd like to admit about the cops down here."

"You've got every reason to be worried. This place hasn't exactly been healthy for you. I still don't see why you came down here this weekend."

"Aside from the opportunity to see you."

"Okay, aside from that."

I shrugged. "It's the last weekend of the festival. If anything more is going to happen, it's going to happen this weekend."

"And you need to be here?"

"Yeah."

"You got any idea what might happen?"

"I admit I'm a little hazy about the whole thing."

"Hazy is good," Naomi said. "Better than being completely in the dark anyway."

"I don't know," I muttered. "Things might get dark again."

I turned to face her as she drove. "I mean, I can't get a handle on how everything fits together. Jason Gilroy is killed. He doesn't seem to have any real enemies. He was just an inoffensive little guy who tried to look cool by hanging out with the drug-dealing Dirk LeGrand. Then Gregory Eckels gets separated from his head. Now this guy is truly well liked—a real straight arrow. As near as I can tell, Eckels was perfect for the role of Lancelot. He really was handsome, strong, brave, and completely virtuous. Except, like the storybook Lancelot, he betrayed himself by becoming the lover of a married woman. I guess that means his only real enemy was Don Hess. But I really don't think Hess killed Eckels. And I know Don didn't kill Gilroy. Then we got the real villain of the piece, our pal LeGrand. Just when I nearly got LeGrand fingered as the killer, he ends up dead himself. Then I find out that Dick Peterson and Otis McInerny were helping LeGrand deal drugs."

"I didn't know that," Naomi said. "Are you sure?"

"As sure as I am about anything. Anyway, I know that Otis doesn't have the *huevos* to kill anybody and I just don't see Peterson as a killer. Besides, why would he kill Gilroy or Eckels? And what has he got to do with Julia Hess?"

"I don't know, what *has* he got to do with Julia Hess?"

"Beats me. But Peterson and Julia got together to discuss something the other day and when I talked to Peterson, I got the impression that he's trying to protect someone. Probably her."

"Maybe he's trying to protect himself as well. Maybe they were in on it together."

I rubbed my hand roughly across my forehead. "But in on what? Okay, say that Peterson killed LeGrand because of something having to do with the drug business. Happens all the time. Why would he kill Eckels? Because Eckels threatened to expose him? Maybe. But why kill Gilroy? And how does Julia fit in? And what about the cops? They're involved in this thing somehow."

"According to the paper, the cops have been protecting drug dealers. Maybe they killed Eckels when he tried to turn in LeGrand and Peterson."

"Only we have no evidence that Eckels wanted to turn in anybody. It's pure speculation. We don't know anything for sure."

"Well, you're a professional. How do you usually solve murders?"

I laughed. "I have a great system for that. I let the cops solve them and when I read about 'em in the paper,

I claim that I knew the answer all along."

"Maybe you can do the same thing this time," Naomi said.

"I hope so, sweetie. I really do."

Chapter Twenty-four

Concerned as I am about the "franchisification" of America, of the two motels we had to choose from in Little Crow, instead of the Motel 6, I insisted on a place called Hidden Oaks. The "independently owned and operated" Hidden Oaks was aptly named. Situated along a stretch of highway that cut through a tract of flat, treeless, former farmland, if there were any oaks in the vicinity, they were hidden but good. But no one questioned our lack of baggage or the fact that I had checked us in under the names Detective and Mrs. Steve McGarrett, so I was happy. Book 'em, Danno.

Naomi and I got up early the next morning, made love again, and checked out with enough time to grab a couple of breakfast sandwiches before she had to be back at the festival. After extracting a promise from her to let me pick her up for lunch, I walked her to the Cock and Bull, gave her a quick peck on the lips, and watched her turn to go into the tavern. She took one step before turning back toward me. "Take care, Lyle," she said, trying awfully hard to make it sound nonchalant.

I smiled and shrugged. "What could happen?"

Naomi returned the smile, but a tendril of doubt wriggled in her eyes. Alone, I proceeded toward the armory.

There was still an hour before the festival opened, but the buildings and the stalls were all aflutter with activity as the festival's tradespeople made ready for their customers. As I neared the armory, on the low hill beyond the Irish Cottage, I spotted Clan Highland's tent slowly rising. A large black crow circled over the field but skittered away at the sound of a loud and very moist-sounding sneeze. I turned to the direction of the sneeze and saw Dick Peterson's elephant tied to a stake near the elephant track. I didn't see Peterson.

When I reached the armory, I found Edgerton sitting by the remains of the previous evening's fire. He glanced at me as I approached but didn't say anything in greeting. "You upset with me for some reason," I asked.

He shook his head. "No. But I guess this whole thing is still getting to me. You know, Jason's death, the others, your involvement. The whole thing. I need something to take my mind off it."

"The festival closes tomorrow. That might help."

"Yeah. But other things go on. For instance, I'm still stuck with you."

"I thought you said that you weren't pissed at me?"

"I'm not. Can't you take a joke?"

I grunted. I was pretty sure that he wasn't entirely joking.

I watched Don Hess climb up to the balcony to ready the cannon charge while Julia arranged weapons on the display counter next to the cash box. Then she turned her attention to the weapons on the wall. She was making a kind of bouquet out of arrows and was fixing it to the wall next to a crossbow that hung there. A cold, creepy feeling ran up my spine.

"Stephen," I called. "How many crossbows have you guys made?"

"Several. They're a bit complicated and woodwork

is not our specialty, but we've managed to turn out a few."

"Good," I said.

"Why?"

"It's nothing really. It's just when I saw that on the wall, I—"

"What on what wall?"

"That over there," I told him, pointing to the crossbow.

"Shit!" Edgerton exclaimed. "Don! Don! Get down here!"

Hess came bounding down the staircase from the balcony.

"Look there!" Edgerton shouted, pointing.

Julia was still standing near the wall and the crossbow that had so attracted Edgerton's attention.

"Now, how did that get there?" Hess asked, betraying no emotion whatsoever.

Julia looked at both men, concerned and puzzled at the same time. "What is it?" she asked. "What's wrong, Stephen?"

"You didn't bring another crossbow out here, did you, Don?"

"No. No, I didn't."

Julia drew back suddenly from the wall as the entire meaning of what the two men were discussing struck her. "You think that's the bow that killed Jason?" she asked.

"Got to be," Hess said.

Julia moved slowly toward him and stepped into his embrace.

"None of you put that there?" I asked.

Hess looked first at Edgerton, then at Julia. "No."

"And you were all here last night?"

Hess nodded.

"When did you turn in?"

"We all went up about the same time. I guess it was maybe eleven thirty."

"And nobody heard or saw anything suspicious? You've got no idea how that thing got there?"

"No."

"I guess we better call the cops," I suggested, not exactly thrilled at the prospect of again dealing with Little Crow's finest.

"Not a good idea," Hess said.

"Why not?"

Hess let go of his wife and turned to face me. "I think they're the ones that planted it."

"What makes you think so?"

"You've seen what they're like. First, they arrested me for murder and then they tried to pin it on you. Now they're in a bunch of trouble with the media over civil rights and drugs and all that. It'd look pretty good for them to solve the Ren Fest Murders while they still have their jobs. You and I both know that they don't care who the real murderer is. They only care about arresting somebody and bragging about it on the TV news."

"So, you figure they planted the murder weapon here so they could show up later and arrest one of us for Gilroy's murder?"

"For Gilroy's murder, probably for Eckels and LeGrand too. That's the only way it makes sense."

I studied Hess' face. He looked earnest enough, but nothing in his manner suggested that he was either afraid or even particularly concerned about the imminent arrival of the cops. He could just as well have been discussing a new pair of shoes as the instrument of his friend's death. "What do you guys think?" he asked Julia and Edgerton.

"You may be right," Julia ventured.

"You've a strong argument," Edgerton agreed, staring narrowly at Hess.

"Okay," I said. "No cops. What do we do with the bow?"

"Well," Hess said, "we can't keep it here. Even if we hid it, the cops could search the place, and if they found it, we would look even guiltier than we would with it just hanging there. I'll sneak off and hide it out there somewhere." He motioned to the field and woods beyond the festival walls.

"Good idea," I told him. "But I'll do it."

"No, really," Hess insisted, "It's my idea. It's my risk. If you should get caught—"

"We all agree," I interrupted. "We all think we should hide the thing. We all share the risk. Besides, the festival is about to open. You're going to have to fire your cannon like you do every other morning. If you're not here, you might be missed. We don't want to arouse any more suspicion than necessary. You can see that I'm right. Right?"

Hess took a couple of steps toward the bow. "I really can't let you take responsibility for this, Lyle. I'm the one who should hide it."

"I don't agree," I told him, taking a couple of steps of my own toward the bow.

"But I insist," he said.

"No. I insist."

With that we both raced toward the bow. Hess was the first to get his hands on it, but I wrenched it from his grasp. As Hess was about to try to take it back from me,

Edgerton cried out, "For God sakes, knock it off you two! You're acting like children. If it will get you two to stop fighting, I'll hide the damn thing."

Hess took a step away from me.

"You don't have to do that, Stephen," I said. "I'm the logical one to hide it. That's okay, isn't it, Don?"

Hess gave me a half smile. "Yeah. That's okay."

I returned his smile. "You guys got a bag or something that I can use to cover this thing with? I'm gonna look a little conspicuous lugging this crossbow around."

"I'll get you something, Lyle," Julia said.

As we waited for Julia to return, Hess, Edgerton, and I shuffled about the armory, eyeing each other. Julia soon emerged with a giant plastic bag from a Target store.

"This is all I could find, Lyle," she said.

I held it in front of me. "It's just perfect," I told her, tracing a finger along the large target emblazoned on the bag. Edgerton snorted as I headed out the back door.

I walked as nonchalantly as I could across the strip of parking lot outside the armory wall and into the grass beyond. I quickened my steps as I reached the edge of a clump of woods only about fifty yards away. Since I didn't really want to go off walking down the road with it, looking for a better place, the woods were really the only place close to hide the thing. It would have to be good enough, I thought.

The truth was, I hadn't really wanted to hide the crossbow in the first place. I just didn't want Hess to hide it. The reasons that he gave for wanting to ditch the weapon were lousy. If the cops were going to plant the murder weapon on us, they damn sure wouldn't give us the opportunity to find it and get rid of it before arresting us. And they sure wouldn't plant the thing in plain sight. Besides, Hess was a bit too insistent that he be the one to do the hiding. Hess wanted to hide something, all right. But it was more than the bow. At least now, I thought, as I set the bag next to a large rock and began to pile vegetation over it, I was the one who knew where the murder weapon was. Now all I needed to figure out was who put it in the armory and who used it on Gilroy in the first place.

I was nearly back to the armory when the twin cannon shots signaled the opening of the festival. When I arrived, Edgerton and the Hesses were making ready for the customers who were already streaming in the front gates. Hess gave me a questioning look and I gave him a thumbs up sign. He nodded, then turned and his face broke into a broad grin as the first customers reached the armory. The first guy to reach him pointed up at a sword hanging on the wall and asked, "How much does that thing weigh?"

Watching Edgerton and the Hesses work the crowd, I was struck by the enormity of the fact that although there was a killer on the loose, I'd just hidden a murder weapon, and every fiber of my being thrummed with a need for action, there was simply nothing for me to do but wait and see what would happen next. It was maybe a half-hour before I couldn't take it any longer and I decided to wander over to the Clan Highland tent.

On the way, I was drawn by the sound of a fiddle accompanied by what sounded like chains rattling. Following the sound, I came upon a clearing where one man was fiddling furiously as six other men dressed all in white with green suspenders, some wearing berets, and all with rows of bells strapped to their legs were cavorting to the music, waving hankies over their heads. It was highly choreographed cavorting however, and I watched with great interest and amusement as they capered about, at times leaping in unison impossibly high into the crisp autumn air. After several minutes of what must have been exhausting frolic, the dancers took a break, and I headed over to the Scottish encampment.

I milled around with a large group of kilt-wearing strangers until I spotted Wiseman placing an iron cooking grate over a cold fire pit. "You guys gonna be making some chili?" I hollered by way of a greeting.

"Hey, Dahms," Wiseman answered, coming over to me. "I figured you'd be out here. No. No chili for us today, I'm afraid. No, today we're going make haggis. It's just expected, you know."

"No, I don't know. What's haggis?"

Wiseman smiled. "Oh, my poor ignorant, laddie. Why it's the national dish of Scotland. The dish before which all others pale. Or is it just that those eating the thing pale before it?"

The men around Wiseman chuckled.

"Well, what *is* haggis?"

Wiseman clapped an arm around my shoulders and walked me over to the fire pit. "Haggis is made from sheep's offal," he told me. "You know, the windpipe, heart, lungs, liver, stuff like that. First you boil that all up, then you mince it, mix it with some toasted oatmeal and a few spices. Not too much. You don't want to cover up the taste. Then you stuff all this into a sheep's stomach and boil it for like another three hours."

"Good Christ! What then?"

"Then it's dinner time."

"You're making this up."

"Not at all. You want to join us?"

"I'll pass," I told him. "But I'll tell you what, if you're planning stewed entrails for dinner, then you'll be needing something decent for lunch. Why not eat with Naomi and me? We could meet at the tavern and then head out…wherever."

"Sounds like a plan. What time?"

"Say…one o'clock?"

"One o'clock."

I turned to leave but Wiseman touched my sleeve and moved over close. "You're not gonna get me in any more jams, are you? I mean, since I've met you, I've been threatened by a madman, been assaulted by the police, and arrested on suspicion of murder. I mean, it is just lunch, right?"

"Right," I smiled. "But just in case, bring a haggis with you. You know, in case you need to defend yourself."

Chapter Twenty-five

After departing Clan Highland, I strolled around the festival grounds a while longer, then thought maybe I'd try and find Otis. I hadn't spoken with him since he'd set me up with LeGrand at the Irish Cottage and I had plenty that I wanted to discuss with him. I wandered over to King Henry's castle, but the place was deserted. I figured that the entire kingly retinue was out parading somewhere, so I decided I'd just walk around until I spotted them. Instead, I spotted Edgerton, heading toward me.

"You're not working today?" I asked.

"I'm on break. I figured this is the last time you'll be out here, and I thought maybe we could do something. You busy?"

"Not really. But if you see Otis, let me know. I'd like to speak with him."

Edgerton led me slowly through the festival site, occasionally stopping to examine a piece of leatherwork or pottery in one of the many stalls that lined the circuitous lanes, but he didn't say anything. I followed behind, also silent. In his right hand, Edgerton held a rolled-up sheet of paper, but I didn't ask him what it was.

I wasn't surprised that we didn't do much talking. The strain that had come between us since Gilroy's death had become glaring enough that it was only in silence that we could pretend it wasn't really there.

We came out of one of the lanes and passed the open field where I had earlier seen the men dancing with hankies. Now they were dancing with sticks—staffs really—leaping and clacking them together with practiced precision. "What are they doing?" I asked.

"Morris dancing," Edgerton said. But he didn't elaborate.

We continued on, at last stopping to join a clump of festivalgoers that had gathered around a small, raised platform in a clearing surrounded by various food stands. On the platform, a young man with a long feather in his cap was cajoling the crowd. Next to him was a set of stocks. The stocks consisted of a pair of elevated, parallel boards, hinged on one side, that, when brought together, had a large hole in the center and two smaller holes on either side. The large hole was for clamping around a person's neck and the smaller holes were for hands. A large padlock kept anyone unfortunate enough to be sentenced to the stocks confined between the two boards. Next to the stocks was a rack, and on the rack were hanging small wooden signs, each one emblazoned with the name of one of the seven deadly sins. The young man was laughing as he asked those gathered if they knew someone who might benefit from some time in the stocks.

"Ladies! Ladies!" he shouted. "Surely there is one among you who, from time to time, has had to take measures to keep your man's eye from wandering. Surely, you've seen how your sometime good man's glance has knavishly strayed to gaze upon the bosom of another. Perhaps, in so observing, you have bethought yourself, how can I keep my man's eye affixed to my bosom alone? This is your opportunity, my good ladies!

Time spent in King Henry's stocks will make him think twice before letting his attentions stray from where they should be. Come! Who will propose a candidate for the stocks?"

Those in the crowd giggled nervously and cast glances among themselves. A couple of women poked elbows playfully at the men beside them, but no one stepped forward.

"And gentlemen," the young man declaimed. "Perhaps your good woman has of late neglected her duty to you in either board or in bed. In that case, this is your opportunity to administer a correction. And gentleman, I've oft heard it said that each minute in the stocks will yield several minutes of rousing sport between the sheets—so wanton does the fairer sex become after submitting to such punishment."

A few of the men in the crowd laughed and fixed lascivious grins on the women with them, grins which were returned with stares of cold fury. Still, no one stepped forward. A group of teenagers at the edge of the crowd were poking each other and giggling loudly, and I figured that eventually they would offer up one of their number as a candidate, but before they could settle on who would be volunteered, Edgerton spoke up.

"Milord," he declared. "It seems that the crowd before you is unable to find even one worthy...or should I say *unworthy*...candidate among itself. And yet it defies reason that amongst such a goodly crowd there be not one whose actions warrant some chastening. Alas, I must confess that I, myself, have oft examined my actions and found them wanting."

"Are you, then, offering yourself for public chastisement, sir?" the young man asked.

"With all humility, and knowing that such chastisement is surely warranted, I am not. There is another with us here that I think is more in need of the curative powers of good King Henry's stocks."

"Prithee, good my lord, make this individual known to us."

Edgerton clasped a hand on my shoulder. "It is my large friend here," he declared.

The young man threw his head back in laughter and the crowd followed his example. Edgerton on the other hand didn't even smile. "Bring him forward, good sir," the young man prompted.

I looked hard at Stephen, but he ignored me. I shrugged his hand from my shoulder. He smiled at me wryly, moved in close and whispered, "Sirrah, bring me my fool."

I stepped back, but several in the crowd lightly pushed me toward the platform. Then someone put both hands on my back and pushed hard enough for me to stumble forward. I whirled around, enraged.

I'm not good at much, but I'm good at looking pissed. I found myself face to face with a woman of about fifty who had gotten too wrapped up in the frivolity of the moment. And she was simply not prepared for my reaction. She stared at me as her sloppy grin melted away. Her expression stiffened with shock and fear. Almost immediately, my anger turned to embarrassment. I hung my head and smiled a crooked apology to the poor woman. Then, I allowed myself to be pushed forward.

Once I was atop the platform, the young man opened the stocks and said something to me about being a good sport. I rolled my eyes at him, but meekly placed my hands and head into position. The two pieces of the stocks were brought together around me, and I heard the padlock snap decisively. It wasn't terribly uncomfortable, but I wouldn't want to make a weekend of it. I half-heartedly tried to pull my hands free, but quickly realized that I wasn't going anywhere until they released me. Edgerton had joined us on the platform and said something to the guy in charge. The young man nodded and stepped back.

"It is truly a sad case that you see before you," Edgerton began, addressing the crowd. "It is, indeed, difficult to know where to begin." He walked the length of the rack where the seven deadly sin signs hung, and as he walked, he fingered each sign. He picked one up and showed it to the crowd. I couldn't see which sign he had chosen, but the crowd roared its approval.

"Ah, but perhaps it is unfair to attribute this particular fault to another," Edgerton said, finally showing the sign to me, before hanging it around my neck. "Lust is, I fear, the most oft committed of sins. But in this sad fellow's case the offense is coupled with a charge of disturbing the peace."

A puzzled murmur passed through the crowd.

"For those of you wondering how lust can disturb the peace," Edgerton continued, "I'll only say that this man's neighbors complain that their barnyard animals have oft made rather an abnormal amount of noise in the night, and he has then been seen on the morrow sporting an unmistakable leer."

As the crowd erupted with laughter, Edgerton removed the sign from around my neck and went to pick out another. He paused thoughtfully before each sign and when he finally chose one, the crowd applauded. "Again, I fear that this is a sin that many of us have too oft been guilty of. But, looking at my friend, you can see that if but one fault needs must be exorcised, it is indeed the sin of gluttony."

As Edgerton hung the sign around my neck, I looked up at him and whispered, "Come on. Enough already."

He glanced at me disdainfully and then slowly unrolled the sheet of paper that he had been carrying in his hand. Then he raised his head proudly and began to read in a loud voice, as though we were in court, and he was the bailiff reading the charges. "Gluttony!" he exclaimed. "Hereby defined as excessiveness in eating or drinking. And gazing upon the overstuffed figure of my friend here, you can see that he has long suffered from this malady. The result—corpulence! Obesity! Portliness! Paunchiness! Gentlepeople, he is simply lacking in firmness. He is chunky—big boned, porcine, thickset. In short, good people...my friend is fat."

Edgerton lowered his gaze and shook his head dejectedly. Then raising his eyes to meet the crowd he called in a loud voice, "Yet, let us be mindful of this poor unfortunate's feelings. Is it his fault that nature has afflicted him so? Is the fact that he is rather less well-proportioned than some to make him a laughingstock?"

Someone in the crowd shouted, "Yes!"

Edgerton laughed heartily, but then cast a warning gaze upon the sniggering crowd. "If you fear not engendering hurtfulness in my large companion, then mind his wrath. For if pushed beyond reason, any man's anger may burn so hot that this very stage be in danger of catching afire. And from the ashes he, like the legendary bird, may arise—a great spherical phoenix. And so, I say, jailer, release him with our applause for providing us such wonderful sport."

Stephen rolled up the paper, then, bowing deeply to the crowd, he descended the stairs. I flushed crimson and the spectators applauded wildly. They were still clapping and shouting as the padlock was removed and I rose from the stocks. As I walked down from the platform, someone clapped me on the shoulder and said something about my friend "showing me." I didn't say anything, but I agreed. He'd shown me all right.

I hurried to catch up with him and together we walked away from the crowd. He turned to me and laughed. But it was a hollow, perfunctory laugh.

"We got to talk," I said.

We stopped and stood in the shade of a large maple tree, the edges of its leaves tinged with red and orange as if someone had touched them with a flame. Edgerton tried to look bemused, but there was nothing in his eyes that even resembled joy. There was nothing there but cold, insular pride. I wanted to smash his face.

"I ought to kick your ass for that, Stephen," I said.

"If it makes you feel better."

"What the fuck is wrong with you? What the fuck makes you think you can treat people like that you self-centered son-of-a-bitch?"

"Hey, it got a laugh. That's what matters, isn't it?"

"What's that supposed to mean?"

"Just taking a page from your playbook, pal," he said, a cool blue light flickering in his eyes.

"My playbook?"

Edgerton shrugged. "If things aren't going right, make a joke. That's your way, isn't it? I don't see what you're so pissed about."

My hands tightened into fists at my sides. I almost hit him. I longed to hit him. But there was something about his manner. He seemed to want me to take a swing at him. He was expecting it. I didn't want to give him the satisfaction. "Fuck you, Stephen. Just fuck you." I turned to walk away.

"What's the difference, Lyle?" he asked. "I made a joke. You make jokes. Remember that joke you made when we found Greg Eckels' head. His fucking head, for christsakes. You're standing there looking down at the guy's bloody, severed head and for you it's hoo-ha time."

I turned back to face him.

"And I'm not just talking about Eckels," he continued. "It's everything. It's all the time. No matter what you're doing, you're cracking wise. Every time I try to tell you something, it's a goddamned joke. When the cops are talking to you, it's a goddamned joke. If you get beat up, it's a goddamned joke. If a friend of mine gets killed, it's a goddamned joke. It's just…Ah, it's just boring. It's boring and it's bullshit."

"I never joked about Gilroy's death, Stephen," I said. "That's unfair."

"Who the hell can remember what all you joke about? Who the hell wants to?"

I held my tongue and let silence rush in and fill the gulf between us. The silence was a palpable thing—the only thing, I thought, that linked us in that moment. I was afraid that if I spoke, it too would shatter.

Edgerton stared at me for some seconds, but as the silence became ever weightier, he cast his gaze to the ground. He kicked a little clump of dirt that broke apart, the pieces bouncing lightly across the close-shorn grass. Finally, he said, "I got nothing to apologize for."

"I'm not looking for an apology, Stephen. I'm

looking for an explanation."

It took Edgerton a moment to respond. "Maybe it's just…Ah hell, I don't know. Maybe it's just all this death. I don't know. Things just seem so damned…so damned empty all of sudden."

"I didn't realize that Gilroy meant so much to you. I'm sorry."

"There you go!" Edgerton shouted. "You don't listen. You don't try to understand. I told you before. It's not Jason. It's not him, or Eckels, or LeGrand or any one of them. It's…It's me, I guess. I just feel empty. Like none of it matters. Like none of our lives really matter."

Edgerton again fell silent, shuffling in a slow circle like a man alone on a dance floor moving to remembered music long after the band and the crowd have gone. As he moved, he looked at everything, everything but me. He watched groups of festivalgoers hurrying past and couples simply strolling across the grass together. He watched children playing with cheap souvenir swords and their wary parents watching that they don't put out an eye.

"What's the population of the earth, anyway?" he asked. "Seven billion people? More? And we're supposed to believe that each of those lives is important. That each life is unique enough to leave its mark on the world. Shit. You know how they say that with each person's death we are all diminished. Well, forgive me, but I don't think that anybody really believes that. We all want to believe it. We wish it were true. But really, what we believe is that our own life is unique. Not those other people's lives. Not your life…but mine. I'm the one who will do something extraordinary. I'm gonna leave my mark on all of you. You remember that Twilight Zone episode? The one where the guy becomes convinced that the whole world and everyone in it is just something that he's dreaming? He becomes consumed by guilt, knowing that when he wakes all the lives around him will simply cease, murdered by the act of waking. I open my eyes. I see the world. I reach out and I feel the world. I listen and I hear. But what if I'm not here? What about after I'm gone? Does the world go on? And how do I know? Maybe death is like waking up. Maybe when we die, the world dies too."

"Stephen, I'm pretty sure that the world will go on. Even without you."

"Of course, it will. Maybe that's the whole problem. The importance of our individual lives exists only in us. Outside, we as individuals barely matter at all. The world won't be diminished by my death. No more than it was diminished by Jason's death or Eckels' death, or the death of anyone listed in the obituaries on any day in any newspaper in the world. You know what rocked me about Jason's death? The fact that I wasn't rocked. He was dead. I realized that although I would remember him fondly, day to day I would barely notice him gone. It just wouldn't matter that much to me. And one day I'll be Gilroy and I'll be gone and that won't make a difference either. That shit just empties me out."

I paused a moment before making comment. When I did, I felt the corner of my mouth crinkle into a smirk. "So, you publicly humiliated me because you feel empty?"

A smile slowly spread across his face. "Yeah. I guess I did."

"Feel better now?"

He chuckled. "Yeah."

"So glad I could be there to help."

Edgerton clapped a hand on my shoulder.

"Your life's got purpose, you know," I told him. "You just don't see it right now."

Edgerton nodded. "Well, I tell you one thing, I don't expect to be standing at the pearly gates."

"What, you're going the other route? Fire and brimstone and all that?

"If only it were that easy."

"Easy?"

"I wish I could envision something else. Something beyond this life. To believe in an afterlife, even one of perpetual torment, would be a great thing. If only I could believe that there was something waiting for us after our lives here are over, then death wouldn't matter so much. You know what I mean? If I could know that when we die, we move on, I could...I could...Oh, hell, I don't know. I don't know what I'm talking about."

"It sounds to me like you do. Maybe you could do something truly radical. Maybe you could just take it on faith."

Edgerton sat down on the ground. He pulled up a few blades of grass, held them up in front of him and watched them intently as they fell, as if using them to check the direction of the wind. Then he cocked his head. I heard the song of a bird coming from a clump of trees not too far away. I looked around, but couldn't tell which tree it was perched in.

"I just can't do it," Edgerton said. "I just can't make my mind go there."

I let my own mind reach back to a stoop-shouldered priest named Finnegan, a chubby Catholic schoolboy, and a dimly remembered catechism. "No," I said. "I don't think you're supposed to. You're not supposed to get there by reason. That's not what faith is. It's believing in something that is unknowable. It's not a place your mind can go. Sounds hokey, but maybe it's only a place your heart can go."

Edgerton looked at me with large, sad eyes. "My heart's here," he said.

He plucked a few more blades of grass and clenched them in his fist. "And your heart?" he asked.

"It's here, too."

"And heaven and hell and all the rest?"

"The rest," I said, "is silence."

Chapter Twenty-six

Edgerton went back to the armory, and I wandered around some more looking for Otis. I had made very nearly a complete circuit of the place without luck when I found myself back at King Henry's castle. This time there were a couple of guys there that I didn't recognize, dressed in period costume and drinking red wine from pewter goblets. When I asked them if they knew where Otis was, they launched into a loud, pseudo-Elizabethan improv.

"Egad!" one man shouted to the other. "'Tis some knave come with designs upon the king! Call out the guard!"

"Nay, my good lord," said the other. "'Tis some knave come with designs upon our libation! Call out the wine steward!"

They laughed uproariously at their combined wit.

"Could you guys just tell me if you've seen Otis?" I asked.

The first guy leaned over and said, in a voice that I'm sure he meant to be an undertone, "No. He was here earlier this morning, but he went missing more than an hour ago."

"That worry you?"

"Hell, no. He does it all the time. We don't really need him until the noon parade anyway."

I looked at my watch. It was eleven forty-five. "He

should be here pretty soon then?"

"Yeah."

"I'll wait."

The guy shrugged and went back to doing his drunk act for the patrons. Only it wasn't really an act. Those two were putting it away pretty good. I found a bench across from the castle and waited. Within a couple of minutes, Queen Candy showed up. She took a seat in one of a pair of little thrones that were set up on what I guess was supposed to be the front porch of the castle. As the minutes ticked by, Candy's face become more and more impatient. More lords, ladies, and knights arrived at the castle and before long, they were all looking mighty restless. I looked at my watch. It was twelve-fifteen. It was nearly twelve thirty before the royal troupe decided to parade without the king. They tried to hide it behind wide, fixed smiles and the tight, figure eight waves they gave the crowd, but these people were seriously unhappy about Otis not being on time. I waited for a few minutes after the royals went on their way, but when Otis still didn't show, I left too.

I began to hike back toward the Cock and Bull, where I was supposed to meet Naomi and Wiseman for lunch, but I decided to detour a bit and swing past the elephant rides before meeting them. I got to wondering if Otis' absence had anything to do with LeGrand's drug business. If it did, maybe Peterson would know something that could help me track down Otis.

As I approached the track, I could see that one of the elephants was tied to a post, while Peterson's oldest boy was leading the other around the track. Atop the elephant, two kids of about five or six were laughing nervously, but with what looked like real joy. A long line of would-be riders had formed in front of the cart where the ride tickets were sold. Peterson's youngest child was selling tickets and talking to the folks in line. There was no sign of the boys' father.

"Jack!" I called to the boy with the elephant. "Jack!"

The lad looked my way but with an expression that clearly said he was too busy to be bothered. I bothered him anyway. I approached and began to walk alongside him, trying to stay as far from the elephant as possible and still be able to carry on a conversation.

"Jack. My name's Dahms," I told him. "I'm a friend of your dad's. Do you know where he is?"

The boy shook his head. "No. We ain't seen him. I mean, he'd been here all morning. We've been having a good day. We were running both elephants. There's a lot of people waiting for rides. We need both to keep up. Anyway, one moment he's behind me letting off some riders and the next minute he's gone. The elephant isn't even tied up and he's gone."

"When did this happen?"

"About a half hour, forty-five minutes ago."

"I wonder if Simon…That's your brother's name, right? I wonder if Simon saw anything."

"I asked him. He said he was busy. Said he didn't see nothing."

"This don't seem right," I said.

"No way this is right. No way we can keep up with this crowd without him. People are getting seriously pissed."

"Has your dad ever left like this before?"

Jack stopped the elephant to look at me. "No," he said, drawing out the syllable slowly. "Do you think something…Do you think something's happened to him? I mean, he was just here. If he'd been hurt or something, we'd a seen. Right?"

"I don't know, Jack," I said. "But I think I'll ask around a bit. See if anybody's seen him. You guys hold down the fort as best you can. You're doing a wonderful job. If people get pissed, fuck 'em. You guys are doing great." I smiled a big, confident smile. Jack managed a weak smile back at me. As I left, it suddenly hit me that I really shouldn't have used the "f-word" with a fourteen-year-old.

Because it was close, I headed for the armory. Edgerton and Hess were busy with potential customers and someone I had never seen before was working the cash box at the counter. Edgerton had just handed a short sword down from the wall to a customer who was wearing a sheepskin vest, open to expose a sunken, hairless chest. When Edgerton pointed the fellow to the cash box, I caught his attention. "You seen anything of Dick Peterson?" I asked.

"What do you mean?"

"I mean, did you happen to see Peterson within the last hour or so? He's not at his concession. Did you see him leave? It may be important."

"Nah. Didn't see him. Sorry."

Hess had moved over near us, and I asked him as well. Same answer.

"Who's the new guy?" I asked Edgerton.

"He's not really a new guy. He works with us at the shop. He just doesn't much like working out here. But we really needed him this weekend, so we drafted him for festival duty. His name's Alex."

Both Edgerton and Hess went back to work, and I approached the guy at the counter. "Alex," I said as if I knew him, "you didn't happen to see the guy that runs the elephant rides within the last hour or so, did you?"

Alex had dull eyes and a slack jaw that didn't exactly inspire great confidence in his intellectual acumen. "You mean that guy with the elephants?" he asked.

"Yes. That would be the guy. Have you seen him within the last hour?"

"He ain't been in here."

"Thanks anyway."

I turned to leave.

"I saw him take off toward the back gate, though," Alex said.

"Within the last hour?"

"I don't know. Maybe about forty minutes ago."

"Was he alone?"

"No. There was a guy with him."

"Was it the guy who plays the King out here?"

"I didn't see no King."

"Who was the elephant guy with, then?"

"I didn't recognize him."

"Could you describe him to me?"

"Yeah. Let me see. He was wearing a pair of khaki trousers and a short-sleeved blue shirt. The kind with a collar on it. You know, like a dress shirt. Only short-sleeved."

"Anything else?" I prompted.

"Yeah. He looked like he pumped iron. You know. A real weightlifter-type."

"Did it look like the elephant guy wanted to go with him?"

"Why wouldn't he?"

I sighed "What was the elephant guy doing before

he left?"

"He was walking the elephant. Then he helped the riders down. Then he left."

"Did he tie up the elephant? Did he go over to say something to his kids?"

"No. He just left with the other guy."

"Did he follow the weightlifter guy or did he lead?"

"He led. The weightlifter guy was right behind him though. Real close."

I thanked Alex for the information and started back toward the elephant track. A thought struck me, and I turned back to Alex. "Hey! Is Julia around?"

"She took off for town. Said she'd be back later."

"When did she leave?"

"I don't know. A little less than an hour ago, I guess."

I walked out into the sunshine with absolutely no idea what to do next. Otis had failed to show up for the noon parade. Peterson had abruptly left both his business and his children with a guy who, based on the description, almost had to be Chief Dunstable. And not only had Peterson taken off without warning, he led the way to the back gate with Dunstable following close. Did Dunstable force him to go? Was he holding a gun on Peterson? It's a sure sign that things aren't going well if your business partner pulls a gun on you and orders you to leave a crowded place.

I looked at my watch. It was time to meet Naomi and Wiseman. At least that was something to do, so I headed for the Cock and Bull.

Wiseman was standing outside the crowded pub. "I'm not going to able to have lunch after all," I told him. "I got a bit of a situation brewing here, I think. People are starting to go missing on me."

"You mean besides your girlfriend?" Wiseman asked.

"What do you mean?"

"I got here a few minutes ago and didn't see either of you. I asked around and it turns out that your girlfriend just took off. Evidently, she didn't say anything to anybody. She just took off."

"Did anyone see her leave?" I asked, trying to remain calm as blood rushed to my head and something strong clenched at my insides.

"Not that I talked to."

"Stay here," I told Wiseman, and I pushed my way into the pub. Within a couple of minutes, I had accosted everyone working there and several of the pub's customers. No one I talked to had seen Naomi leave.

I returned to the spot where I had left Wiseman. I took a deep breath and tried to think of what to do next. "Let's go to the armory," I said. "Maybe Naomi went over to meet us by mistake."

"Sure thing," Wiseman said, a gentle but puzzled look crowding his features.

We walked quickly and quietly back to the armory. On the way, we passed the elephant rides. One elephant was still tied up and Jack Peterson was still giving rides with the other. At the armory, no one had seen anything of Naomi and Julia had not returned.

Edgerton, Hess, and Wiseman formed a semi-circle around me, watching me intently as I took a couple more deep breaths. "Something's wrong, isn't it?" Wiseman asked.

"Yeah. Maybe. I think so."

"What do you need us to do?"

"Okay," I said, steadying myself. "Stephen, Dick Peterson's disappeared, and I think he may be in real trouble. His kids are all by themselves over at the elephant rides and they're probably getting pretty worried by now. You go over and see if they're all right. Maybe you should close down the ride and bring them back here. I don't know. You know them best. Do what you think is right."

"Sure, Lyle," he said.

"Naomi's gone missing too. I'm going to go see if her car is still parked where she left it this morning. I'm really not sure what that will tell me, but it's a place to start."

"What do you want me to do?" Wiseman asked.

"Maybe you could make a circuit of this place and if you see Peterson, Otis McInerny, Naomi, or Julia, bring them back here."

"Okay."

"Why Julia?" Hess asked. "What's she got to do with this?"

I glared at Hess. "I'm not sure. Maybe you'd like to tell me?"

Hess' eyes crinkled with irritation. "What the hell is that supposed to mean?"

I decided it would be a nice release for me if I beat the crap out of somebody right there. Hess was elected. I took a step toward him, but Edgerton stepped between us. "There's a lot going on here," Edgerton said. "We'll sort it out later. Dahms, you go check on that car."

He was right. I went out the back door of the armory.

Having confirmed that Naomi's car was parked where we had left it, I looked all around me, hoping to catch a glimpse of something, anything that would help me find Naomi. Across the field, I saw the clump of trees where I had buried the crossbow that morning. It was something to do, so I took off for the trees at a half trot.

It took me a few minutes to remember exactly where I had stashed the thing. I hadn't taken the time to bury it in the ground, I had merely set it on the ground next to a maple tree and piled leaves on it. I was pretty sure I'd found the right tree. It was hard to be certain. The tree looked the same, and there were plenty of leaves piled around it, but there was no crossbow.

I heard a crinkling sound a few feet to my right and turned to see something white wrapped around the trunk of another tree. When I picked it up, I found it was the plastic bag I'd carried the crossbow in. The wind had come up and must have blown the bag there from wherever it had been dropped. I stared at the red and white Target symbol on the bag for some time. Sunlight filtered through the quaking leaves above me making it seem like everything around me was in motion. A gust of wind swirled through the dry, fallen leaves at my feet and a few skittered across the ground before settling a couple of yards away. I watched the leaves come to rest, nestling against something purple on the ground. I knew what it was even before I approached it. It was good King Henry's robe.

I found Otis kneeling, but slumped forward, his face in the rustling leaves. The back of his head was a mess of blood and bone and brain. I felt for a pulse, not because there was any chance that he was alive, but because it was what you were supposed to do. There was no pulse, and he was still warm.

Otis had been gagged with what looked like linen and lace torn from his costume, but he had not been bound. That probably meant that someone had covered him with a gun but didn't shoot him because of the noise. Instead, the killer had bashed his brains in. I crouched down and began looking around for the weapon, figuring the killer had used a rock or branch or something else that had come readily to hand there in the woods. I hadn't looked long when it occurred to me that maybe the killer was still hiding close by. I decided maybe I should go.

I rose slowly and started to make my way past the trees. Only a few feet from the clearing, I found Dick Peterson. Like Otis, he was dead, face down in the fallen leaves, his skull crushed. I didn't bother to check for a pulse. My own pulse was racing as I looked up and saw that only a couple of steps would find me out of the cover of the woods. I thought I might feel safer in the open.

That's when I heard it. The same sound I had heard in the Irish Cottage the night LeGrand had been killed. The sound of a ratchet. The sound of a bullet being chambered.

"Don't make me shoot you, Dahms," Dunstable said, stepping out from behind a tree, blocking my way to the clearing. He had a handgun in one hand and a fist-sized, bloody stone in the other.

"Nice gun," I said. "A 9mm semi-automatic. Peterson here give you that?"

Dunstable smiled thinly. "No. I had to take it from him. He pulled it on me once, you know. That evening in the cottage. I wanted to kill you right then. But Peterson wouldn't have it. He pulled out this here gun. So later that night, I made him give it to me."

"You killed LeGrand with it?"

"You figure that out all by yourself, tough guy? Or did your mommy help you?"

I shrugged. "So, LeGrand was a loudmouth?"

"You don't know the half of it, pal. He kept noising it around that I was working for him. The little shit. People were starting to talk about police corruption and other nonsense. Fucked everything up. Goddamned LeGrand! Everybody was happy. He should've been happy too. He got to be one of a select group of dealers that I allowed to operate. All he had to do was keep his nose clean and do his business in a professional manner. But no. He just had to make more of himself than there was, you know. Kept forgetting who he answered to."

"So, you reminded him."

"And now I'm gonna remind you," Dunstable said, moving the barrel of the gun slightly. "Now, raise your arms, tough guy. I want to see if you're carrying."

"Only a grudge," I told him.

Dunstable smirked as he patted me down under my arms and at the small of my back.

Dunstable let out a brittle chuckle. "That's right. I forgot. We got your .38 down at the station. You never did come in to claim it. I wonder why. It's only a couple of forms. Easy to fill out. Even for you."

I grunted.

"You can put your arms down now," Dunstable said. "And hey…why don't you just kneel down on the ground here. Make yourself comfortable. No reason for this to be unpleasant for you. It's not going to be unpleasant for me."

Dunstable laughed.

I lowered my arms and stared at him. This guy liked killing, I thought. He'd kill me and walk away savoring the rush it gave him. Maybe even with his hand wrapped around his johnson. I pictured Otis and Peterson with their faces in the dirt. I didn't want to be found like that. It was too meek. Too quiet. God, it would be quiet.

I tried to think of some way to escape. Maybe I should just charge him. He'd probably just shoot me in the gut. Christ! Any way it goes down, this was gonna hurt. Then I was gonna be dead. Everything gone. Everyone. My mind flashed on Naomi. Still missing. Missing, but not dead in these woods. Maybe okay, I thought. She'd miss me. She'd be broke up when they told her I was dead. I didn't know if we'd have stayed together. Probably not. It would probably have been over with the end of the festival. This way it would never be over. I'd be the one for her. The one great love lost. Her feeling would never grow cold. I'd always be as I was…even better than I was. Taken away too soon. Like Elvis, I thought.

"On your knees, tough guy," Dunstable ordered. "Take it like a man."

I bowed slightly and bent one knee as if to kneel. "What would you know about acting like a man, you dickless wussy?"

"You know," Dunstable said, anger unsettling his voice, "maybe I'll make you beg a little first. McInerny begged. You should have heard him. He begged like a little girl. I finally had to gag him just to shut him up. I bet you beg too."

I didn't reply at all. Instead, I made a run for it.

I faked to the right, then tried to dodge past him on the left. He simply stepped in my way. I pivoted, turned tail, and ran into the woods, zigzagging through the trees. I knew the woods weren't very deep and that there was a clearing beyond them. I also knew that I was running away from the festival site and any chance for help.

Dunstable knew it too. He was right behind me, moving easily, even unhurriedly. He could have shot me at any time, but why risk the noise? He let me make my way through the woods, following my fleeing figure and the sound of my heavy, labored breathing. But even over the sound of my breathing, I could hear him. He was laughing.

I got through the woods and into the clearing. But the clearing was nothing but a narrow strip of land that quickly fell away into a deep gully. I kept running, but the downward slope became too much, and I stumbled. I fell down and began to roll toward the bottom. I managed to stop rolling, but couldn't help skidding down the slope, feet first, on my belly. When I finally came to a stop, I looked up, and at the top of the gully stood Dunstable, his gun leveled steadily at me, the rest of his body quaking with laughter.

I slowly got to my feet and brushed some of the dirt off me. "You coming down?" I asked.

"You know, I think I'll just shoot you from here."

I dropped to one knee, desperately tugging on my pants leg, trying to slip it up high enough so I could get at the ankle holster I was wearing on my right leg. Dunstable had been sloppy when he checked me for a weapon; I had a pocket-sized .22 strapped to my leg. Now, if I could only get at it and get a shot off before the son-of-a bitch blew me away.

Still groping for my gun, I glanced up. Dunstable had me dead in his sights. I wasn't gonna make it, I thought. It was over. I closed my eyes.

A bullet thudded in the ground a couple of inches in front of me. I thought I heard something else at the same time on top of the hill—a muffled, knocking sound. My eyes snapped open, and I saw Dunstable doubled over, grabbing his leg. Then I heard another sound. Dunstable was screaming in pain. Confused, I forgot about my gun and jumped to my feet. Dunstable was now trying to turn around, trying to aim the 9mm at someone behind him. Then I saw the shaft of an arrow impaled in his left leg. A moment later an arrow hit him in the head, knocking him over and sending him rolling down the slope toward me. As he fell, most of the shaft of the second arrow snapped off before he came to rest some three yards distant. He ended up on his back, his arms splayed out on either side of his motionless body, about four inches of arrow protruding from the socket of his left eye.

I took a step toward Dunstable, but an arrow passed just over my shoulder. Damn, I realized, now someone's shooting at me.

I whirled around, looking for someplace to take cover. I didn't see anything that I could hide behind. I was standing in a narrow gully. There were no trees or rocks or anything. I thought about running farther away, but that would mean I'd have to climb the other side of the gully. That would make it easier for someone standing in the clearing above to shoot me. Not a good idea. I could run down the gully, but with no cover, I wouldn't last long. Only one thing to do, I decided. Head back up there and see if I could kill him before he killed me.

I started to clamber up the slope, pausing just long enough to pull the .22 out of the ankle holster. I expected that at any second an arrow would slice into me. But I was wrong. I made it out of the gully. Then I made it into the clearing. And there wasn't anybody else in sight.

I broke into a run. I figured that the shooter had gone

into the woods and was taking aim at me from the cover of the trees. I ran as fast as I could, my heavy footfalls thumping loudly. Sweat was streaming down my forehead, stinging my eyes, and the woods were just a blurry outline as I skirted the edge of the stand of trees. Running toward the festival wall, my heart was beating so hard I figured if an arrow didn't take me out, I'd be dead of a heart attack before I reached safety.

I felt my pace begin to slow. I tried to push myself, but there was nothing I could do. I opened my eyes and found that I was nearly back to the festival wall. Nearly to safety. With the last of my energy, I reached the back door to the armory, slamming into it. I groped for the door handle, pulled it open, then fell inside. The door that led out into the main part of the armory was closed and the back room was filled with a comforting darkness. My eyelids were heavy with exhaustion and my legs quivered as I settled to a sitting position on the stairs that led up to the bedrooms. There was enough light leaking in around the door that I was able to make out Don Hess' jar of green olives sitting on the floor just inside the room. I leaned back and a step creaked beneath me.

"I need you to give me that gun now," a voice said softly.

I was so tired that I couldn't even manage surprise when Julia Hess stepped from the shadows, the crossbow in her hands.

I looked down my lap. I still held the little gun weakly in my hand. I couldn't see Julia's face, but I made out the bow clearly enough. The tip of the arrow was an ugly thing—shiny silver glinting in the dim light. With effort, I handed the gun up into the darkness.

Chapter Twenty-seven

Julia preferred the crossbow. After taking the gun from me, she slipped it into an embroidered bag that hung over her shoulder. She cracked open the back door, glanced in all directions, then turned back to face me. Her eyes were patient and gentle. The tip of the arrow was pointed at my throat.

"I'll take you to her now," she said.

It took me a moment to realize who she was talking about. "Is Naomi okay?" I asked at last.

"Yes. She's okay."

"I'd like to see her."

"I know."

We went out the back door and along the festival wall. Julia walked behind me, making no attempt to hide the crossbow that she aimed at my back. I glanced around and saw several people in the parking lot some distance away. A couple of them stopped to watch us as we walked. I wondered what they thought. It must have looked strange—a woman holding a crossbow, prodding a fat guy along the outside of the festival walls. Maybe it looked too strange. So strange that the people in the parking lot thought it was just part of the show. No one called out to us. No one shouted an alarm.

Finally, Julia prodded me away from the festival and out across a field of tall grass. We walked slowly and deliberately, and except for terse directions on which way to walk, Julia said nothing. I was glad of the slow march. Some of my strength was beginning to return. I still wanted to collapse, but now it was more of a preference rather than an immediate danger.

We walked until we reached a dirt road that cut through the field in front of us. It was really just a path that seemed to come out of nowhere and go no place. But on its way, it passed a weathered, gray shack listing noticeably in the shade of some tall, white pines.

I turned to look at Julia.

"It's okay," she assured me, "nobody uses it anymore."

"Good. I do hate to bust in on folks unannounced."

Julia smiled at me and motioned with the crossbow for me to enter. The door still hung on the dilapidated structure, but with the entire frame of the building slanting to one side, it no longer closed all the way. As I pushed the door open, it shrieked on its hinges. As the door opened, frenzied scratching sounded from inside. Rats, I thought, instinctively backing up out the door and into the crossbow behind me.

"Careful, Lyle!" Julia cautioned, real concern in her voice. "This thing is cocked. You bump into it, and it could go off."

"Sorry. I'll be more careful."

"See that you do."

I stepped into the shack in time to see the tail of a squirrel departing through the glassless pane of a double-hung window. Along the wall under the window was a bench, crudely constructed of two-by-fours, and next to the bench was a large stack of yellowed, bundled newspapers. There was little else inside the one-room building except a wooden chair with one leg considerably shorter than the others, and a metal bucket with a large hole eaten by rust in the side. And Naomi. She was kneeling in a corner, her mouth gagged, her arms behind her bound at both the elbows and the wrists, her legs bound at the knees and ankles. Her eyes were wide.

"I know it looks uncomfortable, Lyle," Julia said, "and I didn't want to have to do it, but…You see, I had to go find you and I had to make sure she wouldn't leave. I wish I'd had some other choice."

Her voice was so gentle, so genuinely apologetic, I felt like I needed to reassure her. "That's okay, Julia," I said. "I'm sure she understands. Do you think that we could release her now?"

"Certainly, Lyle. Could you do it? There's a knife on the bench. You'll never be able to untie those knots. Do be careful with the knife, please. I mean, don't do anything thoughtless that might get you hurt."

I glanced at the crossbow. "I'll be careful."

Julia pulled the chair into the middle of the room and sat down, covering me with the crossbow. Then she took my gun out of her bag and laid it in her lap. I turned my back on Julia and felt a tingle run up my spine. I squirmed a bit as I went to the corner to release Naomi.

As I was cutting the ropes, Naomi's eyes first showed relief, but then she glanced toward Julia, and her eyes appealed to me for an explanation. All I could do was shake my head. Having cut the cords that bound her, I removed the gag before carefully placing the knife back on the bench. I took Naomi in my arms. She said nothing. She just held me tightly as we both turned our attention to Julia.

"I suppose you're wondering why," she said,

sucking in her lower lip in a pensive expression. "It's one of those things, you know. It all makes sense as you're going through it, but when it's over, you have trouble remembering just why you did everything you did. Do you know what I mean?"

"Sure," I said. "Happens all the time."

"I knew you'd understand, Lyle," Julia said, relieved.

"And I do. Well, part of it anyway. It's like you said, looking back, not everything is always clear. Maybe you'd like to talk about it."

"I'd like that very much. You don't know how lonely it's been for me. I'm used to being able to tell Don everything. But I couldn't very well tell him about all of this."

"No, I suppose not."

"But I tried to give him a hint," Julia said, her expression brightening. "That's why I went to all that trouble with Greg Eckels. That's why he was at the armory. I wanted Don to find him. I wanted Don to be able to figure it out. You know, without my actually having to tell him. But you found him instead." Her expression clouded over. "Oh! I don't like thinking about that."

"If it's too hard for you now," I said, "we could try another time."

Julia looked up at me with moist, patient eyes, a comforting smile on her strong, beautiful face. "Lyle," she said, chiding me gently, "there won't be another time."

"I suppose not."

"I have to end this thing today. I can't let it go on any longer. It's been so hard. Hard on me; hard on Don.

Hard on everyone."

"Okay," I said. "Would you like to tell us what happened?"

Julia frowned. "I'd like to tell *you*," she said. "I hate to be impolite, but I don't think this person has any right to be here. She's not the kind I particularly like talking to about my problems."

"Uh…Ah…" I stammered, "um, maybe we should talk alone, then. Maybe you could—"

"Oh, Lyle," Julia interrupted, "I can't let her go. I had to bring her here. You understand. Don't you?"

"To be perfectly honest, Julia, no, I don't. Not that part of it, anyway."

"Maybe I should start at the beginning."

"Please do."

"Some of this, I'm sure you know. You know, for instance, that Don has not always been entirely faithful. I don't really blame him, though. He would get busy and be away and we wouldn't be together for weeks at a time. Then some woman would come along…"

Julia paused and glared coldly at Naomi. Then she continued.

"Some woman would come along, and he would briefly succumb. It never lasted. How could a thing like that last? Don and I belong together. What we have is strong. It can weather a great deal. I know that. I have proof. We stayed together after…after I…Well, you know, after Greg Eckels and I met."

Julia looked down at the crossbow for a moment, taking her eyes off Naomi and me. I thought about rushing her, but she looked up, fighting back tears in her big, soulful eyes. I waited.

"That nearly ruined it. But Don stayed with me.

He'd been weak himself and that helped him forgive me. It took a while, you know, waiting to know if he'd forgive me. For weeks I wondered. It was torment. I tried to kill myself. Down in Texas. They had to put me in an awful place. Just for a while. Just until they were sure I wouldn't try to hurt myself again. But once I knew that Don would forgive me, I didn't want to hurt myself anymore. It was like we were whole again. Do you understand?"

"Sure," I told her. "He filled up the empty places."

Julia smiled and nodded. Then a shadow passed over her.

"Only it wasn't quite like before. Don tried to hide it, but I could tell. I could tell when he looked at me. He saw the stain. I'd stained what we'd had. He tried not to look. Not to let me know how it bothered him. But I knew."

"How did Gilroy become involved?" I asked.

"That was my other mistake. I couldn't talk to Don about what I'd done. I didn't want to dredge it all up again. But I had to talk to someone. When we got back home from Texas, I tried to stay close to Don. I didn't go out without him. I didn't see any of my girlfriends anymore. I didn't want him to worry when I was away from him. I didn't want to give him cause to think that…" Julia paused, staring past me at the memory. She nodded her head, almost imperceptibly, several times before proceeding.

"But I did see the boys at the shop. More and more they were becoming like a family to me. It sounds funny, but it was like they were the kids that Don and I haven't had. Jason, Stephen, even poor, slow-witted Alex—they were my boys. And one day when Don was busy, Jason and I went out for lunch. Jason mentioned that I had seemed unhappy lately. It all came pouring out. I told him all about it. Jason was wonderful. He listened. He reassured me. He was wonderful. But…"

"But he betrayed you," I said, nodding sympathetically.

"Yes. He told that awful LeGrand all about it. At first, I couldn't imagine why he'd done that. I confronted Jason. But he wouldn't tell me. But I think now I know why. He wanted to impress LeGrand. He wanted to get close to him. So, he told him a secret. Jason told me that LeGrand swore he would never tell anyone. But his word was nothing. Do you know what LeGrand did? He came to me. He was all smooth smiles and smooth lines, and he told me that he knew about Greg and me. He said he also knew about Don, how Don slept around, and didn't I think it was time for some more payback. He thought he could have me that easily. I slapped his face. But he just laughed at me. Said I was pathetic. He said I had no backbone. He said that I just let everyone push me around and all I did was take it. He said I was too weak to do anything for myself. That I would never take a stand. So, I took a stand."

"I don't get it," I said. "Why didn't you take out LeGrand? Why Gilroy and not LeGrand?"

"I didn't care about LeGrand. He was all words. His words couldn't hurt me. What hurt was Jason. His betrayal. I couldn't bear to see him, day after day, pretending he still had a place with us after what he'd done. I had to get rid of him. I had to…Oh, you know."

"I think I do, Julia," I said. "Excising Gilroy would help keep you whole."

"Yes. That's what I thought."

"Only it wasn't enough."

"No. No, it wasn't."

"Did Greg Eckels try to rekindle what he'd had with you?"

"Oh, dear, no. Greg knew it was over. He still had feelings for me. But he knew that I would never leave Don."

"Then what—"

"It was me," Julia interrupted. "It was me. I just couldn't face him. Every time I saw him, it was like I was burning. Like I was being punished again and again for what I had done. I could never be free of my...my sin...my awful sin. Not until I was free of him."

"So, you killed him."

"I killed him," she admitted, a steely calm settling over her. "I went to him and got him alone and when he turned his back to me, I hit him with a war hammer. I killed him with something Don, himself, had forged. I hid the body and then, when I thought it was safe, I used one of our knives and I-I guess you'd say I carved off his head. Then I brought it to my husband."

"Grisly stuff," I said.

"Sometimes only blood will wash you clean."

"Hasn't there been enough blood?"

"Nearly enough," she answered, looking hard at Naomi. "Nearly enough."

"What about Dunstable? Did you know he killed LeGrand?"

"No. I didn't know and I didn't care."

"Why did you kill Dunstable?"

Julia looked truly bewildered. "Why, to save you, of course. He *was* trying to kill you."

"But then you tried to kill me. You shot an arrow at

me after Dunstable was down. Remember?"

"That's entirely different."

I nodded. "Peterson's dead," I told her.

Her faced flushed and contorted with pain. "No!" she cried. "How?"

"Dunstable killed him. Peterson knew some things about Dunstable that he didn't want to come out. So, he killed him."

"Dick knew a lot of things," Julia said.

"Like the fact that you killed Gilroy?"

"And Greg. He knew about Greg, too."

"You told him?"

"About Greg? Yes. But he saw me kill Jason. He saw me standing in that shed he uses. The one by the cottage? He saw me, and I saw him, and he let me get away."

"Why didn't he turn you in?"

"I asked him that. At first, he said that he didn't want to go to the cops because of something that he'd done. Something they could arrest him for. But the more we talked, the more I came to understand that Dick just knew about loss. He'd lost his wife. His hope. Just the way I was afraid that I would lose Don. He understood. He was a good friend. Now, I guess his kids will get another lesson in loss. So much loss. So very much loss."

"Why don't we put an end to it?" I asked. "Why don't we just walk away and pick up the pieces that are left?"

"I'd like to, Lyle. I'd really like to. But sometimes things just have a way of moving forward. No matter what you do. You just can't stop them. You gotta just follow them through.

"I really don't find that to be true," I said.

"Sometimes it's important to stop and let things make sense before proceeding."

"Nothing makes any sense, Lyle."

"Why is Naomi here, Julia?"

"Naomi?" Julia asked, lowering her eyes.

"Yeah. That puzzles me. I can't imagine that she posed any kind of threat to you?"

Julia's eyes snapped up to meet mine. They were flinty with hate.

"Oh, you can't imagine it, can't you?" she asked, her lips tight, her mouth barely moving. "That kind is always a threat. You don't know. She's blinded you. That's what that kind do."

"What kind are you talking about, Julia?"

"She's a whore, Lyle. She's less than nothing. She slept with Gilroy. You heard her say so. You must know she slept with LeGrand, even if she won't admit it. Now, she's sleeping with you. Tomorrow it's some other guy. She's the kind that tries to break up decent relationships just to hurt other women. Other women she can never be like. Decent women, who love their husbands and lose them to the arms of sluts like her."

"Husbands like Don?"

"Yes. Like Don."

"So, you snatch up a woman you barely know, label her, and drag her out here to kill her?"

"She is what she is, Lyle."

"That's true, Julia. But she's not what you say she is. No one is. That's the thing about the labels we tag on people. None of them really fit. They say more about the person doing the labeling that those they are used against."

"What are you saying, Lyle?"

"Julia. We both know that you are a good person, just trying to cope. And it's been real hard for you. You've made some bad decisions and I think if you take the time to step back and look at the situation, you'll find that there are other ways to approach your problems. Things aren't the way they seem to you. You got the labels wrong."

"Lyle," she said, chiding me again, "I'm as close to eliminating my problems as I've ever been in my life. Now, I know that this is going to be hard on you. But, really, it's for the best. First, I'm going to remove this woman. And then, I'm sorry, but you're also going to have to go. You know, you're lucky really. You're going to a better place."

Julia laid the crossbow in her lap and raised my gun. Aiming it directly at Naomi, she said to me, "You might not want to watch this."

I lunged toward Julia, hoping that the gun wouldn't go off before reached her. I was too slow. The little gun made a big noise in the small room. I didn't look to see if the shot had been true. I slammed into Julia and crushed her against the wall. I thought I heard the door to the shack screech open behind me, but I didn't turn around. I couldn't see it, but I assumed Julia was still holding the gun. I moved back from Julia just enough to give me room to cock my right hand, hoping to drive a fist into her abdomen. But before I could deliver the punch, something came down on the back of my head.

Whatever it was hit me pretty hard. Not so hard that it would normally do any real damage, but I'd been hit on the head a whole bunch the previous couple of weeks, so the blow made the room swim blurrily before me. I wasn't even sure that I was still standing when someone grabbed me by the shoulders and turned me around. It was Don Hess. Hess reared back and slammed his right fist squarely into my face. There was a great *thunging* noise in my head as my body gave it up and slumped to the floor.

I managed to raise my head in time to see Hess towering above me, hands clasped and raised high, preparing to hit me again. I tried to raise an arm to block the blow, but the blow never came. Edgerton was there. He came up behind Hess and punched him hard in the kidney. Hess left out a moan and turned to face Edgerton. Both men were staring at each other with a mixture of anger and disbelief when the gun went off again. Julia had fired a shot into the ceiling, and for an instant, the room was deadly silent.

A pair of arms closed around me, and lips lightly kissed my forehead. Naomi was alive.

A voice I couldn't immediately place, said, "It's over. Let's end this thing."

I turned to find Wiseman standing just inside the door of the shack. I chuckled weakly and with Naomi's help, I rose to my feet. Julia was still against the wall, the gun still in her hand.

"He's right, Julia," Don Hess beseeched her. "Please, let's just end this thing."

Julia looked first at her husband, then at each of us, standing before her. Her customary warm and generous smile returned to her lips. Then she nodded. "It is a bit much, isn't it?" she said at last.

"We can deal with it, Julia," Hess said. "We're all friends here. We can deal with this. It's going to be all right."

Julia laughed lightly, then closed her eyes and

slowly opened them. "I don't think anything's going to make this all right, Don. But it's sweet of you to lie. Even noble."

"We can do it," Hess insisted. "Together. You know how strong we are together."

Julia nodded. "And we'll be together again. We just have to...how did I put it earlier? Lyle, you remember. We just have to wash it clean. The stain. We just wash it clean."

"We can do that," Hess promised. "We can do that."

Julia looked directly at me. "How's your Shakespeare, Lyle?"

"Sub-par, I'm afraid."

Julia nodded and in a soft, singsong voice said, "The Thane of Fife had a wife; where is she now? What will these hands ne'er be clean?" Then she looked at her husband and mouthed the words "I love you."

I saw it in her eyes. In that instant, I knew.

"No!" I exclaimed, stumbling towards her. But it was too late. With a smooth, fluid motion, she turned the barrel of the little gun toward her and placed it in her open mouth. She brought her lips together and pulled the trigger.

I felt Naomi shudder beside me as Julia slumped to the floor. Edgerton stiffened, then turned around, unable to look at the dead woman, at the bloodstained wall, at the grisly, ignoble death. Wiseman stared resolutely at his shoes. Something wet hit me in the face and dripped into my eye. I wiped at it with the heel of my hand, but it continued to burn. I used the sleeve of my shirt, dabbing the sting from my eye. I stared at the stain on the shirt sleeve, then at Julia. Then I turned to look at Don Hess.

Hess was frozen, his arms at his sides, his face drawn and lifeless. And the look in his eyes. They were glazed, like the smooth, marble eyes of a bust in a graveyard, focused on something far away. Something beyond the corpse, beyond the death, beyond the loss. Something that we all hope we will never gaze upon, but something that waits for us all.

Chapter Twenty-eight

We missed the last day of the festival. Instead, we all spent the day at the Little Crow Police station answering questions. Both the investigating officers and the media thought it awfully suspicious that the Ren Fest murders were committed by two different people and that both of the murderers were now dead. But acting Police Chief Thompson needed to do some immediate damage control and having the case officially closed was going to help him a great deal. He hoped that the cloud of suspicion that had enveloped his department would begin to dissipate as he went about, pinning all the talk of corruption on his dead predecessor.

When I got back to the Bijou late Sunday evening, I caught Thompson's act on the TV news. He appeared almost tearful as he pleaded with the camera to try to remember Dunstable for the good things that he had done during his many years in law enforcement, and to try not to focus on the mistakes he made at the end of his career. He also called for sympathy for the confused, mentally ill woman who had killed her husband's co-worker and her former lover in a misguided attempt to hold her family together. Thompson concluded by saying that he would try to keep his family together as well. His family was the Little Crow police force—a family now in mourning for its fallen leader and having to deal with the shocking revelation that the man in whom they had once had so much faith, had betrayed their trust. It was a beautiful speech. I wondered who'd written it for him. Maybe, I thought, they've got image consultants for small town police departments now.

The news broadcast also included a story on how the festival had dealt with the shock of losing its titular head, King Henry. A festival official in a gray, pinstriped suit was interviewed standing next to a stage where a belly dancer was performing. He spoke of the great personal loss that he felt at the death of Otis McInerny. But, he stressed, Otis' whole life had been devoted to entertaining people and it would be a great disservice to his memory if the festival did not go on providing the type of wholesome, family entertainment that Otis had been such a big part of. He concluded that he found it a great tribute to Otis and his legacy that the festival was estimating that they would, that very day, break all previously existing attendance records. "People need to make merry," he said, "perhaps, particularly after suffering a terrible loss."

The story concluded with a shot of Queen Candy, smiling winsomely and waving to a crowd gathered at her castle. She was now dubbed Queen Elizabeth, and she bravely promised to carry on in the great tradition of her fallen friend and mentor. I confess I had a bit of trouble with the notion of Candy as the Virgin Queen, but then I didn't need to be convinced. She only needed to play to festivalgoers, and there was damn sure no way I was ever going out there again.

It wasn't until Wednesday that I saw Naomi again. She'd told me that she needed a few days to herself to get over the thing that we had witnessed together. I'd really wanted her to stay with me. I'd hoped that I could offer her strength, someone to lean on. But when we parted, I could see in her red-rimmed eyes that she was already marshaling her own strength. She'd be fine, I thought. It made me wonder about myself.

Naomi agreed to meet me for beers at McCauley's. I'd mentioned it to both Edgerton and to Wiseman. I hadn't exactly invited them to join us; I'd just told them where we'd be, at what time, and that if I saw them there, I'd say hi. It's not that I thought I needed someone else there, it was just that the festival was over and maybe Naomi wanted to tell me something about moving on. Maybe, I thought, I could get her to put that off if we weren't alone. In any case, when Naomi arrived, I was sitting in a booth sharing a pitcher with Edgerton and Wiseman.

Naomi settled in the booth next to me, and Skip brought over a glass. I introduced her to Skip, who smiled knowingly and looked at me with his eyebrows slightly raised in approval. Naomi smiled, and exchanged pleasantries with both Wiseman and Edgerton, but turned a concerned gaze toward me after greeting Stephen. I shrugged slightly. I'd noticed it too. Edgerton was looking quite drawn and haggard, as though he hadn't been sleeping much since Julia's death. His room at the Bijou was next to mine and I'd heard him stirring in there quite late the previous three nights. But I hadn't questioned him about it. I figured he would tell me what he wanted me to know when he wanted me to know it.

The four of us talked about anything we could think of besides the horror that we had shared in that little shack under the pines. Despite his fatigue, Edgerton managed a moderate level of excitement as he talked about a new, high-speed copier that he was being trained on at his copy center job. Wiseman joined in, talking about the copy machine that he used at his office. Naomi and I pretended to be interested in their conversation, but I kept sneaking glances at her, looking for signs of how she felt about continuing our relationship. She caught me looking, and when she smiled at me, her eyes smiled with her. I figured that was a good sign.

Finally, Wiseman and Edgerton, having discussed copies per second, paper jams, hopper capacity, and toner intensity, seemed to have exhausted the topic of copiers, and we lapsed into an awkward silence. Edgerton broke the silence by taking a deep draught of his beer and nodding his head at Naomi and me. "So, how you guys doing?"

I waited for Naomi to answer. She looked around the bar dramatically, shaking her head, her eyes crinkling into a distasteful squint. "I suppose this place is part of the package," she said. "I mean, this is where you hang out. I'll probably have to hang out here too."

"I guess," I said. "What do you think?"

"A person could get used to it. A person can get used to almost anything."

"Yeah?"

"Yeah."

I smiled up at Edgerton. "I guess we're doing just fine."

He nodded. "That's good. I guess I'm doing okay too. A little tired."

"I'd noticed that," I said.

"No big deal," Edgerton replied.

Wiseman nodded. "I'm okay too. But I'll never forget that image."

We all nodded.

"Not just the blood, you know," Wiseman continued. "Although there's that. No, it was the gun in her mouth." He paused. "Did you get that reference, Dahms? That 'Thane of Fife' thing?"

"Yeah. Macbeth"

"I don't want to quibble," Wiseman said, "I mean, her reference was apt and all. But it wasn't Macbeth that I thought of. It was Othello. You know what I mean. Othello's death scene. It was the way her lips seemed to caress the barrel of that ridiculous little gun. Othello's last words, you know. 'I kissed thee, ere I kill'd thee— no way but this, killing myself, to die upon a kiss.' " Wiseman shuddered. "I can't lose the image."

"So, you're saying that she 'lov'd not wisely, but too well?' " Edgerton asked.

"Something like that. Yeah. That's how I'm going to remember her anyway."

Naomi stiffened and took a sip of her beer. "Excuse me, but I'm going to remember her as a crazy bitch that tried to kill me."

Edgerton looked up at Naomi but didn't say anything.

"That might be a bit unkind," I said.

Naomi smiled, "Yeah, but then you're the one who told a confessed killer pointing a crossbow at you that she was a good person who'd made some bad decisions."

Even Edgerton chuckled at that.

"Well," I said, "it's important to see the best in everyone."

"Well, as far as I'm concerned," Naomi continued, "all of your quotes from Shakespeare and your decisions about how you're going to remember her are nothing more than…well, nothing more than words."

True," Wiseman said, pouring himself another beer, "but in the end, that's really all that's left. Just words. Words spoken in memory, written in a book, or etched on a gravestone."

Edgerton sipped at his beer. "I'm still trying to wrap my head around it is all. Julia was more than just a killer. She was a wife, and a friend, and a confidant. Inside each of us, a whole invisible, unknowable, inner life is playing out and no one outside can fully grasp it, or understand it, or label it, or sum it up with a pithy quote. We want to. We may even need to, but we can't. It just don't work that way."

Wiseman nodded. "But what we do is what people know and what they'll remember. And those memories are our legacy. The scary thing is that no matter your accomplishments, no matter how you strive, no matter what you achieve in this life, death robs you of the ability to defend yourself. Your legacy is consigned to those left living. And they may pervert it terribly. Or focus on one thing to the exclusion of everything else. It doesn't seem right. A life is too precious to leave to the memory of others."

"Well, if we're still talking about Julia," Naomi interrupted, "and I'm not sure we are, I still say that she was a crazy bitch that tried to kill me."

"See what I mean," Wiseman said.

We stayed at McCauley's long enough to finish off another pitcher of beer. Wiseman and Edgerton's conversation drifted to other topics. I didn't really pay much attention. Naomi was warm next to me, and the beer was nice and cold. My life, for the time being, had balance.

Unfortunately, Naomi had to work the next morning and before long she told me that she had to go home. Wiseman looked at his watch and said that he'd better be getting home as well. I kissed Naomi goodnight, a kiss that lingered for a couple of delicious seconds.

"Maybe I could come over tomorrow night," she suggested. "Maybe we could get some take out. Eat in. What do you think?"

"I'd like that."

She nodded her good-byes to Wiseman and Edgerton, then turned back to me. "Now, Lyle," she said, wagging a finger at me with mock concern. "Don't stay out too late. You need to get home. Get some sleep. Rest up. You're going to need it tomorrow night." Then she turned on her heel and left smiling.

Wiseman followed after a couple of minutes, and Edgerton and I left after one last beer.

We stepped from the warm bar into the cool, autumn night. As we walked away from the bar and the concentration of streetlights that bathed the block in their yellow glow, a few stars became visible in the cold sky above. The sound of our footsteps on the pavement merged with the rustle of leaves stirring in the gutter alongside us. Music played softly and indistinctly from one of the rooms in one of the rooming houses we passed on the way home. I felt peaceful.

Peaceful, a little tipsy, and sleepy. Not tired in the sense of being exhausted, but the good kind of sleepy that you feel just before being enveloped in a welcome slumber. I'd gladly take Naomi's advice, I thought. I would sleep well.

I glanced at Edgerton as we neared the Bijou. We still hadn't spoken directly about it—about how he was holding up—but he appeared to be handling it. And although he was weary and his face was care-worn, he did not seem overly grave. He'd soon work it out for himself. And I'd be there if he needed me. He'd soon put the last few weeks behind him, stored in memory, like a book you've finished and placed on a shelf, perhaps never to be opened again. Then he would sleep, I thought. And how splendid it is to put away your cares and lose yourself in the sweet balm of sleep.

A word about the author...

Brian is a graduate of the University of Minnesota whose Dinkytown neighborhood provides the setting for his mystery series featuring private investigator Lyle Dahms. The Dahms novels spring from his lifelong love of mystery fiction, especially the works of Dashiell Hammett and Raymond Chandler, as well as more contemporary masters like Robert B. Parker and G.M. Ford.

He is a three-time finalist in the Pacific Northwest Writers Association mystery and suspense contest. Brian spent much of his professional career working to alleviate domestic hunger serving as the operations director of the Emergency Feeding Program of Seattle & King County as well as the manager of the Pike Market Food Bank in downtown Seattle.

Married with three beautiful daughters, Brian now lives and writes in Ocean Shores, a small city on the Washington coast. www.brianandersonmysteries.com

9 781509 250912